PRAISE FOR D. D. SCOTT:

"One of the top Romantic Comedy/Humorous Mystery writers out right now." —ENT (Ereader News Today)

HOLLYWOOD HOLIDAYS

(Home for the Holidays, Book 1)

By:

D. D. Scott

Copyright © 2013 by D. D. Scott. All rights reserved.

This book is a work of fiction. Names, characters, places and incidents are either products of the author's imagination or used fictitiously. Any resemblance to actual events, locales, or persons, living or dead, is entirely coincidental. All rights reserved. No part of this publication can be reproduced or transmitted in any form or by any means, electronic or mechanical, without permission in writing from the author or publisher.

First Electronic Edition: October 2013
First Print Edition: November 2014

ISBN - 13: 978-1503268784
ISBN - 10: 1503268780

This time of year, it's all about going home for the holidays. But what if you're not sure where home is?

In this Romantic Comedy, think The Grinch and his Desperate Housewife.

Socialite Harper Cantwell wants more out of life than being Briar Creek, Tennessee's philanthropic queen. Her husband Grant is a financial stud, but he's also an emotional dud. Tired of being nothing more than his glorified event planner, she leaves him. Hoping to find herself in the creative excitement and sizzle of the holidays in Hollywood, she meets Jake Benton. One of Tinsel Town's ultimate players, Jake doesn't waste any time letting her know he's interested—very interested. In spite of Jake's hot advances, it's Grant she can't forget. But sacrificing herself for any man is no longer part of her party plan.

Ultra-conservative businessman Grant Cantwell III doesn't completely understand why Harper left. He misses her terribly but is clueless how to get her back. He gets a real wake-up call when Harper's best, gay friends tell him he's an idiot for losing her. Under the tutelage of their company Chick Tricks Inc., Grant is soon on their fast track program, "How to Please a Woman." But Grant needs more than just a few tricks. He must learn to open his heart instead of his wallet, before Harper gives up on him forever and runs into the open arms of Hollywood's premier gigolo.

CHAPTER ONE
(Briar Creek, Tennessee)

A HEART FOR SALE

Harper Cantwell wrapped her fingers around the thick barrel of her husband's Mont Blanc and wiped away a runaway tear before it stained the embossed seal of the Cantwell crest. Closing her eyes, she begged the heavens for the right words. As she moved the tip of the pen against the fine grains of stationery, her hand trembled. No amount of time or thought could ease her burden.

She tucked the gilt-edged parchment inside its accompanying envelope and addressed the front surface. Her first inclination was to leave it on the desk in Grant's study since that would be the first place he'd go upon arriving home. But she didn't want her correspondence treated in the same dutiful vein as the rest of his business mail.

With that in mind, she closed the door to his office and forced one foot and then the other toward the master suite they were supposed to share.

She'd taken second seat to his vast empire for the last time. Tonight, she would be the final thing he thought of when he turned off the lamp on his bedside table.

Propping her note against the antique Tiffany's base, she extended the handle on her suitcase and reached for her tote bag. Checking the outer front pocket for her flight confirmation, she turned her back on life as she knew it before she changed her mind.

•••

Grant entered his code into the security pad, waited for validation, and then opened the front door of the primary residence on his estate. As the rest of his household slept, only late-night darkness greeted him.

He set his computer bag on the floor. The click of its brass feet against the marble tiles chilled him.

Just once, he'd like to make it home before Harper drifted into dreamland. But with the deals he had pending, it wouldn't be any night soon.

The ancient grandfather clock chimed midnight…as if he needed a reminder of the insane hours he worked. Loosening his tie and unhooking his cufflinks, he made his way in the dark through the foyer and up the staircase.

The stairs creaked, aching with the same added weight his head did from digesting all of the relevant title code changes that had been presented at his annual broker's conference.

He was so glad to be home. Not really wanting to, but knowing he should, he stopped in his study to sort through the mail.

No sense in hurrying to bed, he supposed, splitting the bundle into personal, business and social stacks. Harper wouldn't be up waiting for him. And who could blame her? No decent spouse continually came home as late as he did. He'd have to wait until morning to give her the art glass necklace he'd purchased for her at one of her favorite SoHo boutiques.

When his Movado read two-thirty, he struggled to keep his focus on a bid from his new builder. Rubbing his eyes, he tried to stave off sleep long enough to review the blueprints attached. He had to get to bed soon, or he'd never make it to the chamber breakfast by seven. He scrawled a quick note in the margins regarding the changes he wanted and headed for the master suite.

He undressed quietly so as not to wake Harper and climbed into bed.

The cold sheets startled him. He reached for her, but she wasn't there. He flipped the switch on his bedside lamp. As his eyes adjusted to the bright light, he saw her handwriting on a note propped against the base of the lamp.

He retrieved his glasses from his dressing table, opened the seal, and ran his fingers across his family's crest.

Not until he read her note a second and then a third time did he fully understand its contents. Placing the letter back onto the nightstand exactly where he'd found it, he slowly sat down on the edge of the bed, waiting for air to refill his lungs.

His body went numb. Never in his life had a feeling of such complete inadequacy overcome him. His emotions eluding him, he struggled for a plausible explanation. She'd shredded his heart into unrecognizable pieces.

CHAPTER TWO
(Playa del Rey, California; 6 months later)

HOLLYWOOD

Damn him, Harper fumed. What did Jake Benton not understand about a date? In her mind, it was fairly simple. You called a girl. Asked her out. Then, you either met her at the designated place or picked her up at the arranged time.

In Jake's case, he'd called her—two hours after he'd said he would, but he'd called, which was a huge improvement. In the not-so-distant past, he hadn't bothered. Now he called, but then failed to show seventy percent of the time. Tonight must not be one of her lucky thirty percent draws.

He always had some excuse. Logical, but an excuse. And every one, no matter how reasonable, was starting to piss her off.

Still feeling naked without her platinum-banded three-carat solitaire with surrounding two-carat baguettes, she stared at the tan lines making a perfect circle around her left ring finger.

The drops of condensation sliding down the sides of her glass mirrored the raw emotions spilling out of her heart. It was her. It must be something about her. Neither the man of her past nor the man she thought was her future was there when she needed him.

As tears threatened to come, she closed her eyes and forbid them to fall. No way would she cry by herself in the middle of The King of Whales.

Her new favorite bartender, Stokey Abrams, poured her another Crown and Diet. She twirled the straw around the circumference of the glass. Tall ones tonight. He hadn't even asked, probably why he was the best bartender in town. He was kind enough to just keep pouring.

She took the first gulp and shivered, a stout pucker forming across her mouth until she shook off the stiff concoction. At the K.O.W., there was no such thing as alcohol conservation.

"Hey, Stokey, bet you're wondering where our friend Jake is tonight," she said.

Harper caught the bartender's concerned look.

"I figured you'd tell me when you were ready," he said, wiping down the perfectly clean surface of the bar top, probably so he wouldn't have to see her disappointment yet again.

After spending quality time with Stokey during the last six months she'd been in Playa, she'd come to think fondly of him. Much of that quality time spent was at his bar, crying in her Crown, waiting on Jake.

She'd inadvertently become the queen of stand ups—not as in stand-up comedy, which was best in the clubs in Hermosa Beach—but as in stood up, dateless.

"Hell, Stokey, it's only a quarter till twelve. We still got another two hours before last call."

"That we do, my dear. You're not driving tonight, are you? I've never seen you drink more than two. You've got me a little worried, girl."

"Drive the whole two blocks to the inn? No, but thanks for caring."

"Then drink up, friend. The next one's on me."

She held up her glass to salute him and took another long pull. The liquor numbed her teeth and gums but didn't drown her heart. The muscles there still pumped pain.

Men. Damn them all. What was it about having a penis that entitled a man to screw her over—and not in the manner that felt good?

She'd left Grant, and she'd leave Jake too, before she even had him. She was tired of being a man's support stick and emotional punching bag. Giving up on them entirely might be her best option.

Grant had almost completely deflated her ego. He'd sucker punched her, and those bruises were still yellow. According to her divorce attorney, she wasn't mentally or emotionally ready for the final round of that fight, which meant she was horribly ill-prepared for a match-up with another heavy-weight heartbreaker.

She motioned for Stokey to hit her again and smiled graciously as he prepared her fourth serving from his liquid courage café.

Organic chocolate-covered strawberries used to be her elixir, but since she'd been in Hollywood, whiskey had replaced them.

Taking a swig from her glass, she recalled the night nine months ago when she'd met Jake. It was Valentine's Day, of all days. Typical Cantwell family style, she wasn't spending the day on a wonderfully romantic date with her husband. Instead, Grant was away sealing another huge business deal, and she was fulfilling her philanthropic duties as President of the Performing Arts Council that she and Grant funded. It was midway through their winter season, and they were hosting the sixties and seventies musical sensation The Sapphires.

Arranging glass bottles of designer cappuccinos, she'd checked the contract rider one last time before a limo delivered the vocal group hall of fame members from the hotel to the theatre. Her caterers were placing a meal on the banquet table in the green room—as specified in the rider's instructions, and load-in was just about complete. Sound check would begin as soon as the group was dropped off at the backstage door.

She'd heard the door open. And as soon as she'd turned to welcome the group to Briar Creek, the brisk February air rushed against her cheeks. Her body had quaked so unexpectedly, she'd almost toppled over the edges of her Louboutin spike-heeled booties. But it wasn't from the sudden drop in temperature. The last Sapphire who'd climbed out of the sleek luxury sedan looked like a demigod who only had eyes for her.

Once thinking love-at-first-sight was a phenomenon reserved for storytellers, she couldn't deny their instant attraction.

The youngest—and by ten years—of the three performers in the group, his muscular build and rugged youth defied his forty-one years. His piercing blue eyes matched the finest tropical oceans. His hair—a shorter, trendier version of Fabio's famous locks—fell in loose waves around his sun-kissed face. And his arresting persona emptied the theatre's scene shop of all its charm.

When he walked onto the stage, a whirlwind of energy followed him and trapped anyone within its reach. His presence demanded, and he received, undivided attention from all who stood in his midst.

Tonight, nine months later, Harper sat in the K.O.W., in Playa del Rey, California, separated from Grant, hooked on that same feeling that Jake produced in her every time they were together.

Hearing the door to the bar open, she turned her head, preparing herself for yet another Southern Cal hottie who wasn't her date.

But, miracles aside, Jake had made it. An hour before final call, while hoarding all charisma still left in the room, he blessed them with his presence.

His windswept waves of blond hair reflected the light of the blue neon whale that hung in the front window, giving him an ethereal glow as he rushed past the bouncer.

In artfully torn Armani jeans and a black leather jacket, he received an obscene amount of attention from the other female patrons in the bar. Harper didn't blame them. He had the same effect on her.

"There you are, missy."

Feeling his warm breath across her face while she finished off drink number four, she struggled to swallow the straight whiskey left in the bottom of her glass.

Jake slid up behind her and wrapped his strong arms around her back and shoulders. Placing a swift kiss on her cheek, he claimed the stool next to hers, rubbing his hands along her thigh.

"Sorry I'm a little late. You won't believe who I ran into in Hollywood. Then, with traffic, and showering off…"

Harper's mind glazed over. She used to ask whom he'd coincidently bumped into, but not anymore. She knew his routine, one of his character traits she'd never adjust to. He claimed it was A.D.D. She thought otherwise but hadn't finished her analysis.

Regardless, she'd sat alone half the night…again. If she was smart, she'd have given up an hour ago, at the latest, and already be asleep on her couch. But instead, she'd suffered through the added humiliation of being the only woman alone at the bar, prompting Stokey to serve his other patrons while also having to soothe her crushed spirits.

Despite her irritation, and considering the number of drinks she'd already consumed, she didn't have the energy or the appropriate vernacular to call Jake on his ridiculous behavior.

Taking a deep breath, forcing her sweet nature to the surface, she looked into his expectant eyes. "So, how was your day?"

"Great! God, I love being home and off the road. Got two whole weeks this time. What are we going to do?" He pinched her cheek.

Sometimes she took pride in the fact that she could always make nice with someone no matter how they treated her. Other times, she made herself sick with her candied-toned bullshit. Her friends didn't call her Golden Lips for nothing. She'd worked hard to earn and maintain the title.

Jake nudged up against her and tucked a piece of loose hair behind her ear.

"You look great tonight. I think you've lost a couple more pounds too! She'd a hottie, isn't she, Stokey?"

"Jake, what'll it be tonight?" Stokey asked, not hiding his irritation.

"How about a Black and Tan? And a compliment here to Harper for looking so hot."

Heat flushed Harper's cheeks.

Stokey removed a glass from the overhead rack and grabbed a bottle of Jaegermeister.

"She's hot every night, Jake. You better quit leaving her in here alone. I have to pay the guys around here to keep their hands off her. Hell, if I wasn't of another orientation, I'd take her myself."

Stokey winked at Harper before setting Jake's glass on the bar on top of a cocktail napkin with a cartoon of a well-endowed topless waitress.

Why did most of the great guys in her life have to be gay, Harper thought, blowing Stokey a kiss.

"Aw, Stokey, Harper can take care of herself. She's a big girl."

Pointing to the perfect breasts of the purple metallic maiden on his napkin, he laughed and whispered, "Not as big as these, but I'll help you with that. Have you thought any more about getting an enhancement? You know I think you'd look great with them, and remember what I said about the sensitivity thing. I'm telling you, you'd luuuvvv 'em."

"I know you'dlike 'em. But, I'm still thinking about it."

"That's my girl. Keep thinking."

Harper silently considered the breast enlargement issue, although she wasn't about to get a boob job just because a man wanted her to. That said, she wasn't opposed to the idea of plastic surgery. And she had read that following the augmentation many women reported that their nipples were more easily aroused, which could be fun. But she didn't need them to be more aroused, she simply needed someone to arouse them.

"May I ask what fragrance it is you're wearing, my dear?"

William, the K.O.W.'s pain in the ass schmoozer, asked while sidling up next to her. He put his head inches away from the side of her neck and inhaled with the dramatics of a Shakespearian player. "It compliments you beautifully."

"Jesus," Jake muttered. "Not this again."

Harper politely addressed William, as she always did when he was schnookered and unaware that he'd repeatedly used this line on her as well as most of the rest of the women in the bar. "How kind of you, William, but it's the same French perfume you asked me about last Friday night."

"Beat it, Will." Jake brushed William aside and rolled his eyes at Harper. "You know I can't stand that guy. Why don't you just ignore him?"

"C'mon, Jake. You think if I don't acknowledge him, he's just going to go away? It'd be nice, but I doubt it. Besides, I like his line."

"It's your decision, I guess."

"You're right. It is." She leaned in and kissed him on the nose. "But thanks for claiming me."

"That's what friends are for."

When they show up, she growled to herself, despite the smile she pressed on her lips.

And 'friends' my ass. None of her other friends touched her body like he did. They were definitely friends, with benefits.

"You haven't asked me about who I met today." He downed the rest of his Black and Tan and motioned for Stokey to refill his glass.

"I don't have to ask. You always tell me anyway," she said, knowing that little dig would go right over his head.

"You'll never believe it."

Probably not.

"I was sitting at Café Med on Sunset Strip with a friend of mine. I use her for various film projects. Drop dead gorgeous Asian gal. Anyway, just as we got our food, in walked an old agent of mine, Richard."

Harper guzzled down half the golden liquid left in her glass, needing the extra comfort to get through Jake's latest excuse.

"Richard proceeds to ask me about The Sapphires' gig and how it's going. Then, out of nowhere, he asked me if I was still into filmmaking. After I told him I was, he asked me if I had any projects ready to go."

He turned to her, touching her arm as if making sure she was all his for the telling.

"I told him that I'd recently found an investor, a friend of mine who was interested in getting into films and who loved my work—that would be you, Luv. Then, I fibbed a bit, of course, and told him we were ready to roll with our first feature."

"So now what?" She pressed him for details, anxious to move forward with their first feature film. She'd read the treatment and what was finished of his script and had been hooked from page one. The guy didn't know how to treat a woman, but he could write a helluva partial script.

"Well…the rest is up to us, hon. Richard has a distributor ready to buy as soon as we can get a reel or two done. I told him we'd have something great in no more than six months. That means we should really start filming next week while I'm off."

"Okay. Let's do it. Just tell me what you need me to do."

As many times as he'd scheduled to roll the film and then backed out, she'd never thought they'd get to this point. And yet she hadn't lost hope. She'd always wanted to be part of the movie business.

"Hey, Stokey, you think I could film a few scenes for our new movie here in the K.O.W.?" Jake asked and slapped his hand against the railing as if the idea were coming to him from divine providence.

"Jake, man, you asked me that about six months ago, and I said yeah then and hell yeah now. Are you finally ready?"

Harper saw excitement slowly building in Stokey's eyes. He'd told her, on one of the many nights she'd sat alone waiting for Jake, that his first love was acting. Bartending paid his bills while he pursued his Hollywood calling. He'd landed a couple of decent commercials—one for a pet food company and one for a Swiss bank—but that was it. He been anxiously awaiting the small typecast role Jake had promised him.

Yet despite Stokey's apparent enthusiasm, he still remained cautiously optimistic.

"Just let me know the date, and I'll get it arranged. You've actually got the script worked out now?"

Stokey looked at Harper as if seeking her confirmation of the status of the screenplay.

She wished she could say she'd seen a completed script, but she hadn't. She threw her hands up in the air signaling surrender.

"Almost, Stokey. Harper here has agreed to be my financial angel."

Jake played with her hair, winding the ends around each other.

"I just have a couple of scenes to rework, and it's action time."

"Sounds good. Keep me posted." Stokey nodded at Harper and flipped the towel he'd been twisting over his shoulder.

She swore she saw him raise his eyebrows as he backed away from them to wait on a new customer at the other end of the bar.

Jake got up from his stool and headed for the boys' room while she ordered another drink for both of them. "Put it on my tab, Stokey."

"No can do, sweets. You need to let Jake buy you a few. He can afford it. I don't think you should spoil him like you do. You deserve better."

She swayed on her barstool, definitely having exceeded her limit.

"You think Jake likes me, Stokey? You know, for more than a friend?"

The whiskey was definitely getting the better of her, otherwise she'd never have had the nerve to ask that question. A question she darn well knew the answer to. And it wasn't in her favor. She wasn't stupid. She knew when she was being used. Hell, after being Mrs. Grant Cantwell for ten years, she was a pro.

Before Stokey could answer, Jake returned from the bathroom.

Her world was moving at dizzying speeds, first supersonic, and then in slow motion. Circles of light were followed by long, never-ending spirals of darkness.

"You okay, or are you drunk?" Jake asked, his tone more than a little condescending.

"I'm okay, but I think I'd better go to the little girls' room." She stumbled slightly off and then around her stool, bumping into Jake before making her way slowly and cautiously across the bar.

Entering the bathroom, she looked into the large mirror hanging above the sink. Feeling like she was searching for her own ghost, she wiped away an imaginary mist on the mirror, trying to get a better view.

After becoming Mrs. Grant Cantwell, she'd lost sight of who she was without that label. She had no idea who she was looking at right now.

How was she supposed to start a life without Grant? For all his blatant disregard of her, she loved the man buried somewhere beneath the hard shell of the one he'd become during their marriage. Why wouldn't he let her in? Why did he care more about his work than about her?

She pulled a paper towel from the holder mounted on the wall and dampened it with cool water. Pressing it to her hot cheeks, she reveled in the coolness it sent throughout her whiskey-warmed body. Her heart rate slowed to a less nauseating rhythm.

She gave her lips a shot of shimmering gloss, spritzed on her favorite perfume and shook her cleavage back into proper position within the confines of her plunging neckline.

Willing and able to work what she had to get what she wanted, she pulled herself up tall. Although Jake definitely wasn't her ideal man, his non-consistent attention was better than none at all. Plus, all sound reasoning aside, she couldn't ignore their physical connection.

She walked back into the bar, teetering on her Versace platforms, and took her seat.

Jake whistled and licked his lips, the Black and Tans making him louder by the minute. Good thing it was almost last call. Both of them should call it a night.

"Come here, you."

He beckoned her with his finger like a child being chastised for being naughty.

He kissed her deeply, tantalizing what was left of her composure.

"I can't stand seeing those lips so perfectly drawn and untouched. Plus, when you lean toward me like that, I catch a glimpse of that fine cleavage. By the way, nice scent you're wearing. It compliments you well."

She playfully swatted at him and squeezed the inside of his thigh.

"I think we'd better be going before we both get ourselves into trouble," she said while digging around in her bag for her credit card.

"Stokey, my Luv, could I please have my tab?" she asked.

Jake kissed her again.

"I'm your only, Luv, and, your money is no good with Stokey. It should only be spent on me. You know how badly I want to be a kept man."

He threw his head back, laughing with unrestrained ease.

Stokey didn't hesitate before handing Jake a receipt for his signature.

"Jake, Harper, I thank you and good night."

Harper winked at Stokey and looped her arm through Jake's for the walk back to the inn.

"Night, Stokey. See you next Wednesday. We'll usher in Thanksgiving Eve together," Harper said, so glad she wouldn't be alone.

"No she won't, my man. I'm taking her on a real date that night."

"You are?" she asked, loving it when he surprised her. He often took her on adventures to parts of Hollywood she'd yet to experience. "Where are we going?"

"You'll see."

Jake opened the heavy wooden door of the tavern and ushered her out into the early morning air. Even in late November, Southern California weather was resplendent. A slight chill blew in with the Pacific mist nothing Jake's leather jacket around her shoulders couldn't withstand.

Huddled together, laughing the happy tunes of two well-polluted night owls, they stumbled their way to the inn at the end of the avenue. Reaching into her pocket, she pulled out her key to the front door, dangling it in front of him.

She'd been a guest of the bed and breakfast for the last six months. And since her arrival, Jake also frequently called it home.

Until certain that Los Angeles could comfortably be her new, primary residence, Harper planned to stay at the inn.

"Need some help with that?" Jake ventured, brushing his arm against her breasts as she struggled with the key.

Taking in an unexpected tug on her senses with his touch, she grabbed for the door handle as the night attendant buzzed them through. Pulling it open too fast, almost losing her balance, she turned her attention back to Jake, who caught her before she tumbled completely backwards.

"Coming in?" she asked.

"You know I…we…shouldn't. I'm trying to be a good boy and do the right thing for once. But, damn, you're looking hot in that shirt. Did I tell you that yet?"

"You did. Yes. But carry on."

She closed the door quietly behind them and headed toward the elevator leading to the main floor.

As soon as the door slid shut, he reached for her, burying his face against her chest.

"You smell so good."

He raised his eyes to hers.

"Why did you get me drunk tonight? You know how much I want you."

In an inebriated bliss, she hoped to lose herself deep inside the kisses he stole from her lips.

She couldn't deny it. They had a chemical flame that never disengaged from full throttle. The heat from their physical connection attempted to swallow them whole every time they were in the same room. So it had been on Valentine's Day when they met. And it had yet to be extinguished. Fires of desire raged inside each of them.

They reached the long, narrow hallway ending at her room, barely breathing freely of each other. Their hands explored the lengths of their bodies and searched for what lay beneath their clothes. Feeling Jake's hardness throb against her, she thanked Fate for being on her side of the fence.

She broke away from his hold long enough to unlock the door, her heart catching an unexpected thrill as he shoved the door closed with his foot, scooped her into his arms, and carried her to bed.

The darkness brought them freedom, but she couldn't remember who passed out first. Regardless, as the alcohol overtook them and beckoned them to sleep, their fires were left to kindle.

CHAPTER THREE
JUST A GIGOLO

Refreshed and raring to go, Harper dressed in a jogging suit and went down to the inn's breakfast room. Being as it was almost noon, she found herself alone…the other guests well into their days.

All that was left on the antique buffet were coffee and blueberry crumb cake. She poured herself a much-needed cup of Colombian, grabbed The Times from the stand in front of the fireplace and cut a sliver of cake. She was too famished to count the carbs and consoled her guilty conscience by promising to run off the extra grams in a little while.

She took her usual seat at the small table placed against the window looking at the wetlands out back of the inn. The autumn sun gleamed brightly, catching the tops of the sails of several boats leaving the marina that cut in behind the wetlands.

In the distance she could see the pristine stone walls of The J. Paul Getty Museum glistening in the midst of the Hollywood hills surrounding them. Further to the north, she could barely make out the letters that spelled HOLLYWOOD. The smog wouldn't totally burn off those puppies till mid afternoon, if at all.

Some days she pinched herself to make sure she was really here, so far away from the rural town of her past. She'd thought Briar Creek would always be her home and had looked forward to creating a family there with Grant.

She'd also thought that Jeffrey, her personal assistant, and Reggie, her decorator, would always be her best friends. Instead, she now lived across the country from all of them, looking for replacements.

She'd never dreamed of calling Southern California home. But as each day passed in Playa, she was less hesitant.

She topped off her coffee with the half and half from the small pitcher on the table and fought the urge to have another bite of crumb cake. Winning the battle against the cake, she pushed her plate back and opened the calendar section of the paper, perusing the arts and entertainment headlines.

"Well, good morning, sleepy head. Late night with our favorite entertainer?" Stacia, the inn's manager, greeted her.

"You could say that, Stace. Not only late, but rather inebriating as well. Sorry I missed breakfast again."

"No problem. I saved you a plate. I can heat it up now, if you'd like."

"You're the best, but I'll get it."

Harper followed Stacia into the kitchen.

"Why don't you eat in here with me while I get some reservations ready on the computer? No need for you to sit out there alone, unless you want to," Stacia said.

"You sure you don't mind? The company would be great."

"Of course, I don't mind, or I wouldn't have suggested it."

Harper placed the plate of spinach and feta quiche in the microwave and pulled out a stool at the large oak worktable that formed the center of the inn's kitchen.

Running this afternoon was no longer an option but a must after she settled in to devour the quiche.

The check-in desk and computer sat directly across from the table. Although she found this a bit odd at first, she'd changed her mind after Stacia had explained to her that the inn's proprietors designed it in this manner so guests were immediately charmed by the fabulous aromas greeting them.

Noticing the next time she'd paid her monthly rent how much more appealing signing her credit card slip was amidst the smell of chocolate chip cookies cooling on the baker's rack next to the oven, Harper considered the design a brilliant success.

"So what's on your agenda today?" Stacia asked as she sorted the mail.

"Not much. Since you were so kind to save me this plate of sin, I'll be pounding the pavement here in a bit. Then I have a bunch of reading to catch up on since Jake says we're going to start filming soon."

Stacia looked up from the mail pile, gave Harper a once-over, then went back to sorting.

"Oh, and get this...he's taking me on some surprise date next Wednesday night."

Harper rolled her eyes at the absurdity of that plan ever making it to fruition.

"I'm going for the big no-show. Care to bet?"

"A little feisty this morning, are we? Want to talk about it?" Stacia asked.

Harper pushed the last few bites of quiche around her plate.

The Inn at Playa del Rey had offered her so much more than a place to rest following her separation. The friendships she forged with the staff were priceless.

An only child, Harper had found sisters in the girls who served as hostesses as well as wonderful acquaintances in the cleaning and security staffs. Without their concern and companionship during this low point in her life, she was unsure where she'd be.

Stacia was a bulldog, though when she wanted information, so Harper threw her a bone.

"It's the damn 'friend' thing."

"What do you mean?"

"Well...one minute he's all over me and the next he's 'all-holier-than-though,' with the 'that's-what- friends-are-for' spiel. I just don't get it. What does he want from me?"

"You want my personal opinion? Or the one I should give you to make you feel better?"

"Spill it, Stace."

"I don't think he knows what he wants. Face it, Harper. You're the only non-boob job he's ever been interested in, not to mention the only one he's been with that has brains. He's probably confused."

Despite the seriousness of her predicament, Harper laughed.

"You're too available and way too frickin' sweet to that gigolo. You need to teach him a thing or two. Set your standards higher. Make him work for it."

"I don't know, Stace. I know what you mean, but I don't think he means to let me down. I think it's because no one in his life has ever not shit on him—including his parents. Since he was fourteen, he raised himself and his brother. He's been touring off and on Broadway, then Vegas, and with The Sapphires ever since. He's never had stability and has never committed to anyone."

"You can try, Harper. But I'm not so sure you can tame this beast. Just remember, I'm going to kill him if he craps on you much more, so you may want to warn him."

"I'll do that," Harper said, squeezing her friend's hands. "And thanks for listening."

"Anytime."

Harper washed off her empty plate and placed it in the dishwasher. She pushed in her stool and started for the kitchen door.

"Hey, wait a minute. Save me a trip later, and take your mail with you."

Stacia handed her a small envelope.

Harper wasn't expecting anything from either her attorney or Grant's. And she rarely heard from anyone else by mail.

She grabbed the envelope and turned it over to read the return address. Seeing Grant's handwriting in the upper left corner, she almost dropped it.

CHAPTER FOUR
SACRED GROUND

After opening Grant's note, Harper could think of nothing but escaping the confines of the inn. She craved the strong sea air, open space and absence of familiar faces.

Headset in place, she began to run.

Out here she felt free, even if for only the forty-five minute duration of her jog.

A warm misty haze swallowed her, leaving a residue on her sweat-dampened skin. Licking her lips, she tasted the combination of salt and sand mixing with the air. The tidal breeze whispered in her ears, beckoning her to pick up her pace.

No postcard had ever prepared her for the view on this path. Always one to extol the handy work of the gods and goddesses, she figured many of them resided at these coordinates. Her search for the great immortals' playground ended on this western edge of Playa.

After going west the final three blocks of Pacific Avenue, she stood on a small bridge. It connected Playa to a jetty leading out of the marina it protected and into the ocean.

The jetty not only connected her with the Pacific, it connected her with the threshold of her soul—a connection she thought had been severed.

With the first pounding of her shoes on the asphalt surface, her breath deepened, and her pulse slowed. Without willing her body to relax, nature simply took over and claimed her for its own. The soft ruby glow permeating her skin wasn't a reaction of melanin to sun or blood to muscles. It was a reaction originating inside the walls of her heart.

Her first glimpse of this panoramic jewel resulted from Jake's suggestion for a scenic jogging route. His directions had been easy…run toward the sunlight, following the wind's pull.

The land, once sacred Indian ground, had been purchased by a developing company in 1902 and christened Playa del Rey, meaning The King's Beach.

Harper understood and appreciated the sovereign solitude elicited by this narrow strip of land reaching out into the Pacific.

She cranked up the volume on her headset, setting her pace to the music as well as to the speed of the water vessels racing beside her. Gliding sails with names like The Muse and La Mer sliced rhythmically through the channel.

Passing the American flag that whipped in the crosswinds at the end of the jetty, the horizon was her finish line. The emerald fronds crowning the palms gently waved her on to victory.

Gulls circled, soaring on the restless air currents, hunting their next meal, diving mercilessly once they spotted a target. If she could escape their deluge of discarded shells and droppings, no problem was beyond her ability to resolve.

Silver fish, hooked by multi-national families while they picnicked on the rocks, flopped desperately in their white bucket prisons. Harper silently cheered for the lucky few that flipped themselves back into the ocean.

She watched life move around her. It wasn't a nauseating rush like watching the world fly by from a passenger window. It was as if she were alone in a cinema watching a film in slow motion, pressing pause and then rewind, viewing one still shot at a time because she had the power of the remote.

People were everywhere. Walking. Running. Biking. Roller-blading. Kissing. Touching. Reading alone or to each other. Tossing soggy tennis balls into the waves while their chocolate labs retrieved them and begged for one more throw. Pushing children, lucky to be cruising the coast in high-dollar, aerodynamic strollers.

Couples strolled hand in hand, planning their futures or healing their pasts. Golden-skinned elders walked side by side, lost in sweet recollections.

Taking time to rest her muscles and catch her breath, Harper stopped and sat on one of the large, flat rocks that tumbled into the ocean at the end of the strip.

The serenity of the view, however, didn't vanquish Grant's letter from her mind.

His request seemed simple. He wanted to know her plans for the holidays. Specifically, he'd ask that she spend them with him.

He reasoned that since they'd both probably be alone, they might as well share the time between Christmas and New Year's. He'd even offered to come her way if she didn't feel comfortable coming back to Briar Creek. She was to get back with him and let him know her thoughts.

He'd signed off with a salutation that had always irritated her— "As Always, Grant". What the hell was that supposed to mean? Perhaps, "As Always I can't seem to say anything remotely emotionally endearing."

Maybe she was being a little harsh. After all, she'd been dreading the holidays, certain they'd be even worse for Grant. And he was accurate that he had no one to spend them with. He never took time to make friends, and he had no family left. Now, he'd lost her too.

They'd always spent the holidays at the estate—the only place Grant had ever called home. It was the one-week of the year that she had him to herself. He closed the office and tried his best to enjoy their time together.

Retying her running shoes, she shook her head. Even at Christmas and New Year's, both magical occasions for her, Grant couldn't let go of his pretentious nature.

She'd accepted his lack of compassion toward her years ago and attributed it to his endless hours at the office. But after the last several holiday seasons, feeling more alone with him in the room than if he were gone, Harper was beginning to think that he'd arranged for a wall to be built between them for reasons she had yet to identify. All she knew definitively was that the wall became thicker with each of her social achievements.

Grant was plain lousy at living life. He didn't know how to express joy or love unless it was in the form of gifting some exquisite material object.

Standing up to stretch out her muscles before the jog back, she looked once more at her new surroundings. Grant would appreciate Hollywood with all of its power, wealth and success neatly packaged around the edges of the marina and nestled in the hills.

Lavish houseboats every color of a painter's palette and condominium units built in the likeness of Medici villas spanned this tiny beach town. Life shouted out that it should be lived with the sophisticated and adventurous glamour of Hollywood's Garbo and Dean.

The barren and desolate side of life also spoke to Harper along this stretch of coast. But it would be inaudible to Grant. A shelterless man she jogged by every day called a single bench on this sacred ground home. Covered in soiled, ragged clothing and dust, sun-bleached dreadlocks brushing the middle of his back, his dark eyes still registered hope.

Rested and ready for the final trek to the inn, Harper turned her back on the sea. Lifting her face to the sky above, sunlight filled her with warmth, entered her soul and relaxed her mind. The earth smiled on her, and she smiled back.

She'd discovered in a brochure at the inn that the Gabrielino Indians, also known as the Tongva (people of the earth) Indians, were the first to settle Playa. They were a people, like their name implied, who celebrated the earth as a sacred means to life.

Each day as she ran this stretch of sand, she understood why they settled here and why they celebrated the earth on the king's jetty.

The jetty did have magic, and it was sacred not only to the Gabrielino Indians, it had become sacred to her.

Her body arrived back at the inn way ahead of her mind. Despite her cool down routine, an emotional surge threatened to overwhelm her.

Her fingers hesitated over her iPhone's keypad before she summoned the courage to dial Grant's private line at the Cantwell estate.

CHAPTER FIVE
THE INVITATION

Grant moved the ring between his fingers so that the descending rays of the late autumn sun bounced off the precision-cut facets. He had surprised Harper with it on their fifth anniversary. He still marveled at his master jeweler's craftsmanship creating the piece from the design Grant had given him. He'd wanted it to be flawless, like Harper, and it was.

Five carats of dazzling brilliance—one for each year of their marriage—rested in his hand. The white ice it radiated speared his heart. The cold metal, once warmed by Harper's body heat, matched the chill that had descended over his life without her.

He'd been her husband for twelve years. And he couldn't begin to conceptualize that his time with her had run out.

Cantwell Realty Group had amassed a vast fortune throughout the United States. As the sole heir of the third generation, Grant may have been handed a silver platter, but he worked countless, exhausting hours to keep it polished. Nothing mattered to him more than leaving the closing table with both a satisfied buyer and a well-compensated seller. That philosophy ensured his firm that those same customers would come back the next time they bought or sold or needed an investor.

The first year of their marriage, he'd asked Harper to help him take the company to the next level of his strategic plan. He wanted to make The Cantwell Group a socially responsible, community-minded entity. With her extraordinary ability to show compassion toward people of all kinds, as well as her talent for event planning, she was the natural choice for executing his plan.

Using his name as a threshold and his checkbook as added leverage, he'd secured seats for her on the boards of the most elite philanthropic organizations in Briar Creek and throughout Tennessee.

For a small berg on the west edge of downtown Nashville, Briar Creek was on its way to becoming the artistic center of the region. As a Main Street, USA town, it was in the middle of a renaissance.

The socially coveted positions were those on the Performing Arts Council and Fine Arts Council, so he'd started her there. A few years of her exemplary work, and his investment began to show positive returns. As president of both councils, it was because of Harper that The Cantwell Group's SOLD signs hung outside each new gallery opening on the downtown square, and it was both their names that graced the golden benefactor list on each performing arts program.

He was proud of her accomplishments on The Cantwell Group's behalf. Evidently the community of Briar Creek was as well, because, to his knowledge, she was the only person to have won the Spirit of the Community Award two consecutive years.

He used to accompany her to all of the fundraising soirees she hosted. In fact, since they rarely had time to go out together otherwise, the events had become their weekly date nights.

He soon realized, however, that Harper always had the occasions more than under control, and with his schedule so full, he could easily skip attending. In general, the patrons seemed much more interested in talking to her than him, so he felt comfortable staying behind his checkbook. Eventually, she stopped telling him which functions she was attending.

The evenings she was out, he often thought of her while he worked late in his study. He wondered what she was wearing and how she'd fixed her hair but wouldn't know the answers till he read the next day's newspapers. By the time he arrived home, she would already be gone. And by the time he called it quits for the night, she would be asleep.

He reminded himself frequently how lucky he was to have such a beautiful and talented wife. She turned heads in every room she stepped into. And it wasn't just her gorgeous strawberry blonde hair and svelte figure. She had the quirkiest sense of style. She called it artsy. He called it a bit odd, but really fun. With her smile, warm spirit, and genuine interest in the people around her, she easily captured everyone's attention.

Harper understood his need to continually push the massive amounts of paper that passed through the firm. But when it was all too much and she seemed uneasy and disappointed by the demands of his schedule, he would make a note to buy her something special at one of the newest galleries or boutiques.

His gifts seemed to please her, and he wanted her to know how much he loved and appreciated her. Not being adept at finding the right words to express his feelings, he'd learned to show his consideration with the finer things he could buy.

Placing the ring back in the safe—recessed into the wall of his study behind his favorite Ansel Adams original—he took a deep breath and settled back into the leather depths of his office chair. He powered up his laptop and opened the file containing a purchase agreement he was drafting.

As he typed in the specifics for the purchase of the historic building Harper had chosen for the site of the new performing arts center, he felt sick to his stomach. She was to have been in charge of its renovation. The council was going ahead with the purchase but had yet to find a project chair to replace her. He wasn't the only one missing her.

The dull buzz of his private line forced him from his screen.

It was odd he'd receive a call this late on a Saturday afternoon. Even though he worked seven days a week, most of his business calls were done by noon on Saturdays. He then used what was left of the weekend to catch up on paperwork.

Stranger still was that the call was coming through on his private line. Few used this line or even had the number, which was why he'd disregarded the caller ID option. He made a mental note to have his secretary upgrade the service first thing Monday morning.

He picked up the phone from its cradle, a little annoyed that the caller was interrupting his thought flow.

"Grant speaking."

There was a brief silence, almost as if no one was on the other end of the connection.

"Hello, Grant," Harper said.

Grant lost all focus on anything except her, and he tightened his grip around the receiver. His Mont Blanc slipped from his grasp and hit the glass surface of his desk with a heavy clank.

She must have received his letter. This was probably the call that would end all hope for him. Suddenly feeling too weak and lost to continue to fight with her, he prayed she'd let him down easily.

"I got your letter this afternoon."

He knew it. This was it. Her final rejection.

"Glad it made it there."

Jesus. This was awkward. She was still his wife, and yet he couldn't express himself in more than five-word sentences. He had so much he wanted to say, but he didn't know how.

"About the holidays, Grant…"

"I know what you must be thinking, Harper, but I…"

"No," she interrupted, "you can't begin to know what I'm thinking. You haven't been able to for quite some time."

"Oh."

As he leaned back in his chair and prayed to the man upstairs to have mercy on him, his hands shook.

Tortured by her words and the silence that followed, he had no idea how to bridge the gap between them. He heard the hesitation in her tone. He felt his heart breaking all over again.

"I don't know why I'm offering this."

She paused again.

Grant placed his just-manicured index finger between his front teeth and bit down hard, hoping the pain would compensate for the shards of regret slicing through the walls of his heart.

"You are welcome to come to Playa for the holidays."

As his head spun trying to convince his mind that he'd heard her correctly, he nearly dropped the phone.

Christ! Maybe he still had a chance!

"Thank you, Harper. Thank you. You don't know how much this means to me. I didn't want to, couldn't stand to be here alone. I've missed having someone around…I've missed…"

"Grant, that's just…never mind."

He was grateful for her intrusion but wary of the resignation in her voice. Had he said something wrong? Luckily, he'd caught himself before he'd forced her to renege on her offer.

Jesus. He was really going to see her. It had been six months since she'd left. He wondered if she'd changed.

He had so much to tell her and only four weeks to figure out how.

"Grant, are you still there?"

"Yes, I'm here. When did you want me to come out? Anytime is fine. I'll arrange my schedule accordingly. Really, anytime would be great."

He hoped he didn't sound too eager. His heart was racing faster than his championship thoroughbreds.

"Okay. How about Wednesday, December 22? That will give you Thursday to adjust to the time change before Christmas Eve on Friday."

"Great. Sounds great."

Easy boy he chided himself.

"Call me with your flight plans, and I'll pick you up at LAX."

"Will do."

"Well, I'd best be going. I've got plans tonight."

His breath caught in his throat. The thought of her with another man was more than he could handle.

"Okay, I don't want to keep you," he said. "Thank you. Thank you, Harper."

"You're welcome. I'll see you soon. And please give my best to Jeffrey."

He thought he heard her voice crack and shake like his own.

"I will. Take care, Harper."

"You too."

The line went dead.

CHAPTER SIX
ANYBODY'S FOOL

What in the hell had she done?

Harper had attempted some fairly foolish things in her lifetime, but this one was the topper.

There was no way in Hades she could spend the holidays with Grant. First of all, there was the obvious fact that he was soon to be her ex-husband. Hell, she'd moved across the country to start a new life that did not include him. So why did she still care about him enough that she couldn't stand the thought of him being alone for the holidays?

And what about the awkward situation that left her in with Jake? What happened if he decided to show up for Christmas Eve, Christmas Day, New Year's Eve or New Year's Day? She knew better than to count on him for all four, but one or two was a distinct possibility.

The way her luck was running, Jake would probably be ready for more than his weird version of friendship by then. So what was she supposed to do with Grant, who was still, legally, her husband? Throw him a blanket and pillow for the couch while she went to her bedroom with Jake?

She nestled into the stack of pillows on her bed. After talking to Grant, her body was still coiled in bundles of twisted nerves.

She picked up the magazine on top of her "to-be-read" pile and buried herself in the business of movie making. There was nothing like the Hollywood Reporter, Entertainment Weekly and Screenwriter to keep her company on an otherwise lonely and long Saturday night. Hurray for Hollywood.

• • •

By Wednesday night, she was too rattled to do anything requiring finesse.

She grabbed a pair of well-worn jeans from her dresser drawer and pulled on a fitted tee. Good thing her clothes tightly hugged her body because she'd given up on a man providing comfort and fit.

What a mess. Jake would be here in as little as ten minutes to take her on a special date, and all she could think about was Grant and the feelings she still had for him.

He'd sounded absolutely miserable on the phone Saturday afternoon. She'd never heard him that unsure of himself.

She was used to his confident, all-business persona. Hearing his hesitancy tore her to bits. Since when did he feel anything?

When the phone in her room rang, she jumped.

"Harper, it's Stace. Looks like you lost the bet tonight, sweetheart. Jake just pulled in downstairs. He should be at check-in in a few."

"Surprise. Surprise. Thanks, Stace. Please send him to my room."

"You got it. Have a great time tonight."

"Thanks. I need it."

After extending her asinine holiday invitation to Grant, she craved the diversion Jake offered on her otherwise companionless night before Thanksgiving.

Normally, she'd be well into the process of preparing Thanksgiving dinner. Not this year. No Grant. No turkey.

Jake arrived at her room with a playful knock on the door before Harper barely had time to finish dressing, freshen her perfume and slide some gloss on her lips. What was it with musicians that they always had to be tapping out some idiosyncratic beat instead of using a normal, dignified thump?

When she opened the door, she couldn't see Jake behind the wall of calla lilies he carried. Not only did their fragrance overwhelm her senses, but Jake's kindness knocked her off her feet.

How did he know those were her favorite flowers? She didn't recall telling him.

She couldn't remember the last time she'd received flowers. Come to think of it, she wasn't sure Grant had ever given her something so wonderfully basic. He preferred Tiffany's.

It wasn't the flowers that got her most, but rather the thought behind them.

"Oh my goodness, Jake. How did you know how much I love these?"

She grabbed the bundle from his arms and rushed to get a vase from the kitchenette.

"These are wonderful. You've outdone yourself."

Harper swore she saw him blush. Every time she began to lose hope in him, he surprised her.

"Glad you like 'em. But Robert's the one that outdid himself on these."

"Ah ha. That's how you found out about my calla lily fixation. And that's why Robert is So Cal's premier florist. He remembers what his customers like. I should have known he would come to my rescue."

"Robert, as well as all of the rest of the gay men in LA, have been rescuing you since the day you arrived. I can't figure out why they're all so ga-ga over you. Actually, you'd think they'd be drooling over moi."

Jake swished his arms through the air with a saucy bravado and did his best to strike a queen's pose.

"You, my dear, have way too much testosterone for the gay man. You're just jealous."

"Yeah, that's it, Luv."

"Let me put these in some water and we can get going. By the way, where are we going?"

"That's for me to know, Luv, and you to find out."

He patted his hands against his pants to dry off the water from the ribbon-wrapped lily stems.

"After you, my dear."

He grabbed her fur poncho from the coat closet next to the door and ushered her to lead him out into the night.

"I take it our destination might be a wee bit chilly?"

"No questions."

He kissed her on the cheek and nudged her out the door.

• • •

"I'd like to propose a toast." Jake raised his glass and motioned for Harper to do the same.

"Ok. Let's hear it."

She lifted her wine glass to his. The reflection of the lighted palm trees in the marina's outdoor Italian bistro was a stunning special effect. Perfect for a Hollywood night.

She waited patiently as he cleared his throat, evidently choosing his words carefully. She couldn't remember him ever being speechless.

So far this evening, he'd blown all of her impressions of him to smithereens. First flowers, and not just any flowers. Her favorite. Then, a quiet, quaint dinner for two at the posh, Italian villa-style restaurant he knew she'd been dying to try. Now a toast that started with his inability to find the right words.

What had she done to deserve this? She wished she could pinpoint it. That way, she could make sure his actions continued along this line. She could get used to this type of treatment.

"To you, Harper, who never ceases to amaze me with your uncanny ways of knowing how to make me happy. You make me laugh. You make me think…"

"That's scary."

She couldn't let that one slide. He sure as hell wouldn't have.

Between laughs, he asked her to be still so he could continue.

"You make me look at the world in ways I never have before. And most of all, you're always there for me. I am more thankful this special holiday than I can ever remember—thankful I have you in my life. I hope you know how much you mean to me."

He clinked his glass against hers and finished his remarks with a well-composed smile. "To us."

'To us.' Now there was a scary thought. Intriguing, but scary. As much as she wanted to believe in the possibility of sharing a future with him, she knew a tomorrow with Jake Benton couldn't be guaranteed. In the meantime, she'd made up her mind to live for each night on its own merit. A guy like Jake contemplating anything beyond twelve hours from now was too unpredictable and usually too painful.

She toasted him and noticed a sparkle and depth to his eyes that she'd not seen before. Before she could formulate a motivation for his over-the-top behavior, he stopped the waiter and requested tiramisu with two forks and coffee for each of them.

"That sounds good, doesn't it?" he asked.

He must have noticed the look of bewilderment on her face.

"It sounds great."

Before she drove herself crazy with wishes of a long-term relationship that could never be with a man like Jake, she had to get to the bottom of his indulgence. He always discouraged her from having dessert, claiming she'd ruin her fitness progress by consuming the added sugar.

"What is up with you tonight?"

"What do you mean?"

He fiddled with his napkin.

"Well, don't take this the wrong way, because I'm beyond flattered and loving every minute of this, but you've kind of blown me away with thoughtfulness tonight. Is everything ok?"

"Everything's great."

His voice caught in his throat.

"Does something have to be wrong for me to spoil you?"

"No, not at all. You can spoil me rotten, but..."

She wasn't sure how to say what she was thinking.

"But what?"

Judging by the way he shifted in his chair, while continually raking his wind-ruffled hair with his fingers, he seemed to be getting more uncomfortable.

"But..."

Oh, what the hell, she'd just say it. Maybe it was the wine talking, but Jake needed to hear it.

"You usually don't spoil me at all. I mean, sometimes, like this week, I don't hear from you for days. And most of the time, you call or show up a couple of hours after you've promised. But not tonight, Luv. You're on it. I must say, I'm shocked."

He looked away for a moment, as if he were intently watching one of the yachts sailing out of the marina.

She fidgeted in her seat, waiting him out for a reply. She had all the time in the world and wasn't about to give up on seeing her question through to an answer. She wasn't good at playing games, and it was time he knew it. Spoiling her didn't jive with Jake's MO. She wanted an explanation for his deviance.

He suddenly turned back toward her and, like an unexpected gust of wind, grabbed her hand.

"I've got an idea. Let's get out of here."

"But what about the tiramisu? Don't even think I'm leaving without that slice of ecstasy. Plus, you haven't answered my question."

"Ecstasy it is then, a la mode with questions to be answered soon."

He asked the waiter to box the dessert and put their coffees in to-go cups.

"C'mon, Luv. I've got something to show you."

He slipped the valet a folded twenty and asked him to bring his Hummer.

Her poncho around her shoulders warmed her from the chill of the ocean breeze while they waited. But his actions tonight had left her warmer than she'd been in months. The heat he stirred in her was intense, and if she wasn't careful, she'd scrap the dignity she had left in favor of satiating her burning desires.

They drove in silence and parked in a lot reserved for members of the California Yacht Club.

"I didn't know you were a member here," she said as he opened the door and helped her out of the truck.

"There's a lot you don't know about me."

He grabbed the sack holding the tiramisu and coffees out of the Hummer's backseat.

"Touché."

He dug around in one of his jean pockets.

"There it is," he said, pulling out a small key. "I wasn't sure I had it on me. C'mon."

He took her hand and led her to the docks.

"I'm on Pier 57."

"What are you talking about?"

"It's been awhile since I've been out here, and I can't remember how far down my slip is. So help me look for Pier Number 57. That's the one we need."

"You have a boat?"

"Don't sound so surprised. Yes, I have a boat. I do live close to the ocean, after all. I just don't have anybody…I mean, I don't take the time to use it."

Harper didn't know what to say to that, so she kept on the lookout for Pier 57.

She'd never seen such huge yachts. Most of them were at least fifty-five footers, and many were sixty or better. Intermingled among them were sailboats of various sizes as well as a couple of catamarans. She'd always wanted to learn to sail but had never had the opportunity.

Speedboats were common in Tennessee, and she and Grant had one, although they'd never put it in the water. With Grant's schedule, and his preference for remaining indoors, boating wasn't on their must-do list. Like many of the big toys they had, it was simply a status symbol, another corporate write-off.

"There it is. I knew we were close."

Jake fit his key into the padlock and pushed the gate open. Locking it securely behind them, he took hold of her hand and led her down the pier.

About two thirds of the way to the end of the slip spaces, he stopped.

"My Luv, as Captain of The Slacker, I welcome you on board," he said with a grand sweep of his arms and a mocking bow.

Harper focused her gaze on the navy blue and white sailboat that bobbled in the water. She looked up at Jake and saw the hesitant but proud look in his eyes. He looked like a boy showing his mother a project he'd made in shop class, his pride mingled with a strong fear of rejection.

To catch her heart in her hands, she touched her chest.

As if hypnotized by the sound of the boat lightly rubbing against the dock, neither one of them spoke for several seconds.

"Well, do we want to gawk all night or should we take her out and see how she handles?" Jake asked, breaking the uneasy silence.

"Really? You'll take me sailing? Now? Tonight?"

"Of course, silly. Why do you think I brought you here? You're not afraid, are you?"

Despite the slight tease to his tone, she could tell he was seriously concerned about her seaworthiness.

"No, I'm not afraid. I've never been seasick."

"But have you been out on the open ocean?" he asked, raising his eyebrows.

"No, I haven't. Just lakes. I'd sure like to try though."

"Okay then. Shoes off."

He handed her the tiramisu bag, pulled his loafers from his feet, jumped over the railing, then reached back to help her.

"Careful, Luv. I'm not ready to lose you or the tiramisu."

"Nice. We'll see who throws who overboard first."

She took his hand and followed him onto the teak decking of The Slacker.

Jake removed the coffees from their holder and put them on top of a small wet bar on the deck and tucked the tiramisu inside a built-in icebox under the bar. He opened the latched door to the cabin below and stepped down into the darkness.

"Wait just a minute until I get a lantern turned on, and I'll help you down."

Harper waited on the deck, glad Jake had grabbed her poncho from the back seat of the Hummer. The chills that covered her body weren't from the breeze. They originated from the anticipation of what the night held for her.

Jake shined an old lantern along the steep stairs that led into the cabin and called for her to join him below.

Tentatively descending the steps, she found herself chest to chest against him. He pulled her close and kissed her with an intensity that took her for a wild roller coaster ride—first upside down and then around one helluva corkscrew.

"I'm glad you're here." He kissed her again. "You're the only person…the only woman who's been on board The Slacker. She's honored and so is her Captain."

"I see. You don't bring your girlfr…"

As soon as she'd started to spit it out, she wished she could have sucked it back in.

The girlfriend concept was probably listed as a phobia in his medical records.

"Something like that," Jake said, shifting away from her, but then leaning back into her and kissing her on the forehead.

"Let's get this thing out to sea. What do you say?"

"Sure. Just tell me what to do," she said, willing to do just about anything to divert attention away from her racing mouth.

"Why don't you go back up on deck and have a seat. I should be able to motor her out of the marina."

Harper climbed back up the stairs. She swore she felt his eyes boring into her backside. When she turned around to follow up on her suspicion, he had a frozen, stupefied look on his face.

"Jake, is everything all right?"

"Oh, yeah, just a little preoccupied. I'm on it."

Too bad he wasn't on her, she thought. His willingness to let her into this part of his world made him even more irresistible. She could get used to sharing this kind of quality time with him.

Harper settled into the thick navy cushions that covered the bench seating surrounding the upper deck. After taking a swig of coffee and placing the cup in a recessed holder, she prayed to whichever gods and goddesses were watching over her tonight that she'd never wake up from this fantasy.

She watched Jake as he adeptly made his way around the deck. He adjusted various lines and managed the steering device with the expertise of a man who had regularly been at the helm. He was relaxed in a way she'd never seen. She had a feeling she was getting a glimpse of the real man behind the glare of spotlights. And she liked what she saw.

Why he didn't show more of this attractive, unassuming manner frustrated her. His normal, high-strung, 'I'm-all-about-me' mode was the reason there was no Mrs. Benton. If only he would be this guy and not the "superstar" version on a daily basis, maybe she would lower her heart guards and warm to the possibility of sharing some kind of a future with him.

It wasn't long before they were cruising the marina causeway with nothing but The Slacker separating them from heaven, the ocean beneath them and the star-filled sky above.

A full white moon illuminated the water and danced off the Pacific's night-blackened mirror.

"Pretty spectacular, huh?"

Jake stood at the wheel, resting one leg against her back as she faced the vast expanse of ocean ahead of them.

"God, Jake, spectacular doesn't begin to cover it. You're showing me a piece of heaven on earth. I really don't know how to describe what I'm feeling."

"I know what you mean. Part of me comes alive out here like it never does anywhere else. I don't know how to explain it either. It's like I'm free. Free to be me. I wish I had more time to do this."

Harper knew that if she wanted to keep him willing to open up to her, then she had to tread carefully. There was so much she wanted to know and share with him. Starting the process now was at once both exhilarating and frightening. The more she knew, the more attached she would be, and she just couldn't shake the feeling that the result of that could only mean heartbreak.

Momentarily distracted by what looked to be millions of diminutive silver fish wildly surfacing over one another in the wake of The Slacker's motor, she got up on her knees and leaned over the stern to get a better view.

In the light of the moon, the fish looked like tiny, silver torpedoes cutting and darting through the churning waters, which had a green phosphorescent glow, at times replaced by a fiery, orange-red.

"It's a red tide tonight."

Jake slipped his hand across her shoulders, and they watched the majestic dance in the water beneath them.

"The perfect night to sail."

"What's a red tide?" Harper asked.

"Ready for a science lesson?"

"Shoot."

"In certain conditions, the phytoplankton populations reach a growth explosion, which is called a bloom. You are witnessing one of these blooms. The water is so thick with them that it takes on luminescent colors. Normally, in Southern California, November is late for this phenomenon. It usually occurs in the spring, summer or early fall."

"Mmm. Why all the fish? Are they feeding off the plankton?"

"Probably. I guess we're seeing it now because the ocean has been unusually warm and calm, which I think is a favorable condition for a bloom."

"Very interesting. Thank you, Professor Benton."

"Anytime. You think it would be inappropriate for the prof to kiss his student?"

"Not if it's consensual, and she's of legal age."

Jake turned her head away from the red tide and with a sinfully erotic kiss, shifted the currents swirling inside her. She drowned in his every pleasure.

"Let me get this sail popped, and then we're free for the night. You didn't have any other plans, did you?"

He knew better. And if she did, they were now canceled. She'd give anything to be all his for just one night.

Maybe on the ocean, without anyone in sight besides her, he'd finally give her his heart along with his body.

"Looks like I'm your captive," she said, sitting back along the starboard side of the boat and watching as he trimmed the motor and prepared the sails.

After a few minutes, the sails burst forth with a loud "pop" and caught the wind.

"You weren't kidding when you said pop, huh?"

"No, Ma'am."

Jake laughed.

"Now, where were we?"

He moved onto the bench seat where she sat and laid her down, covering her body with his own. He settled on top of her, resting his weight on his arms.

All she could see were the hottest stars in the sky and Jake's movie star handsome face, half-lit by the white chrome moon. As his groin pressed hard against her, her body moistened, hoping to welcome Jake into its inner harbors. She'd never wanted anything more.

Her heart raced with the rhythm of the water as it separated to accommodate their vessel.

As Jake's intense gaze searched hers, he pushed a few loose strands of hair from her cheek. It was almost as if he were silently seeking her permission. All he had to do was ask, and he could have whatever he wanted from her.

Trying to capture the moment in her soul for eternity, she closed her eyes but was awakened by what she thought was ocean spray landing next to her lips. When she opened her eyes and reached her hand up to wipe the wetness away, she realized it was Jake's tears that were dampening her skin, not the Pacific. She was overcome by emotion.

She'd never seen a man cry, and seeing Jake share his emotions so freely made her feel even more distant from Grant. Grant sure as hell would never have given in to what he perceived as one of mankind's greatest weaknesses. She'd tried so hard to have a close connection with him, but he'd refused to allow her to get so much as a glimpse of what caused him pain and made him human.

Jake moved his thumb across her lips and soaked up the tears.

"I'm so sorry, Harper."

"For what? It's ok. I'm here. It's just you and me. What's wrong? Tell me."

"I can't do this to you. I can't make love to you no matter how much I want to."

"Why? You've got to know how much I want you, and how much I want you to love me. I want to share that kind of connection with you. In whatever capacity you can give me. I'm not asking for tomorrow, or the day after that. Just tonight."

"That's just it, Harper. I don't think I can keep giving you one night here and there. I'm afraid that once I love you, I won't be able to let go. And I'm no good at relationships. I can't risk hurting you like that."

She wound her fingers through his soft locks of hair as they fell around her face. She stayed quiet, giving him time to get all of his feelings out into the open night air. Not wanting to close the opening between them by saying too much, she simply listened.

"I've never made love to a woman, Harper."

When she started to speak, he put his fingers gently across her mouth.

"No, I never have. I've had sex with too many to count, but I've never loved one of them enough that I couldn't get up and leave in the morning without feeling a thing."

He traced his index finger over the apple of her throat and down the rest of her neck.

"You're different. I feel things for you that, frankly, scare the hell out of me. I'm just not ready for any type of commitment. Hell," he said, raking his fingers through his hair like he did when he was uncomfortable. "I'm not sure I ever will be. It's just not in me."

"Oh," she managed to whisper, feeling as if she were suffocating on account of his brutal honesty.

~ 46 ~

"Yeah, oh. Guess I killed the mood, huh?"

He lifted himself off of her and pulled her up on the seat next to him. He rummaged in a storage bin under the deck boards at their feet and found a blanket. Wrapping the damp, musty wool around them, he held her between his firm arms.

"I'm so sorry."

"Me too."

She rested her head on his shoulder and stared out into the ocean.

After a few minutes of silence, he pointed toward the horizon. "Do you see 'em?"

"Yes, I do."

She sighed as they watched two dolphins arch up out of the water and disappear once more into the dark depths. "They're always in perfect unison, aren't they?"

"That they are."

He turned her to face him, and this time he wiped the tears that were falling from her eyes.

"I do think I might love you, Harper. I just need time to figure out what that means in my life."

Harper had no idea what that meant in her life either.

Jake opened the mini-refrigerator and pulled out the carryout bag. "Tiramisu?"

She nodded. When in doubt, eat tiramisu.

He filled the fork with the sweet confection and fed her, letting his tongue flicker across the remnants on her lips.

CHAPTER SEVEN
PUT A RING ON IT

Harper tossed and turned in her bed. After the tumultuous evening with Jake, she couldn't succumb to sleep. Her mind refused to shut off the pounding thoughts of the emotional Sit-and-Spin defining her life.

The yo-yo string Jake kept bouncing her on was starting to wear thin. As much as she wanted to believe him when he said he thought he loved her, she was terrified he'd decide he couldn't act on that love. She couldn't handle another man unable to show her his feelings.

Finally giving up on sleep, she turned on the bedside lamp. Her eyes caught the Tiffany blue of the small suede jewelry pouch she kept on the nightstand. With hesitant fingers, she pulled the pouch by its drawstrings to her bed and loosened the knot.

What the hell? Why not torture herself a little more.

As her fingers slid into the folds of the pouch and over the cold platinum bands, she sucked in a deep breath. Her wedding set. She'd treasured it over the years, as she did now, not for its grandeur, but for the thought the jeweler had told her that Grant put into designing it. Grant had never told her how hard he'd worked on it or described the diligence he'd used picking out each stone. He never shared those kind of intimate details with her.

The light from the lamp sharply ricocheted off the polished surface of the center stone. Small twinkles of colored prisms jumped from the surrounding baguettes. The value of the karat weight she held in her hand would support an entire village in many parts of the world. And that's probably what she'd do with it. She'd sell it and donate the proceeds to one of the international aid groups she often contributed to.

To his credit, Grant had never been closefisted. In matters of money, he was beyond generous. He had always provided well for her as well as numerous causes around the world. But his heart was sealed. When it came to sharing his emotions, he was The Grinch.

She gently pushed the bands over her ring finger and into the smooth recesses still marking the spot. The feel of the metal settling back into her skin echoed the presence Grant still held in her heart. She couldn't forget him. No matter how hard she tried to move on, he, like the ring he'd designed for her, was holding onto his claim.

She hadn't healed from his decade plus of dismissing her emotional needs. She'd loved him with everything in her. And because of that, the harder she tried to block his connection to her heart, the more she felt his resonance there.

She wanted a man who showed his love for her every day, not just when it was convenient or desirable for his own needs. She'd walked away from Grant's superficial, material comforts, tired of not having him to share them with.

The recognition that Grant had irreparably stifled her sense of self made her shudder. She reached for the quilt on the end of the bed and pulled it up and under her chin.

If she could find her soul, she desperately wanted to nourish it. But more than anything, she feared that the warmth of an intimate connection was beyond her grasp. How could someone else love her when she wasn't sure how to love herself?

Jake could actually be a step backward. She wasn't dismissing how far he'd come tonight. Maybe he had begun construction on the bridge that could span his normal, noncommittal love 'em-and-leave 'em with a strong, steady relationship. And it wasn't as if she wanted to become the first Mrs. Jake Benton. She wasn't even sure she truly liked the guy, let alone would marry someone like him.

Besides, she had serious doubts he would ever make that title available.

Damn though if she could deny how strong she physically reacted to him. She couldn't quiet the restless need he stirred in her body any more than she could silence the warnings he set off in her head.

Grant had never caused the dizzying desire that Jake brought to life inside her. But her head told her heart that there'd be rough roads ahead under Jake's spell.

A relationship with Jake, justified only by her need to be passionately desired as a woman, was far, far away from the emotional connection she craved. But could she fulfill her physical desires and then wait for the crapshoot of a chance that he'd ever want more than that?

She fluffed and re-fluffed her pillow and stuffed it once more behind her overactive head. No sense dodging the issue. Could she have great sex with Jake, preferably on a regular basis, and be okay with nothing more ever developing between them? That was the question she had to answer.

His ardent arousal on the boat was inescapable evidence he wanted her as much as she wanted him. But she feared that, even though he claimed otherwise, he was reacting to nothing more than their animal-like attraction. Shouldn't she be running, not walking, the opposite way?

She supposed though that she should be counting her blessings that such a white-hot desire existed between them. Grant rarely expressed such a proclivity. 'Making love to his wife' wasn't one of the items on the consent agendas he routinely emailed to the over-tasked notes app on his iPhone. And even if it were, by the time he got home and wrapped up the additional work he did in his study each evening, he was out cold.

On the rare occasions when he did allow time, it was wham-bam, thank you ma'am. He had the urges, like any normal man, but as with the rest of his life, the action was devoid of all tenderness. None of Harper's joys or pleasures were ever taken into account. She was the only appointment he always failed to prepare for, research or analyze.

As the pain of her rejection over the course of their marriage surfaced, tears tumbled down her cheeks.

She grabbed a tissue and blew hard. And then another. And another. Until she started to feel very Meg Ryan in the scene where Harry met Sally in a totally new and almost devastating way.

Tired of feeling sorry for herself, she threw back the covers and shoved her feet into her slippers. Glancing at the clock, she couldn't believe another sleepless night was on her. It was two A.M., and she was still wide awake.

She grabbed the canister of ground coffee Stacia kept filled for her and started a fresh pot. The rich aroma, as well as the dribbling sound of it brewing, gave her at least a partial sense of tranquility.

Tapping the calendar app on her phone, she opened up the full view of each of the next few weeks, panicking when she realized Grant would arrive in less than a month—twenty-eight days to be exact. Turning back to today's date, she sighed. Today was her first Thanksgiving without Grant.

To add to her misery, she would be spending the day alone.

Jake was to fly out in just a few hours for The Sapphires' Christmas Tour kick-off. According to the schedule he'd given her, she was due to drive him to the airport in three hours.

After that, the lines on her calendar pages were devoid of electronic ink. Glancing at the rest of this holiday weekend again, in the unlikely event she'd missed something, she was once more reminded of all the blank spaces.

Hell. She didn't need to use her calendar at all. No use making herself miserable every morning with the emptiness of her life neatly glaring on screen.

She poured herself a mug of the dark Columbian blend The Inn favored and curled up on the sofa. Just as she reached for the television remote, a knock at her door nearly caused her to dump the hot coffee into her lap.

Who on earth could that be? And how did he or she get past the night guard at two thirty in the morning?

Maybe Stacia was in early for the holiday. Normally she didn't arrive until around six, but the place was full for the weekend, so perhaps she'd changed her schedule.

Harper wrapped her robe around her, smoothed down her bed-head and went to the door.

Looking through the peephole, she couldn't believe it. Jake. He stood there, evidently not long out of the shower, judging by the wet imprints his long locks had left on his shirt. His arms were full, and he wore a grin that didn't stop.

She unfastened the deadbolt and opened the door.

"Happy Thanksgiving, Luv."

As she stood in the doorframe, momentarily unable to function, he moved past her.

Gulping in a much-needed bundle of air, she closed the door and turned around to face him.

"Happy Thanksgiving to you. I was supposed to be at your place at five, right?"

"Yep. But now you don't have to."

He hurried into the kitchen to unload the packages he was having trouble balancing.

"Give me a hand with this, would ya?"

"What's all that?"

"It's our Thanksgiving meal. Not quite a turkey and all the fixings, but this will have to do. Figured since I'd miss sharing dinner with you, at least I'd make up for it at breakfast."

She helped him empty the bags onto the counter. He'd brought steaming cups of home-brewed Starbucks Breakfast Blend, fixed like they both drank it with half-and-half, raw sugar and a generous sprinkle of cinnamon. The I.H.O.P. sack held ham, bacon and cheese omelets with salsa on the side, along with one piece of wheat toast for each.

She smiled. He knew her better than she thought. He'd brought just what she would have ordered. 'Course she'd shared more meals with him in the last six months than she'd probably had with Grant the last few years of their married life, so he really didn't have an excuse for not knowing her culinary pleasures.

She reached into the bag to pull out napkins and plastic utensils when Jake grabbed her hand.

When Harper realized what he was reacting to, she couldn't swallow or speak. Pulling back her hand in a rush, she felt heat flood her cheeks.

"What the hell is that?" he stammered, dropping the fork she'd handed him onto the floor.

"Oh. Well..."

She struggled to remove her wedding bands from her finger.

Funny how moments before they had slid on with ease. Now, she could barely drag them across her knuckles.

"I'm sorry, Jake. It's just...well...you know...with Thanksgiving and everything..."

She brushed past him in a flustered blur and hurried to her bedroom, where she shoved the bands back into the pouch on her nightstand.

"What does Thanksgiving have to do with you putting that thing back on?" he asked in a way that didn't come close to hiding his contempt.

"It's silly really. Don't worry about it. It's nothing."

"Oh, c'mon, Harper, you don't expect me to buy that line of shit, do you? This is me you're talking to."

He picked up the fork and pitched it toward the wastebasket, but missed.

"I was just reminiscing. Okay? This is the first Thanksgiving I've been without Grant. Until you knocked on my door, I thought I'd be alone most of the day, other than to take you to LAX. Give me a break, would ya?"

She spun around and reached for the fork to throw it into the trash. It was her turn to be pissed. How dare he question her actions. He had no claim to her.

Jake blew his hands back through his damp hair. Placing his hands on her shoulders, he turned her toward him and tried to get her to meet his gaze.

"I'm sorry, Harper. You're right. I have no reason to be angry with you. Your business with Grant is simply that—your business." He placed his hand underneath her chin and gently lifted it up. "Okay, baby? I'm sorry."

Harper removed his hand, took her breakfast off the counter and went into the sitting room. Whistling what sounded like 'Zip-a-Dee-Doo-Dah,' Jake followed close behind her.

As she tried to get comfortable on the sofa without annihilating the cushions with her salsa cup, she flipped on the television. Better to have the diversion of CNN than more time to discuss Grant. She wasn't about to hash out her unresolved feelings for him with Jake. Besides, Jake didn't have anywhere close to the attention span that conversation would require. And his ego was way too big to hear her out anyway.

"So what are you up to today?" Jake asked, stuffing a hearty bite of omelet into his mouth, followed by a long chug of coffee.

"Nothing that I know of except taking you to the airport. Other than that thrill, I'll probably take a run to the jetty and spend the rest of the day cuddled in front of the tube or catching up on some reading."

"Better than hanging out in overcrowded airports and lonely hotel rooms." He finished off his omelet and started on the rest of hers. "I'm tired of life on the road."

"Yeah, it's hell being a celebrity," Harper said and rolled her eyes in case he missed the sarcasm in her voice.

"It is, Luv. You don't understand. For the next month, I'll see nothing but airports, limousines and hotel suites. There's no time to learn the name of one town before I'm on my way to the next. It's such a nomadic existence. I just want to settle down and try a normal life." He moved the last bite of toast through the grease on his plate. "The gigs used to be fun. Not anymore."

His candid remarks surprised her. From the day she'd met him till now, sitting on the couch next to him, she still felt starstruck around him. And she'd grown accustomed to watching him revel in the attention. He was the consummate performer. Always on stage, whether or not one existed. The lifestyle had to be second nature to him. Besides his being a member of The Sapphires, his parents were in the business too. The world of entertainment had consumed his childhood, his adolescence and adulthood, without any time for lapses or alternative lifestyles.

"So how much longer do you intend on staying with The Sapphires?"

She didn't want to push him, but it would be so much easier to get to know him if she didn't have to cram it all into two-week-or-less intervals.

"I don't know, Luv. But not much longer. I'm ready for a break. I'd also like to have somewhat of a family before I'm too old."

"And what exactly is 'somewhat of a family'?"

"Well, you know, maybe a dog or a goldfish. That sort of thing."

He settled deep into the sofa as if he wished it would swallow him whole.

She couldn't suppress a giggle. He was definitely squirming, and she loved the front row view.

"Sounds like a good plan. I hear goldfish make great pets."

He pulled her toward him and started to undo the belt of her robe.
She took a sharp breath and waited.

He pushed the brushed cotton fabric away from her chest and shoulders and ran his hands over her breasts. Her nipples puckered in response to his tease.

"If we're not careful, you're going to miss your flight."

"I'll take my chances."

He ran his hot breath along the side of her neck and nipped at her exposed flesh with his teeth, tempting her further.

"But I still have to shower and dress."

"Better yet." He stopped speaking long enough to roll his tongue across her taught nipples. "How about if I help you?"

"That would be nice. But your hair's still wet from your last shower."

As he lay on top of her and rubbed his hardening length against her, she felt her body open wide to his arousal. He drew his hands down her stomach and slipped them inside her panties.

"I think you're rather wet too."

"Better take that shower then."

She closed her mouth around his and pulled at his tongue with her teeth. She ran her hands along the throbbing bulge in his pants. "C'mon, before we miss your flight."

She wiggled out from underneath him and tried to move up off of the sofa to make her way to the shower. She gently pushed him upright and drew her robe back around her to banish the chills that raced up her skin.

"Who cares about the flight." He lifted himself the rest of the way off of her, swept her up into his arms, and carried her into the bathroom.

As much as she wanted him, Harper couldn't' shake what he'd told her the night before. He'd probably never commit to her.

"Are you sure about this?" she asked.

"I'm sure how much I want you, Harper. And I'm sure that there's no one else I've ever wanted more." He looked deep into her eyes and rested his head against hers.

"I do love you. I just wish I knew what to do about it," he said, running his hands underneath the edges of her robe.

"I'll show you a few things." She wiggled out of his arms and unzipped his jeans.

"Only a few?" he asked.

"Just a few. Not the whole package until you figure out what you're going to do about me."

She released the belt on her robe and let the thick cloth fall off her shoulders.

Jake slipped the soft edges over the curves of her body and finally let it fall to the tiled floor. "Fair enough. Let's see what my limits are."

• • •

An hour-and-a-half later, Harper stood at Southwest Airlines' LAX curbside check-in while Jake got his luggage out of the back of the Hummer. He slammed shut the back door and cradled her face between his hands.

"Happy Thanksgiving, Sweetheart. You're more blessing than I've ever deserved." He kissed her softly on the lips. "Keep your phone on. I'll see you for Christmas."

"Be safe, Jake. Call me when you get in tonight."

Try as she might, she couldn't get the ball out of the pit of her stomach. It was chained there with the weight of the world on top of it.

She wanted to be able to trust his feelings for her. They were intensifying beyond occasional companionship and recreation. But his past behavior demanded that she not count on him.

Leaving him at the airport felt like leaving their future behind before it had even begun. Despite the number of times she'd taxied him to departure terminals, today felt like delivering him to infinity without a return flight. Sure, she'd see him at Christmas. And Grant too.

CHAPTER EIGHT
THANKSGIVING SUSHI

Pulling back into The Inn's parking garage upon her return from LAX, Harper was surprised to see Stokey maneuvering his black Infiniti toward the gate that served as both the entrance and exit. She pulled the Hummer over as far as she could to give him more room.

"Damn, girlfriend, tell Stacia she needs to do something about this parking lot. I don't know how the hell you're going to squeeze that beast into one of these size two spaces."

Harper couldn't help but laugh, even though she didn't feel like it.

All the way back to Playa, she was stuck on the fact she'd be spending her first major holiday without Grant, alone. As if she could forget and needed the play-by-play. She'd be jogging alone. Watching movies alone. And eating alone.

Yeah, she got it. Alone. Alone. Alone.

"Hello? Hello? Flaming gay man calling a soon-to-be-single goddess." Stokey's hellos tumbled among the alones echoing in her mind.

"Sorry. You were saying?"

"Doesn't matter what I was about to say. Are you okay, dear? To be frank, you look rather horrid."

"I feel horrid. It's my first Thanksgiving without Grant. And I just took Jake to the airport for the start of The Sapphire's Christmas tour. So much for company."

"Hell, sweetheart, I'd be celebrating Jake's departure."

"Are you ever going to tell me what it is about Jake that you don't like?" Harper was getting testy over Stokey's frequent but, as of yet, unexplained putdowns.

"Maybe we could talk about it over some sushi and a whole lotta sake." He winked. "What do you say, sweetie? Not exactly turkey and all the trimmings, but a white meat none-the-less."

"With you and Glen?" She couldn't imagine Stokey and his life partner wanting her butting in.

"No, no. Glen is working this evening, so I'm alone as well. In fact, I just popped over here to see if Stacia would be my date. But I'd be thrilled to make it a threesome." He wiggled his brows in wicked glee.

"You're one sick puppy. But I'm honored to be included. I'm a sushi virgin, though. Hope that doesn't change your mind."

"Oh, joy! I love virgins! Be ready around four. Traffic to West Hollywood should be light, and Happy Hour starts at five. The cheaper the sake, the happier we'll be."

"Thank you, Stokey. Your invitation means a lot to me." She met his eyes and registered a flash of concern.

"Don't mention it. Ciao, darling." He kissed the air between them and pulled away.

• • •

Harper's phone rang shortly before four, a welcome interruption. She'd spent most of the holiday feeling more alone than a prisoner in solitary confinement. Not even the jetty had another soul on it. Between Jake's surprise breakfast and dinner, the world had abandoned her.

She'd been lonely in her marriage, but she'd never imagined she could be even more so without it.

Today had been a potent reminder that she'd given up what little companionship she'd had. And for what? Until Stokey's offer, the prospects hadn't looked real comforting.

"C'mon, Harper. The itamae awaits us," Stacia babbled on the other end of the line. It sounded as if she'd already indulged in a glass of something besides water.

"Who's waiting for us?" Harper asked.

"The itamae, Sushi Virgin. That would be the sushi chef."

"Great. Instead of carving a turkey tonight, you and Stokey will have this Tennessee girl spearing raw fish."

"You're not going to spear any fish. Let's hope that's not what you do with your chopsticks."

"Chopsticks? I have to use chopsticks?"

"Wow! This going to be an adventure! Woohoo, cowgirl!"

"We'll just see if I ever get invited again," Harper said, seriously doubting it.

"Don't worry, you will, if only because your lack of finesse is bound to require an encore. Talk about quality entertainment. You ready? Stokey just called and will be in the parking lot in a few minutes."

"I'll be right down."

Harper placed the phone in its cradle. She shut down her laptop, dog-eared the article she'd been reading in the Hollywood Reporter and grabbed her handbag.

She'd never gone out to dinner for Thanksgiving. The thrill wasn't in the sushi. It was all in going out on the town. Hollywood and Thanksgiving were an unexpected combination. Sushi and Thanksgiving were in another lifetime entirely.

Wrapping a shawl around her bare shoulders, she turned on her bedside lamp so the room wouldn't be completely dark when she returned. As she did, she caught a glimpse out of the corner of her eye of the blue Tiffany pouch. Wondering what Grant was doing tonight, she winced. What had he done all day? She'd almost called him but hadn't found the words.

Damn it! This was nuts! She had to quit thinking about him. She'd made the decision to leave him, so why couldn't she accept the consequences?

Luckily, she didn't have any more time to think about it. There were pieces of raw fish with her name on them.

• • •

Traffic moved surprisingly well on the 405, and it wasn't long before Stokey turned onto Santa Monica Boulevard and headed into Hollywood.

"Just a couple more minutes, and we'll be there, my queens. And just so you don't think I'm totally classless, I do realize Fat Fish does not have a sushi bar, so therefore cannot possibly provide the proper first-time sushi experience. However, the owner happens to be an Executive Sushi Chef and is quite the culinary artisan."

"I don't care if there's a sushi bar or not. Why should anyone care?" Harper asked.

"Sitting at a bar watching the itamae prepare your sushi is supposed to enhance your experience," Stokey explained.

"Oh, it'll still be a memorable experience," Stacia muttered with a dramatic flare. "Has our friend Harper told you that she's never used chopsticks and intends to, and I quote, 'spear' the unsuspecting fish?"

"Oh, Gawd. Maybe we should have opted for the quiet evening at home." Stokey flashed his bejeweled fingers and placed his pink-tinted Fendi's over his eyes in exasperated shame.

"Excuse me, Sushi Divas, but did you say the Fat Fish? You're attempting to cheer my bruised ego by taking me to a restaurant called Fat Fish?" Harper asked, unable to ignore the irony.

"Harper, don't be ridiculous. No one thinks you're a fat fish," Stokey said while pulling up to the valet parking line and searching her out in his rearview mirror over the top of the Fendi's.

"Now remember, never dip sushi rice in the soy sauce, only the fish. And only if the fish isn't already decorated. And don't rub your chopsticks together. That would be insulting to the itamae."

"Decorated? The fish is decorated?" Harper was way out of tune with these two sushi connoisseurs.

The valet opened the car door, and Harper stepped out into the late afternoon sun, following her friends into Fat Fish. Stokey stopped to hug the host at the front door, then directed Stacia and Harper to follow him.

Harper fancied the Euro-Asian feel of the restaurant. The interior designers had created both a relaxed and intimate bistro. Grant would love the upscale ambience. But she certainly wasn't supposed to care about what he thought anymore.

Glancing at the number of people already seated as well as the line coming in behind them, she was more at ease seeing that they weren't the only people in Hollywood eating out on Thanksgiving instead of nestling at home with their families.

"How about we start with some sake in the lounge? Freddie, our host, said it would be awhile before a table was available on the patio. Oh, I should have asked you two if patio dining was okay," Stokey said, always trying to be the perfect gentleman.

"Fine with me," Stacia said. "The less the crowd, the better off we'll all be with our sushi virgin."

Harper swatted at Stacia but missed.

"Real funny. So much for being my friends."

"Oh, we're your friends. Otherwise, we would never have put ourselves through this horrifying event," Stacia said while playfully pinching Harper's shoulder.

Harper looked up just in time to catch the neon sign of the lounge. The Fat Lounge.

"Is everything in this place about fat?"

"Relax. It's nothing personal. Besides, thanks to Jake the Gigolo, you're rather svelte these days, darling."

Stokey ran his hands over her well-defined arms.

"At least he can be commended for that effort. By the way, you may not want to tell him how many carbs you'll be enjoying tonight," Stokey said, pulling out two bar stools and helping her and Stacia settle in.

Harper welcomed his sarcastically veiled compliment regarding her weight loss success, but she couldn't take his slam against Jake without more of an explanation.

"Jake the Gig…"

"Sit, Harper," Stokey ordered. "Sake first and then we'll discuss Jake. I promise."

The bartender smiled and nodded in recognition as Stokey took his seat.

"Hello, Franz. Please help me start these beautiful ladies' Thanksgiving feast with something extraordinary. How about gold sake for three, please?"

With another smile and nod, the bartender reached under the bar top and then started to pour.

"Gold sake?" Stacia asked.

Harper was tickled that Stacia asked the first question instead of her.

"Well, my dears, it's a sake or rice wine with real gold flakes added to it. Fabulous concept, huh?"

Stacia took a sip and shivered. "Indeed. It is rather fabulous."

"No Crown and diet tonight, Harper. Soft drinks spoil the taste of the sushi. Drink up, dear."

Harper twirled the glass between her fingers and took a small drink. "Wow! It's terrific."

As she was about to indulge again, her cell phone rang.

"Better catch that, sweetie, and then turn that damn thing off. You must close your eyes and feel the various textures in your mouth without interruption. Otherwise, you won't grasp the ritualistic significance of our meal."

If Stacia hadn't turned her head in the opposite direction, Harper would have lost it. Stokey meant well, but Harper doubted she'd be entertaining her inner spirit while eating sushi. What a thespian.

She glanced at the display on her phone. Jake. She was impressed. Forget impressed. Ecstatic was more like it. Maybe he finally understood that telling her he was going to call meant he should call.

She turned her head away from Stokey, whose eyes were narrowing, probably because he'd figured out was on the line.

"Hey, you," she said, her tone more suggestive than normal, already feeling the freedom of the sake.

"Hello, Luv. I can't talk long because we're getting ready to go to dinner. Just wanted to say hi and let you know I'm in Wisconsin. We'll be getting on the bus right after dinner, so I'll call you when I get settled in."

"Okay. Glad you're there safe." She hesitated before continuing, "Jake, thank you for this morning and thank you for calling. You made my day. I…"

"I know, baby, I miss you too. Got to go," he said, his voice dropping off to a raspy whisper. "Bye."

She hung onto his sultry goodbye, treasuring the fact she'd never heard him use that tone with anyone else. She pushed the end button and then the power off button before turning to face Stokey.

Gigantic green things resembling pea pods sat in a large bowl between them.

"What the hell is that?"

Harper watched as Stokey and Stacia popped small beans out of the pods.

"Edamame. Boiled soy beans," Stacia said between licking sea salt off her fingers. "My favorite part of the art of eating sushi."

"You can't be serious," Stokey piped in. "You like the edamame better than the sashimi and sushi? You're missing the whole point of the experience. It's not the vegetables, it's all in the fish, silly girl."

"Call me silly, if you must, but nothing beats edamame. I eat it instead of chips or popcorn."

"Oh. A chip alternative? I'm in." Harper picked up a pod and tentatively pushed the bean out of its green fuzzy coat and into her mouth. "Delicious. Okay, Stokey, swallow that bean and spill the rest of yours about Jake. What is your problem with him?"

"Could I have another sake, please?" Stacia asked the bartender. "Make that another round for all three of us."

"I'll need two, Franz," Stokey said, twisting in his seat. "Help me out here, Stace."

"Go ahead, Stokemeister. She already knows how I feel about the bas..."

Stacia shrugged as if signaling her apology for the name-calling.

"I know what you think. But honestly, he's starting to come around. He took me on the most wonderful date last night, brought me breakfast this morning, and just remembered to call me when he got to his first gig on this tour. Pretty good, huh?" Harper asked, and for Jake, it was damn good.

"I'll admit, hon, it's better than his normal M.O., but it still isn't decent by a long shot. What color will the star on the refrigerator be tonight?" Stacia asked, downing the gold sake Franz had placed in front of her.

"Stars on the refrigerator? Explain, girlfriends." Stokey tapped Harper's arm and gave her his undivided attention.

She pressed out the napkin under her drink with her fingers, smoothing the edges, as if that would massage her aching heart.

Trying to convince herself, let alone her friends, that Jake was ready to love her and commit to their relationship was going to be next to impossible. She didn't even believe in the bullshit she was about to spin.

"We have this little chart on the frig at the inn, Big Mouth," Harper said, wrinkling her nose at Stacia. "We take bets each day on whether or not Jake will come through on his promises."

"And does he?" Stokey asked.

"Well, not always," Harper stammered and rolled the edge of her napkin around the base of her glass.

Stacia cleared her throat.

"All right. Most of the time he doesn't." Harper flicked Stacia on the ear with her napkin. "Satisfied?"

"Very," Stacia said.

"Personally, I think the question should be are you satisfied, Harper?" Stokey finished off one glass of sake and then took a healthy sip from the second.

"Am I satisfied with Jake? Or satisfied to be an almost-single-goddess?"

Harper was leery of thinking out loud about either man in front of Stokey and Stacia. They were turning out to be rather relentless where Jake was concerned. Wait until they found out Grant would be arriving soon. Maybe she should tell them next week and save herself the additional agony over the weekend. She was all into grief management.

"Let's start with Jake," Stokey volunteered. "A good place would be that phone call a minute ago. Let me guess. The chap was in a hurry, just called to say hey and never asked one god-damn thing about you or your day."

Harper looked at Stacia for help but didn't receive any at all. She just raised an eyebrow.

"Something like that. But at least he called. You know as well as I do how many nights I've sat at your bar, and he's never shown up or called. Am I right?"

"Yeah, you're right. But…"

Harper followed Stokey's gaze as it locked onto a passing waiter.

"Speaking of a nice butt," he said.

"Can we please get back to Jake? Or should I call Glen and tell him…"

Stokey sat up straight on his stool.

"No reason to turn all witchy bitchy on me, Cruella Deville."

"But what then?" she asked.

Done playing games with him about his disdain for Jake, Harper wanted answers, and she wanted them now.

"Harper, please don't take this the wrong way, and I don't know your exact financial status with your divorce. But I'm guessing that you're pretty well off, judging by your wonderful taste in clothing, handbags and hotels. And you know how I'm always telling you to let Jake buy once in awhile."

Stokey twisted his napkin into contorted origami-like shapes.

"I'm worried that in Jake's mind, you're his ride. I mean, it's like he wants to be a kept man at your expense. Thus, I toss around the gigolo thing, and…"

With the acceptance of Stokey's perception, Harper's body stiffened. He'd crap if he knew that Jake often mentioned to her that he wanted to be just that—a kept man. Odd that Stokey had pegged him as such as well.

Without warning, a desperate urge rushed through her to defend Jake.

"I know how it used to look, but Jake has changed. He's…"

"Harper, let me get this out before my nerves leave me one synapse behind the curve," Stokey said, reaching for her hand.

Stacia put her arm around Harper's shoulders and squeezed tight. "You need to listen to Stokey."

"You already know all of this too?"

Stacia nodded.

"Oh." Harper held onto her sake glass with a quiet intensity, bracing herself for what she had a feeling was going to be more information than she was prepared to deal with. "Go on."

"Think back to the nights at the K.O.W. when you, Jake, and I have talked about his film production schedules. I know you've seen the looks on my face when he announces yet another shooting date."

She remembered the occasions all too well.

"He has yet to shoot a film, any film, Harper. Have you even seen one finished screenplay?"

Stokey reached for her like a brother shielding his little sister from the ogling eyes of strangers.

"Have you? Because I haven't. He's always finishing the last scene, and then it'll be time to roll the cameras. And what about his knowledge of the film industry in general? I've heard your conversations with him. You know more than he does."

Harper had to give Stokey that point. When she'd proudly told Jake she was devouring all the material she could find on the production process, she couldn't believe that he didn't read any of the industry publications. She'd tried to explain it away that he probably knew and had done all there was to do in the industry. The books and magazines were for the newbies, like her, who hadn't experienced the lifestyle firsthand.

"Jake knows about your financial wealth. Right, Harper?"

Stacia stopped her from her onslaught of excuses.

"Well, yes, he knows that I can more than easily back his film productions, if that's what you're after," Harper said, unable to let go of her defensiveness.

"To the tune of about $1.5 mil?" Stokey asked, polishing off a swig of sake with a vengeance.

Harper pulled at her neck to try and dislodge the air stuck in her windpipe. She forced her vocal chords into action, despite their preference to falter.

"What are you talking about? A couple of weeks ago, I did add his name to my account. But we agreed that he'd ask me first before any money was withdrawn."

A panicking heat rose within her.

"Jesus, are you telling me he spent the entire credit line I gave him without so much as mentioning it to me? And worse, how do you know?"

"I'm sorry to have to be the one to tell you this, Harper, but Jake came into the K.O.W. last night, evidently after your date, and had a couple of Black and Tans. Wasn't long before he was pretty loose lipped about his new 'sugar momma'. I could only assume it was you."

Stokey pulled her toward him without her slightest resistance.

"For what it's worth, I do think he cares about you," Stacia said, trying to lighten the blow. "Stokey said that Jake said as much when he was bragging about your relationship. But you are going to have to nip his spending in the bud before he drains you."

In spite of her friends' concerns, Harper wanted to believe in Jake's feelings for her. But if he cared about her, he wouldn't take her money without asking. And as much time as they'd spent together the last few days, it wasn't like he hadn't had the opportunity to mention it. Did he think she'd just figure it out when her next bank statement arrived in her inbox?

Shit! Grant would get the statement too. How was she going to explain going through that kind of cash in a month? Not to mention that the large withdrawal would put a substantial dent in the monthly living allowance Grant generously supplied her without being asked.

Jake may have left her in a position to have to ask for more from Grant.

Before she had time to respond further, Freddie let them know their table was ready.

"Perfect timing. Thank you, Freddie."

Stokey grabbed both of his sake glasses and practically ran after Freddie.

"Gee, if I didn't know better, I'd think he was glad for the interruption," Harper said, following Stacia to the patio. "Honestly, I'm not sure I'm even hungry anymore."

"Don't worry, once you see what we order you, you might lose what little appetite you have left."

Harper did appreciate her friend's sense of humor, but she wasn't in the mood to laugh.

Once they had all been seated, their waiter turned up the heat lamp flanking their table and set a white towel and chopsticks at each of their table settings.

"Oshibori. A hot towel to cleanse yourself between each type of sushi," Stokey said.

"After I attempt to use these chopsticks, you'll need that towel to cleanse yourself from the fish I fling on each of your faces," Harper warned.

"You wouldn't dare," Stokey said, fanning himself in mock horror. "But just in case, I plan to start you out easy. Even though I feel it's a tragedy of seismic proportion, we're going to skip the sashimi—raw fish slices—and go with sushi for wimps, California rolls. Then on to unagi and finish off with Spider rolls."

"I don't know anything about any of them, but the deletion of the raw fish sounds wise."

Harper perused the menu while Stokey penciled in the order for the waitress.

With their order in, Harper thought she'd better get back to their previous topic for fear Stokey would avoid it like the sashimi.

"About Jake. I want you both to know that I appreciate your concern. And as much as I think that what you've implied—about him being nothing but a gigolo—could be a possibility, I want to believe otherwise. You don't know how far we've come. Well, except for the money issue. He told me he thinks he loves me and is ready to try a more exclusive relationship."

Stokey and Stacia exchanged glances.

"Please, whatever you do, don't both congratulate me at once," Harper said, hurt that they couldn't support her feelings. "If you only knew how tough of a time I'm having without Grant. I'm lost. I need this closeness with Jake. He makes me feel needed and wanted."

She poked at the hot towel with the tips of her chopsticks. "Okay, so he hasn't been very consistent. But at least he's there for me part of the time. Grant was never there. Never. Why I agreed to have him here in Playa for the holidays…"

"Whoa, tiger. You what?" Stokey stopped her cold.

Stacia spit a chunk of tofu out of her mouth.

"I haven't had a chance to fill you both in. But the letter you gave me at the inn the other day, Stace, was a request from Grant to visit Playa over Christmas and New Year's."

"Good God, girl! If you said yes, you do still love him! Thank Jesus," Stokey said.

"Harper, that's terrific news, right?" Stacia gave up on her miso soup and went back to sipping sake.

"I wouldn't call it terrific. Terrifically horrific, maybe. I don't know what the hell I was thinking. Now I've got Jake, the gigolo, to contend with too. I was counting on him ignoring me for most of the holiday. I'm not so sure he will now. And if he planned on dumping me, that's an even bigger problem now that I'm apparently 'invested' in his actions. What am I going to do with both of them?"

Harper tried to ignore the waiter, who'd placed a plate of paper-wrapped rolls and a sadistic dark glob on rice with seeds on top in front of her.

"I'm sure as hell not interested in Jake, but I might be willing to take Grant off your hands," Stokey said, adjusting his barely buttoned shirt to reveal more of his buff chest.

Harper stoically pulled her chopsticks from their wrapper and broke them apart while giving Stokey the stink eye.

"Okay. Okay. I get the hint. No 'queer eyes for the straight guy'. Your ex is off limits. My. My. Pretty protective for a woman who doesn't care about him anymore. What do you think, Stace?"

"I think we'd better show her how to use those things."

Stacia motioned at Harper's chopsticks, "Or else we'll be wearing the fresh water eel."

Horrified, Harper stared at her plate. "That's what that dark, slimy shit is?"

"It's unagi, you ingrate." Stokey broke apart his chopsticks. "One of the most delicious fish you'll ever taste. It's been lightly grilled with teriyaki sauce and sprinkled with sesame seeds."

"Fine I'll try it. But how do I do that?"

"First, put those chopsticks down. You're making me nervous. This is a brand new Armani shirt." Stokey arranged the small square dishes between the three of them.

"I'll have our waitress jimmy-rig your sticks with a rubber band and some wadded up wrappers," Stokey said while putting a blob of green paste in one of the ceramic trays. "Here we go. Dab a tiny bit of this paste, called wasabi, in a tray."

After pouring soy sauce in another, he continued, "Add some soy sauce and blend it with your chopsticks. Then pick up the unagi and dip it, fish-end only, into the sauce."

"So would this be a decorated fish?" Harper asked.

"Yes. Excellent observation. The seeds are the decoration on the eel."

With his chopsticks, he placed pinkish-beige strips in the third dish.

As Harper mixed a generous helping of wasabi into the soy sauce, she noticed that Stokey and Stacia were nudging each other.

Harper waited for their waiter to bring her the special chopsticks and tried to load up the eel.

"What do we do with that pinkish junk?"

"Oh, you'll be using that to cleanse your palate between the unagi and the spider rolls." Stokey picked up his first piece of eel. "And it's not pink junk. It's pickled ginger. And I see that look on your face, girlfriend. No. We're not eating real spiders."

Harper squeezed her new cheater sticks together as she tentatively put her mouth around one end of the piece of eel and rice. She must have squeezed too hard. Once the wasabi lit up her tongue, the rest of the eel flew across the table and landed on Stokey's chest.

Harper grabbed her water glass and didn't stop drinking until it was half empty. "Why didn't you tell me that green paste was so damn hot?"

"I said to dab it, not shovel it."

He picked the eel off of his chest and reached for the hot towel.

"Good thing you missed the Armani, sister."

"Maybe you should just use your hands," Stacia offered between giggles. "That is acceptable for newbies."

"Now you tell me."

Harper consumed a single piece of ginger and tried to hose down her mouth with the last of her sake. She was quickly tiring of the sushi game and definitely going for the blueberry crumb cake when she got back to the inn.

"Since you've been such a great sport, how about we skip the spider rolls and go for some banana soufflé cake?"

Stokey's eyes sparkled merely suggesting it.

"Is that part of the sushi experience?" Harper teased.

"It is at Fat Fish."

Stokey ordered a piece of cake for them to share and coffees all around.

Harper had to admit that the meal was wonderful and despite its small size, she was more than full. The crumb cake at the inn would have to wait for another jog or two.

"Well, there's only one thing left to do, and that's figure out how I'm going to handle both Jake and Grant over the next month."

She poured half-and-half into her coffee and added a packet of raw sugar.

"With all due respect, I think you need to learn how to handle yourself first. And I don't mean in a kinky way either," Stokey said and looked at Stacia as if begging her for a relief pitch.

"What he's trying to say, but can't, because of his sexual hang-ups, is that we think you need to concentrate on yourself first. What is it that makes you happy, Harper? What do you want out of your new life? Have you taken time to think that through?"

"This is your moment," Stokey said. "Come out of your own closet and learn who you really are. You're a beautiful person that I would guess is lost between, and because of, these two idiots you call 'men.' The way they've been acting, they don't deserve to be labeled as such. I'd like to propose a toast."

He lifted his coffee cup.

Harper and Stacia lifted their cups to his.

"To you, Harper. I'm so blessed that you walked into my bar. I only hope my friendship serves you as well as my aperitifs. I also hope that you never again allow yourself to be a kept woman. Jake may want to be a kept man, but both he and Grant have been your keepers. Think about that, sweetheart, and cheers."

"Cheers," Harper said and swallowed the warm coffee, which did little to stave off the chill of Stokey's words.

He was right, though. She'd worked so hard to be everything Grant wanted her to be for the Cantwell Group. But in the process of taking the title of Mrs. Grant Cantwell III, she'd lost herself. Who was she? What did she want from life? She'd gone from being nothing more than Grant's wife to being used by Jake.

How was she going to win herself back from both of them? She needed to be her own keeper. Long before she was Mrs. Grant Cantwell, she had an identity. It was time she rediscovered that woman.

But how? Where should she look first?

CHAPTER NINE
BLACK FRIDAY

Grant perused the headlines of The Wall Street Journal. It was the Friday after Thanksgiving. Black Friday. Unlike the retail register totals, expected to be in the black, his Black Friday bled a dark emotional red from the breakup of his marriage.

He folded the paper precisely along the creases his paper boy had predetermined and pushed it aside. There wasn't any use trying to capture its contents because his mind wouldn't leave Harper's empty place setting at his breakfast nook.

For the last twelve years, he'd never spent the day after Thanksgiving without her.

Their personal assistant, Jeffrey, must think he was crazy to insist her place still be set for every meal, but Grant didn't give a damn what Jeffrey thought.

He picked at his eggs with his fork, and then gave up his manners in favor of drowning his toast in the runaway yolks. If only he could drown his pain as easily.

He should have called her yesterday to wish her a Happy Thanksgiving. But it had been less than a week since she'd called to invite him to Playa for the holidays. He didn't want to seem overly anxious. Other than that call, they hadn't even spoken, except through their attorneys, for the past six months.

He took a swig of coffee. Hearing the fine bone china hit the saucer with a deafening echo, he shuddered. The house was too damn quiet. He missed her all day, every day. But breakfast was the worst.

She was a morning person. He wasn't, which during the early months of their marriage had provided ample fodder for jokes between them. Up no later than five, she was annoyingly cheery, whereas he stumbled to the breakfast table two hours later, his tie still undone and hair not even close to presentable.

Staring at the top shelf of the baker's rack next to the table, his new hobby, he studied every pixel in his favorite picture of the two of them together. Jeffrey had snapped it without their knowledge and given it to them for one of their anniversaries. It was a black and white print of Harper straightening his tie, like she'd done every single day of their marriage.

The image reminded him of the day she'd left. He'd arrived at the office in shambles. His tie hung loosely around his neck, and his hair pointed toward every direction on the compass. She'd always fixed both to precision before kissing him on the cheek and sending him out the door.

He was heartbroken that he'd never again have her sweet kiss at the start of the business day.

He could adjust his grooming habits and was well-suited for fixing his own hair and tie, but he couldn't survive without her kiss, an undeclared asset until now.

He reached up and turned over the frame, laying it on the stack of Jeffrey's cookbooks. Deciding that wasn't far enough out of sight, he got up and stuffed it into one of the drawers in the rack. If Jeffrey saw it lying on the books, he'd assume it had toppled over and he would right it to its regular place. But it would take him a few days to find it in the drawer. And when he did, he'd get the point and be kind enough to leave it there.

Grant tried once more to shake off the silence that permeated the breakfast nook as well as every other room in the house.

He rummaged under the paper for the television remote without success.

Looking again at Harper's empty chair, he realized he wasn't sure what she'd done during breakfast. His nose had always been buried in the fine print. He made a silent vow to find out when he sat across from her in LA.

Come to think of it, he wasn't real sure how she'd spent her days after breakfast either. He could supply a few of the details, but to his consternation, he didn't know much about her daily schedule.

Before breakfast, she used to jog the river walk trail he'd funded. He remembered that she liked to chitchat about various committee meetings while she enjoyed her omelet, water and coffee. But to his complete bewilderment, he couldn't recall the particulars of any one issue that had concerned her.

During the evenings she wasn't meeting some social obligation, did she eat dinner home alone or dine out with friends? He didn't know. He didn't know the frequency of either one either because he'd rarely been home early enough to ask her.

Since she'd always seen to the details of Briar Creek's philanthropic endeavors, he'd kept his mind filled with the day-to-day operations of The Cantwell Group. She'd become the center of Briar Creek's community pride. His heart pitched in his chest as he came to the stark realization that their community knew his wife better than he did.

He got up and pushed his chair away from the table, projecting his self-disgust onto the hand-carved legs of his chair. As he stood, he rubbed the stiffness out of his thighs. Every day that passed without her, his body felt heavier. With the added weight of his raw emotions, he struggled to put one foot in front of the other.

He refilled his coffee cup, tucked The Journal under his arm and headed for the foyer stairs. If he delved into the stack of projects waiting for his attention, maybe he could escape his misery.

Just as he reached the landing between the first and second series of steps, the door chimes sounded. Startled, he nearly dropped his coffee.

Who in the hell could that be on a holiday weekend?

He stepped back and called over his shoulder for Jeffrey. "Are we expecting anyone?"

Jeffrey meandered into the hallway.

"Well, yesss, Mr. C. It is the Friday after Thanksgiving."

"And could you please tell me the significance of that?" Grant forced himself to remain polite.

He loathed the way Jeffrey talked down to him since Harper left. As if it were his fault she was gone! How could he have known she was that unhappy?

Jeffrey may have been accurate in his assumptions that Grant was a total dumb ass when it came to matters of the estate's daily goings-on, but he was the only dumb ass writing Jeffrey's paychecks. So, Jeffrey had best figure that out and suspend with the attitude.

"Mr. C," Jeffrey paused and placed his hands on his hips, "you know Mrs. C always has the estate decorated for the holidays the day after Thanksgiving. If I were to guess, I'd say that, after she left, you never canceled that arrangement, so 'voila'—they're here."

Grant moved around Jeffrey, who was blocking the door. "I'll handle this."

Jeffrey bowed deep and waved his arm in a grand sweep.

"You really do need to treat me with a little more respect," Grant admonished him as he reached for the door handle.

A lot of good that would do. Jeffrey knew damn well he could treat Grant however he wanted to. Harper worshipped him, so his job was secure. And since she'd left, Grant had come to depend on him. Although Grant would never admit as much, he actually rather enjoyed his company.

"I'm working on it."

Jeffrey smiled in his most sincere bullshit mode.

"I'll bet you are."

Grant opened the door but couldn't see if a human existed behind the barrage of greenery and boxes. The strong scent of pine he'd just inhaled was as overwhelming as the number of cartons containing hundreds of boughs.

"Happy Holidays, Mrs. C!"

Coming from somewhere behind the assembly was a tiny elf-like voice.

"We're here bright and early to get started on this year's winter wonderland."

Grant still couldn't see the person speaking. He could only hear his voice. But after clearing his voice, he answered anyway.

"Mrs. C isn't here this year. This is Mr. Cantwell. And who exactly are you?"

Two small but masculine hands parted the greenery. Grant could hardly stifle a snicker when the tiniest of men, four-foot-ten on a good day, peered out. Honest to God, he looked like an elf.

"I'm Reginald Green, owner and design genius of Parties with Jazz. I, along with my staff, decorate your estate every year for the holiday season. We do require a thirty-day notice of cancellation, so it looks like we'll still be putting the fa-la-la-la-la in your about-to-be-decked halls."

Oh boy, did Grant ever need Harper's help. How could she stand working with such a mental case? What was it with creative types? He was way out of his element here.

"Listen, whatever your fee is, I'll pay it. Just please go away. I'm too busy to celebrate the holidays this year."

"Have it your way, Mr. Grinch. Mrs. C always said you..."

The elf stopped cold.

"Mrs. C always said what?"

The idea of her discussing him with anyone left him more than ill at ease. She knew how much of a private man he was and would never betray him that way. Would she?

Grant enjoyed watching Mr. Green's face turn as bright red as his brocaded, crushed velvet shirt.

"Oh, never mind. We'll just get your check and be on our way."

Reginald shifted from leg to leg with the drama and finesse of a Baryshnikov principal dancer.

Grant turned around ready to run up to his study and grab his checkbook. But as soon as he placed his hand on the banister, he thought of the fresh greenery and small white lights Harper always had wrapped from the first step to the railing edging the second-floor landing. He normally cringed at the prospect of loose needles and sap damaging the stained surface. And he'd never been crazy about the pine smell either.

But none of this was of concern to him now. He was so lost without her in the house that anything that would remind him of her was a definite 'go.'

He may have never expressed his love for the holidays, but he thought there could be magic in them too. Although, he hadn't believed in that magic since his sixth birthday.

He stopped mid-step and turned back to the elf. "On second thought, the Cantwell Estate will be decorating this year. So come in and get busy."

"Yes, sir."

Reginald saluted, then immediately started snapping his fingers and issuing orders to his crew, who were lost behind him somewhere in the forest of greenery and garland.

"How long does this take?" Grant asked, having no idea what he'd committed to.

"Oh, Mr. C, we'll be in and out all weekend. But we should be finished no later than Sunday evening."

He clapped his hands into the air and motioned for the drivers of the six vans parked in the driveway to get moving.

"And what do I need to do during all of this?"

Grant watched all of the van doors opening. It was like one of the commercials he'd recently seen with ten clowns stepping out of a Mini coupe. Suddenly, dozens of people were spread across his lawn and driveway, amongst hundreds of wreaths, millions of white lights and gigantic mountains of ribbon and pearls.

"Just stay out of our way. Jeffrey will get us whatever we need."

Reginald winked at Jeffrey, who blushed.

"Okay. Fine. See you all Sunday evening then."

Grant shrugged and retreated to his study, amazed that Harper would give all of these people the run of their house.

As he climbed the stairs and left the bustle in his foyer, he wished Harper could see him now. She'd never believe what he'd given in to. But more than that, she'd never believe the pleasure and excitement he held in check with the anticipation of seeing his 'winter wonderland' complete. She'd be surprised at his unexpected joy. He sure as hell was.

• • •

Grant could hardly concentrate for the racket. If it wasn't a pounding hammer, then it was the screech of ladders being put up and down, or workers sliding across the eaves outside his study windows. How the hell they had the balls to attach lights to the edges of his extremely high, gabled rooftop was beyond him. They really were certifiably nuts.

He had only been in his office for a few hours, but it felt like an eternity. Work was simply more than he could tackle today. Hell, thinking period—about anything other than missing Harper— was useless.

Besides, whatever he tried to focus on, he couldn't, because he couldn't block out Reginald Green's obscenely high-pitched voice yapping orders to his troops. The man never stopped clapping and snapping. By now, his hands must have friction burns.

Grant used to think his walls were sound-proof, but not after today's escapades.

He glanced at his desk calendar. Twenty-six days until he saw her. But then what?

Instead of looking at the blueprints for the performing arts complex that probably wouldn't get off the ground without Harper's leadership, he should spend his time figuring out what he was going to do when his plane landed at LAX and she was standing in front of him.

How was he going to prove to her how much he loved and missed her? Especially when he was struggling to remember what he actually knew about her anymore? How was it possible to live with someone and share the same bed for the last twelve years and not know her?

No wonder she'd left him. He couldn't pass a Jeopardy category with his own wife as the subject.

His intercom buzzed.

"Yes."

"Would you like to come down to the kitchen and grab a bite to eat with us?" Jeffrey was uncharacteristically cordial.

"I thought I had to stay hidden away until Sunday night?"

Grant welcomed the interruption, although he'd never admit it to Jeffrey. So apparently did his stomach as it was growling loudly, due to the breakfast he'd left mostly cold on his plate.

"We're still allowing you kitchen and bathroom passes, of course," Jeffrey supplied in his more easily recognizable snooty tone.

"Be down in a minute."

If his decorator and staff felt bad enough for him to invite him to eat with them, he must be coming off as totally pathetic. He made a mental note to keep himself in better emotional check. He didn't want people feeling sorry for him, especially the hired help.

He clicked off the intercom receiver switch, then double clicked his wireless mouse. He had one task he couldn't afford to leave undone.

He had to book his flight to LAX. There was no way he wasn't going to get a flight out. He'd sleep all night in the airport on stand-by if he had to. Or hell, he'd just book a charter jet. He was worried about availability due to the holidays. He didn't give a damn about the cost.

The transaction completed, he relaxed and clicked the print icon to receive his confirmation and itinerary. Now all he had to do was muster the courage to call Harper with the information.

He picked up the phone but just as quickly placed it back in its cradle.

Would she think he was a hopeless moron calling back so soon after her invitation? She knew he never booked his flights until a few days before a trip. He didn't want her to know how desperate he was to see her. Not yet, anyway.

Maybe after lunch he'd call her. He should probably check up on the hall-decking squad anyway. Besides, if he wasn't down there when lunch was served, Jeffrey would be irate.

As he opened his study door, his ears filled with the Christmas music booming throughout the estate. Nothing like a little "Blue Christmas" to cheer him up.

Leaving his study, he was accosted on the stairway by the smell of the fresh pine garland already wrapped on the railing. The strong stench stung his nostrils, almost bringing tears to his eyes.

He took a handkerchief out of the back pocket of his trousers and wiped his runny nose. He struggled every year with the abundance of forest relics placed in his home, but he knew how much Harper loved it, so he tolerated it and loaded up on his sinus meds.

When he arrived in the kitchen, a blur of swirling activity momentarily immobilized him. Everywhere he looked there were people and elaborate spreads of food. There was a gigantic chocolate fountain on the Italian marble island and two, tree-shaped statues made of strawberries on either side.

"What the…?"

He searched for Jeffrey but ended up with Reginald.

"Oh, Mr. C. Help yourself. These are just a few of the leftover wonderfuls from a Christmas party I catered last evening. If I say so myself, the chocolate covered strawberry trees were sensational hits. Please, do try everything."

"Thank you, Reginald."

Grant reached for a plate and utensils.

The aroma of pastries and pineapple-glazed ham was a welcome respite from the pine.

"Oh, please, call me Reggie." The head elf waved his hand in dismissal. "Pardon me. Jeffrey? Yoohoo, darling."

His shrill voice pierced Grant's aching head.

Reggie then spun around and snapped his fingers as if Jeffrey would magically appear.

He wished he could tell Reggie that Jeffrey took his old sweet time when called to action. But before he could blink, Jeffrey was at Reggie's service.

Maybe he should take to snapping and clapping when he needed him, Grant thought.

"It's bow time, baby." Reggie wiggled his behind, ruining Grant's appetite. "Bring out the ribbons and pearls, people."

Grant had to marvel at Reggie's talents in leading his crew. When he snapped and clapped, they moved. And not only did they move upon his command, but they actually appeared to enjoy doing as he instructed. Unbelievable.

He was about to comment on his observations when Jeffrey interrupted his thought pattern. "Mr. C, I thought you might like to step into the great room for a moment to select our color scheme for the season. Mrs. C always…"

"She does what?" Grant answered with more interest than he could recall having in anything as of late.

Judging by the sympathetic glance he exchanged with Reggie, Jeffrey must have sensed Grant's eagerness to do things the way Harper would do.

"It is sort of a tradition with Mrs. C," Reggie said and shifted his weight while removing an imaginary string from his shirtsleeve. "We choose the accent color together before I embark on directing the dressing of the trees throughout your estate."

"I see." Grant swallowed and took his time replying. "Why don't you just use her favorite one."

"And that would be?" Reggie wouldn't give up and allow Grant a graceful escape.

"Uhmm," Grant looked at Jeffrey for help.

"Mr. C doesn't know." Jeffrey finished his slam with the ultimate challenge. "Do you?"

"Well, no, I guess you're right, Jeffrey. I don't. And thank you for pointing that out."

Grant really was going to have to talk to him about his lack of respect. But now was not the time. And besides, other than Harper, Jeffrey was the only one who knew what the hell happened around this place on a regular basis.

Reggie jumped on Grant's out-of-control wagon and attempted to slow it down before it careened over a cliff.

"I may have just the thing for you, Mr. C. You see, I own this company on the side that specializes in how to please a woman."

Grant started to object, but Reggie shut him down like one of the empty food boxes that littered the floor.

"Don't worry. Many men like you don't get it. In fact, here's my card. Note, I have an 800 number that's staffed 24/7 to provide you with up-to-the-minute advice for whatever your situation. And here, just a minute…"

He disappeared toward the foyer while Grant glared at Jeffrey, who shrugged him off with total disregard.

Reggie came back into the room with a silver box that was marked with a first-aid style red, glittery symbol. Only it wasn't a cross, it was a puffy metallic heart. The large size of the box suggested it held more than Band-aids and anti-bacterial cream. Decadently scrolled across the side in matching metallic red paint were the words 'Chick Tricks 101'.

Grant lifted his arms in protest only to provide the perfect resting place for the box. Seeing Jeffrey cover his mouth to keep from guffawing, Grant was horrified.

"Now, all you have to do is study these materials, use the 800 number as needed, and call my secretary to schedule your one-on-one time with me," Reggie continued as if this gift was perfectly natural and called for.

"But…"

"No buts. It's obvious that what you've been doing hasn't worked, so you could use my help."

Reggie pushed his shirtsleeves to his elbows.

"And since you're already a decorative arts client of mine, I'll forgo the pre-paid plan and bill you upon your graduation from the course. Sound fair?"

"I haven't even agreed to this. And probably won't. But in the interest of your getting back to the 'decorative arts,' which you have been paid for, I'll take a look and get back with you."

Grant handed the box to Jeffrey.

"If you'll take this up to my study, I'll fix myself a plate and leave you to do whatever it is that you do."

"As you wish." Jeffrey took the box from Grant with the reverence required to handle nothing less than a queen's jewels.

As Jeffrey turned to leave, and before Reggie could snap his assistants into work mode, Grant quietly stuttered, "Pink. Harper's favorite color is pink."

"You're right, Mr. C. It is pink."

Jeffrey conceded with his nose so far up in the air Grant could only hope he fell flat over one of the crates of decorations in the hallway.

"Well done, my friend," Reggie said and gave a gallant clap.

Seconds later, the first pieces of pink ribbon were shaped into magnificent bows.

• • •

Grant studied Reggie's Chick Tricks Inc. card, which was silver and covered in metallic red hearts like the box.

Reggie was definitely more in touch with his feminine side than Grant would ever be. 'Call us any time—day or night—1-866-HOW-2LUV.'

He stared at the box. The lights in his study bounced off of the metallic paint, sending laser-like prisms throughout the room.

There was no way Grant was going to participate in private tutoring sessions with that crazy elf. But what harm could come of examining the contents of the box? It did say Chick Tricks 101. And he could use whatever help he could find.

Holding his breath, Grant lifted the lid of the box and offered up a silent prayer to any guardian angel ready to listen. He could pass the state board of realtor's licensing exam in his sleep, but continuing education on how to be a better husband left a cold sweat on his palms.

One-by-one he took out the items in the box and placed them on his desk. By using three books—one on the languages of love, one on rescuing his relationship, and one on how to treat a woman—

along with the top ten chick flicks on DVD, a men's style manual, and a box of tissues (make that two boxes), he was supposed to learn the basics of reconnecting with his wife.

Despite the ridiculousness of the kit, the laminated card in the bottom of the box captivated him more than he thought possible. It was a quote by some guy named Dr. Phil and read: "If a man's worth is reflected in the life and spirit of his wife and family, I am truly a wealthy and blessed man."

For the first time in his life, Grant felt what it must be like to be poor.

CHAPTER TEN
FOR THE LOVE OF CHICK FLICKS

Harper yanked off the cap of her lime green high-lighter and marked a huge 'x' thru another empty day on her desk calendar. With both Saturday and Sunday of the holiday weekend to go, she was beyond desperate for companionship. If she couldn't find something or someone to take her mind off of the confining walls of The Inn, she'd absolutely go nuts.

Sunk into the over-sized cushions of the couch in her room, picking thru a box of gourmet chocolates, she absentmindedly flipped through the television channels, catching a full, HD screen of the world's largest Christmas tree being placed in the plaza at Rockefeller Center. It was one of her favorite trees, the ultimate symbol of the holiday season. But despite how much she loved that tree, she couldn't keep her overwhelming sadness at bay.

She wondered who was doing the tree on Briar Creek's courthouse square this year? She'd done it, with Reggie's help, for the past five years.

Shit. She should have called Grant to have him cancel Reggie's decorating the estate for the holidays. Certainly Jeffrey had taken care of that for her.

As soon as her tongue hit the lemon crème middle of her next chocolate upper, she fired the truffle towards the wastebasket across the room. Yuuuck. She hated the lemon ones. She rummaged through the box trying to find a raspberry crème. So much for the damn diagram on the lid.

Taking a bite, she wrinkled her nose in disgust. Now she had caramel strung across her lips. She couldn't even find a piece of gourmet chocolate that suited her. Not a good sign.

Screw taking Stokey's suggestion to search for herself. She was too pissed at the world to start looking this weekend. She'd definitely moved on from the denial part of post-separation grief and was fully embroiled in the anger phase.

And no shortage of targets existed. Grant had robbed her heart and soul. Jake was stealing—okay, maybe that was too strong of an accusation since her bank account did have his name on it. He was borrowing her money, which she couldn't put a stop to until her bank reopened on Monday, following the holiday weekend. But worse than either of their actions, she'd held herself hostage for both of them.

Grant hadn't so much as called to wish her Happy Thanksgiving. Of course, she hadn't called him either. And they were separated, at her bequest. But neither of those small facts should have figured in.

Still not able to process it all, she felt nothing but an insatiable rage, a level where warning bells should be ringing to keep innocent bystanders out of range.

Last night, she'd removed Jake's chart from the inn's refrigerator and tacked it to her door. She'd started a new page to continue the 'no call' column.

Throwing an orange crème at the basket and watching it splat on the wall behind it, she picked up the box of lick-'em-and-stick-'em stars and smacked a purple one, first on her tongue, and then onto the chart.

With no word from him since last night, he'd run out of room on the first page. Hell. She licked a second purple star and popped it up next to the first one. He'd just earned himself another 'no-calling loser' star.

She looked at the clock. Quarter till midnight. What little sanity she still had left was being stripped away, one star at a time.

Like the salty air eats at the paint on the lifeguard shacks at the beach, the men in her life were eating at her heart, leaving it raw and susceptible to rogue waves.

As wiped out as she felt, she couldn't relax and go to bed. She'd tried around ten or so, only to flip on the light and unwrap the chocolate that Stokey had bought her on the way home from Fat Fish.

Since being in Jake's company, her entire schedule was off balance. Now she crawled into bed around five A.M., the time she used to start her day when she lived with Grant. Maybe over the next month, with Jake on the road, she'd readjust to her old time schedule, just in time for him to get back home. But if tonight was the measure, she was in for a rough change.

Not only was her schedule off, but now her checkbook was too. Ever since Stokey had told her about Jake's huge withdrawal, she'd beat herself up for being so stupid. What had she been thinking adding him to her account? Well, that was fairly obvious. She hadn't been thinking at all.

More importantly though, what was she going to do about it?

"Oh, by the way, Jake, do you happen to have the receipt for the million and a half you spent the night before you left for tour? Let me guess. I bought my own engagement ring?"

Maybe he was so bent out of shape after seeing her wear Grant's ring that he'd bought her one of his own. Like that was ever going to happen. And even if it did, no ring Jake bought was going to cost that much. He'd spend money on his own dreams, but she doubted he'd fund somebody else's.

Thinking about all of these things, she'd laughed until she'd cried. And then she'd cried harder. Why stop now? She'd been feeling sorry for herself all evening. Her eyes would be puffy tomorrow morning, but who cared? She had no plans, no people to please. She'd walked out on all that.

But things were about to get rolling, and if it wasn't Jake's movie cameras, it sure as hell would be his head.

She pulled a tissue out of the box on the coffee table and blew her nose. The sound was horribly un-ladylike, but that didn't matter because no one else was there to give a damn how much noise she made.

She went to the bathroom to get some lotion for her overworked snout, shielding her face from the glare of the vanity mirror. She didn't need the mirror on the wall telling her she wasn't the fairest of all. That's what happens when you don't bathe, stay robed, forget the comb and are still wiping off last night's leftover mascara.

Padding back into the living room in her pink fuzzy slippers, she pulled the comforter off her bed and settled onto the sofa. She couldn't sleep alone in that gigantic nest again. At least the couch didn't have an empty side next to her reminding her there was no one to fill it.

Finding a "Sex and the City" re-run, she welcomed the fictional pain and tribulations. Maybe she should start typing out her dilemmas for the small screen. She visualized herself in a pink tutu on the side of one of Briar Creek's public transportation vans—the closest thing it had to mass transit. Of course, she probably had to have a lot more sex in the city than she was to get a job writing about it. So much for equal opportunity employment.

A phone rang on the show, but when Sarah Jessica Parker answered it, it kept ringing. Huh? Wait a minute. That was her own phone ringing at…what? One A.M.?

Oh yeah! She could tear down the second sheet of Jake's chart and peel off the second purple star in the "no call" section. Although, on second thought, she probably shouldn't throw either away just yet.

"Hey, you."

"Uh, Harper, is that you?"

Harper had to grip the phone with everything she had left in her before her paralyzing shock sent it pummeling to the floor.

"Grant?" Hearing his voice, she took such an unexpected deep breath…and hiccupped.

"Excuse…" She hiccupped again. "…me."

She swore she heard him chuckle, but it was so faint she figured it was only her imagination. It had been so long since she'd heard him laugh, she'd almost forgotten what it sounded like.

"Are you okay?" He asked.

"Yes, I'm fine. You?"

She looked at the clock again to make sure it still said a little after one Pacific Time. Doing the math, she realized it was past four in the morning in Tennessee. What was he doing awake at that hour?

"I've been better," Grant said.

Was that a sniffle she heard? First he'd laughed and then he sounded like he needed to borrow her tissue box? She pinched herself on the arm to try to shake some reality into what had to be a dream. Ouch.

"Welcome to my world," she said and pushed herself up on one elbow. She adjusted the pillow behind her so she could sit up and sound halfway coherent. "What's wrong?"

That was a pretty loaded question for their current relationship, but she'd never been one to dodge the most direct path, and she wasn't about to start now.

"Are you drunk?" she asked, trying to remember the last time he'd had too much to drink.

She honestly couldn't recall him ever being totally out of control. Maybe tipsy, but never out of it.

"It's actually fairly absurd," he said, then laughed with a nervous jitter distinctly not his norm.

"Yeah, I agree. You drunk isn't really plausible."

But what else could it be?

His odd manor having her beyond intrigued, she pressed on, "Believe me, after what I've been through the last couple of days, not much would surprise me, so shoot."

"To answer your question, 'No, I'm not drunk.' Have you ever seen the movie…oh hell, what's it called?"

She heard what sounded like paper and boxes being shuffled about.

"Here it is. 'Message in a Bottle'."

Harper couldn't rationalize what he'd just asked her. But he seemed so damn serious that she didn't have the heart to chide him. The Grant Cantwell she'd fallen in love with, and then sort of out of love with, had seldom watched a movie, and never a love story, a chick flick, a tear-jerker for goodness sake. She had to get to the bottom of this.

"I've seen it a couple of times actually. Even bought it for my collection. But…"

She'd tread lightly, but she had to push him for more information. "You watched that movie? By yourself? Not that you can't watch a movie, and not that you have to answer to me about who you watched it with, but you honestly watched it? Alone?"

She heard him take a deep breath and could almost picture him straightening up his posture and regaining his temporarily misplaced pride.

"A friend of Jeffrey's lent me a few DVDs to watch. I'm not sure that was such a good one to start with. That's some seriously depressing stuff. Great story, but terrible ending. Don't you think?"

To Harper's amazement, Grant's voice sounded anything but dignified. He sounded weak, as if he was struggling.

"You got a point there. It's a rough one. But why would Jeffrey and his friend give you something like that to watch?"

She was certain there was more to it than what Grant was letting on. Jeffrey knew Grant was much more the 'Trading Places' type.

"Oh, it's a long story. And it's late." He hesitated before continuing, "I'm sorry if I bothered you. I called to give you my flight information."

"Grant, you called me at one in the morning just to give me your flight information?"

None of this made sense. Each thought he expressed was stranger than the one before it.

"Well, I was just thinking about it and thought I could always leave a message if you didn't answer. I've got a busy schedule the next few days and was afraid I'd forget to get back with you."

Once he started back peddling, Harper actually felt much better. He normally ran away from any conversation even remotely headed toward sentimentality.

"Okay then. Let me get something to write with."

She fumbled for the high-lighter she knew she'd laid on the nightstand and reached for a small tablet of paper.

As she jotted down his itinerary, she heard the uneasiness in his voice. Why was he suddenly so ill-equipped to deal with her? He never acted like he gave a second thought when communicating with her—or at least any different thought than he used with his best clients.

"Are you sure you're not drunk?" she asked, twisting the phone cord around her wrist.

"I'm not drunk. I told you that before. Sorry I called so late."

She would have bet money that she heard him stifle a sniffle again. Well, maybe not money, being as she had $1.5 million dollars less than she did two days ago.

"It was nice to hear your voice," he said.

Nice to hear her voice? Now she was freaked out.

She reached for the box of chocolate.

"Yours too, Grant. So, I'm just curious, what other movies did Jeffrey fix you up with?"

She stuffed a caramel turtle into her mouth.

"Actually, it was Reggie who brought them over when he was decorating the estate today."

Reggie? Grant had the estate decorated? By himself? Without her input?

She tore the box apart looking for one last raspberry crème.

"Harper? You still there?"

She hurried and swallowed the last raspberry crème, careful not to choke. "Yes, I'm here. So Reggie's working on the estate? I'm sorry. I should have had Jeffrey cancel that for you."

"No. Really. I wanted it done. Jeffrey, Reggie and I discussed it and thought we should go ahead with it. They really did a wonderful job. You should see…"

The silence his suggestion brought punched her square in the gut. Thankfully, the chocolate truffles and crèmes absorbed some of the shock.

"Maybe you could take some pictures and email them to me," she suggested, not sure what else to offer him.

"Okay. That's great. I will. Uh, what's your email address, I don't think I have it," he asked with the hurt of a small child not invited to a friend's birthday party.

She gave him her email address, not sure where it would lead but comfortable enough to take a chance. Surely it wouldn't hurt to email back and forth occasionally.

For some reason, she wasn't in a hurry to bid him goodbye. But she was at a loss for what else to say. And the silence was unbearable.

"Guess I'd better get to bed. Thanks for calling," she said and waited anxiously for his reply.

"Thanks for talking to me. I feel better now. No more movies for a day or two."

He laughed again.

Two laughs in less than twenty minutes.

"Good idea. Hey, you never did tell me what other flicks they gave you."

Dying to know, she couldn't fail one last attempt to find out.

"Never mind. I think I'll start on the books," he said, almost choking on his words.

"Books? What books?"

Since when did he read anything besides The Wall Street Journal and title company newsletters?

"Night, Harper. Sleep tight."

He disconnected their call.

Wait a minute. She wasn't done with this conversation. She'd learned more from him in the last twenty minutes than she'd discovered in the last five years of their married life. Grant Cantwell was willing to watch chick flicks, he cried, and he claimed he enjoyed Reggie's holiday decorating as much as she did. But to top the other oddities, he read books? What kind of books?

Maybe she needed to call Jeffrey and check in. Then again, maybe she needed to butt out. Grant wasn't her concern anymore. She wasn't concerned. Not at all.

She was supposed to be rediscovering herself, not her soon-to-be ex.

Harper threw the empty box of chocolate in the trash and followed it with the lone orange crème she removed from the wall. Pulling the comforter over her head, she tried to block out the dizzying images of Grant curled up on their bed with popcorn, tissues and a chick flick.

CHAPTER ELEVEN
THE TREE OF LIFE

Harper awoke to the sharp rays of the California sun cutting through the sheer white curtains of her room. She sat up in bed and rubbed the last sleepiness from her eyes.

She breathed in the salty sea air filtering through the window screen and wished like hell she hadn't indulged in the whole damn box of chocolates. Her head ached from the sugar rush.

She stared at the glowing red numbers on the dial of her alarm clock. Noon. So much for breakfast. She'd slept through it again.

She stumbled into the kitchenette and started the coffee pot.

Pouring herself a warm mug of caffeine, she shuffled into the living room, balancing the over-filled mug in one hand and her phone the other. She settled into the sofa first, but catching another shot of white light directly in her eyes, she moved to the chair next to it. One more piercing gleam and her head would explode.

At the rate she was going, she'd need to jog twenty extra miles to purge the spears from her head and the sugar from her veins. Her legs felt so heavy she could hardly lift them onto the top of the ottoman in front of the chair.

After drinking half the coffee in her cup, she opened her calendar app and tapped the correct date on the screen. Watching her life pass from one empty day to the next only made her feel worse, but she was such a creature of habit, and checking her schedule had always been part of her morning routine.

Six months ago at this time, she'd have been seated at the café style table in her breakfast nook. Grant would have been physically across from her, but otherwise miles away. With his nose buried in the pages of the Wall Street Journal, he would have left her to her own misery as he grumbled about his worries on the stock exchange.

The difference...her calendar would have been filled with so many To Do's that she would have been figuring out which items she could re-prioritize and reschedule for another day. Walking out the door of the Cantwell estate, and out of Grant's empire, had left her with an abundance of time to spare.

She pulled up her Quote of The Day app, as she used to between bites of Jeffrey's amazing omelets. Half the time she didn't know who the person quoted was, but she often found value in their words.

Reading today's inspiration, she almost ended up with a spray of coffee up her nose.

"in love, one and one are one."
–Jean-Paul Sartre

Dumbfounded, she rolled the words off her tongue and into her mind over and over. Maybe Stokey was right. Before she could love or be loved, she had to love herself.

She had to take care of number one. And until now, she'd thought that was an awfully selfish approach to life. But maybe it had merit.

She'd abandoned herself while repeatedly giving to the rest of the world. Not that she wasn't proud of her accomplishments and the opportunities that she and Grant had provided for others in their community. She was. But where had it gotten her?

She'd blamed Grant for her emptiness, but now she realized he wasn't the only one to blame. She'd played a role in her demise. She was Sartre's one of one, but she had no idea who that one was. And without learning who she was, adding an additional 'one' to her life's equation couldn't possibly balance her soul.

She got it. Thanks to Stokey and Sartre:

She couldn't give a damn about anybody else until she learned to love herself.

She gulped down the rest of her coffee. All this philosophical crap required more caffeine.

Flipping through her app until she reached the calendars showing full months at a glance, she perused her appointments over the past year. She carefully considered each group listed, one at a time, and deleted the ones that meant nothing except added responsibility.

The guilt from discovering that she'd never enjoyed working for these wonderful causes was almost enough to force her to stop the process and return to her philanthropic throne. But she didn't. She kept going through them, one by one.

She believed in and would continue to financially support all of them. But for the first time in her life, she acknowledged the low level of personal joy that her actions in these organizations had brought her. She wouldn't be joining any of these groups and organizations in California.

Banished from her calendar, although not from her heart, were Performing Arts Council, Junior Achievement, United Way, Diversity Dynamics Task Force, Kiwanis, Fine Arts Council, two sororities, the Home Hospital Foundation, and Briar Creek's Community Foundation.

The only item she couldn't delete was the Holiday Chair-ity Ball. Each year, one hundred chairs were auctioned off, designed by local artisans. She and Reggie co-chaired the annual event to raise money for the Briar Creek Arts Festival. The Ball was the talk of the town for the few months before and after the holidays. Of all her responsibilities, it was only this one that she looked forward to.

Noting the theme she'd recorded for this year's event—Mai Tai Madness, her mind was already spinning ideas to turn the old ballroom the event was held in into a tropical paradise. Reggie probably already had most of the evening planned and preparations well under way since, according to her notes, the Ball was two weeks away—the Saturday before Grant was to arrive in LA.

Surely Grant was going. He couldn't afford to miss The Cantwell Group's signature event.

She was more concerned with who he was going with. Maybe Reggie would tell her. She should check in with him to see how the plans were coming along. She made a note to call him later. He could probably use her help with something even if she was on the opposite side of the country.

She missed Reggie and his eccentric crew. She'd always had a good eye—great, according to Reggie—for the decorative arts. But, until working with him, she'd never known the secrets of the trade and how they applied to event planning. He could turn any room into whatever she dreamed of it becoming. After several snaps of his fingers and claps of his hands, any gymnasium, ballroom or outdoor space became a fantasy land with the theme of her choice. They made a terrific team.

No job she'd hired Reggie to help her with felt like a job at all. Working with him was non-stop laughter and fun, mixed with a lot of muscle and sweat as well as large wads of cash. His events were magnificent with gold price tags to match.

Hearing a large delivery truck pull into the driveway of the inn, she closed down her app, set her phone back on the table, and stood up to stretch her chocolate-coated muscles. It was odd for a truck to be pulling up early on a Saturday morning, especially over a holiday weekend.

She wandered over to the French doors that opened onto her balcony and stepped out. She glanced down toward the garage entrance, which was directly beneath her room.

Elegant scrolled letters in a gorgeous, sparkling green paint identified the large white truck as the Robert's Bloom Factory delivery van.

Some lucky guest must be receiving flowers. And it more than likely wasn't her—unless Jake had sent something to make up for the fact that he hadn't bothered to call since Thursday evening.

With his withdrawal from her account, he could definitely afford to send something. Jerk. She'd deal with him later, in the flesh, once she figured out how.

In the mean time, she needed to find herself. What better place to start than a trip to a spa? She'd been meaning to try the one in the Howard Hughes Center in Marina del Rey. Checking the emergency cash reserve she kept in her sock drawer, she figured she could easily cover at least a half-day session.

She took a blistering hot shower, hoping the water would melt the rest of the chocolate out of her system. Anything to cut down the distance of her evening run.

She dressed in her favorite hot yoga pants and the new Juicy Couture T-shirt she'd bought at Bloomingdales the last trip to The Beverly Center. She loved it. Jake hated it, probably because she'd turned more heads in the store than he did when she'd modeled for him outside the fitting room. Even more reason to wear it.

Pulling on her ultra-soft riding boots, she studied her reflection in the dressing mirror of her closet door. Not bad. Definitely LA.

Slinging her Louis Vuitton tote over her shoulder, she placed her sunglasses on top of her head and grabbed a shawl from the chest of drawers. She could do this. She'd never taken the time to pamper herself, but she'd give it a whirl.

She tossed the keys to Jake's Hummer into her tote and closed the door to loneliness behind her.

She could always hock the Hummer to reimburse his debt. Visuals of his learning of that swap tickled her. She added the idea to her mental list of alternatives.

On her way down the hallway to the elevator, she sidestepped a humongous, fresh-cut Christmas tree. About twenty feet high, the damn thing was almost as wide around as it was tall. How the guys wrestling it through the hall's narrow passage were going to get it into the inn's great room would be quality entertainment.

Stranded tight against the wall, waiting for the tree and its hijackers to pass, Harper saw Stacia pacing the kitchen, intermittently ringing her hands and pulling at the loose curls in her hair.

"What's going on in there?" Harper hollered over the large tree bough that now blocked her view. "Are you all right?"

"No, I'm not all right. Does it look like everything is peachy keen?"

"Right now, I'm not sure what anything looks like because this damn tree is out of control." Harper pushed the last couple of branches out of her way and rounded the large, sap-dripping trunk to try and squeeze past the workmen and into the kitchen. "That is one monster of a tree."

"It's a monster about to grow a head and fangs."

Stacia brought up the yellow pages on her computer and furiously typed keywords into the site's search engine.

"I saw Robert's Bloom Factory van downstairs. I can't wait to see what he does with that tree," Harper said.

She leaned her bag against the kitchen worktable and pulled out a bar stool, waiting for Stace to fill her in on the free-for-all.

"You saw Robert's van all right. But have you seen Robert?"

Stacia gave up on her computer, lowered her head between her arms and banged it against the wooden table. "Shit. Shit. Shit."

"Well, no, now that you mention it, I haven't seen him yet. Where is he?"

"He's not here. And won't be. He's sick with the flu."

Stacia lifted her head from the table and looked as if she might cry.

"That's too bad. So I take it his assistants will be decorating the tree?"

Harper felt bad that Robert was sick, and she was super disappointed that she wouldn't get to see his handiwork. Surely his assistants could handle the job, or he wouldn't have hired them.

"What assistants?" Stacia nearly screamed at her.

"His assistant, singular, is doing a party in Hollywood this afternoon," she said, her voice continuing to rise in both octave and decibels. "So here I sit with a huge freaking tree, its worthless delivery boys, an inn entirely booked starting tomorrow evening, and no decorator extraordinaire. What am I going to do? I don't know how to decorate. And where am I going to find a decorator last minute at the height of the holiday season?"

She threw a dirty dishtowel toward the bin in the corner of the room, missing it by a mile.

"Even if I did know how to do it myself, I have extra baking to do for the holiday guests, so I'll be stuck in the kitchen all weekend."

"I have the perfect solution," Harper said. "I'll do it."

So much for the spa, she thought. But nothing pampered her soul like an empty evergreen needing ornaments and bows.

"What do you mean you'll do it?" Even though Stacia's voice was hesitant, her eyes were wide with hope. "You're a guest. I can't make you do my job."

"No, you can't make me do anything…that I don't want to do. But you're not. I volunteered to do it. And I happen to be rather experienced with this sort of thing."

"You are?" Stacia still sounded shell-shocked.

"Would you stop it with the doubting Thomas expressions? You're going to give me a complex."

Harper reached for a pen and paper and started a list of the supplies she'd need. Tearing the sheet from the tablet, she handed it to Stacia.

"Call Robert and have him get his guys to round up these items for me at his shop or wherever else they have to go to come up with them. As soon as they get back, I'll get started."

"Are you sure about this?" Stacia looked worried, but also totally relieved. "I thought you were going out?"

"No worries. I probably shouldn't be spending the money right now anyway. You know what I mean."

"I hear ya."

Harper headed back to her room but looked back in time to catch Stace shaking her head and making the sign of the cross.

"Hey, while we're waiting, could you have housekeeping start to string white lights on that beast?"

"You betcha."

Stacia picked up the phone to summon them.

An hour later, her hair neatly tucked under a ball cap, Harper was all business scanning the boxes the Bloom Factory's crew had returned with. She studied the tree positioned securely in its stand and made her own sign of the cross before giving in to her creative forces.

To set the mood, she set her playlist to Amy Grant's Christmas album and dimmed the light switch on the wall next to the fireplace. With the fake fire blazing and one of her favorite songs from the collection—Tennessee Christmas—piping through the inn's surround sound, she combed through the various boxes removing the items she needed first.

The smell of the fresh pine and Stace's oatmeal cookies baking in the oven transported her into the setting of a Thomas Kinkade Christmas painting. Enjoying a steaming mug of hot cocoa with marshmallows on top, Harper let the energy of the season overtake her.

I can do this. Think like Reggie. With a snap of her fingers and a clap of her hands, she was off and running free.

As the inn's housekeeping staff finished covering the tree with thousands of white lights, working from the inside out as she'd taught them, Harper's excitement built. Muted by the rays of the sun

~ 98 ~

coming in through the over-sized French doors of the great room, the lights took on the red glow of a California sunset.

Using the precision and skills that Reggie had taught her, Harper and the staff crafted no less than a hundred large silver bows out of spools of the hole-punched ribbon cast away by confetti machines. Tying off each bow with floral wire, they tucked,pinched, and popped each one into just the right space between the thick tree boughs.

Struggling with the prickly boughs and sticky sap, Harper's fingers ached. But she welcomed the pain. It felt so good to use her skills because she wanted to instead of being used by others because of her talent.

Stepping back to view her work, she was thrilled to see the sun's effect on the metallic surface of the machine-punched ribbon. The room looked as if it were filled with a magical aura of shimmering, ruby red lasers.

Reggie would be ecstatic.

When she finished, she'd snap several pictures and text them to him back in Briar Creek. He would be most impressed with his protégé's prowess.

After the bows had all been made and placed, Harper attached pipe cleaners to the twelve dozen silver balls she'd requested. With half of the balls covered in mosaic-tiled mirrors and half done in brushed silver, they were sure to look stunning anchored in among the lights and bows.

Harper strategically placed each ball while Stacia and her staff cut strands of gray pearls in three different lengths. Tying together the various strands with floral wire, Harper created chandelier-like ornaments. Taking turns with her newly trained assistants finding boughs to secure them to, Harper gloated at the three dimensional effect she'd designed and executed.

As the sun set late in the afternoon, she stood arm-in-arm with her compadres and toasted the inn's Christmas tree. It was one hell of a tree.

After both she and Stacia thanked the inn's staff, Stacia dismissed them for the day.

"Well, Stace, that does it for the tree. How about we get started on the rest of the place?"

Harper set down her cocktail glass and poured herself a much-needed cup of coffee from the carafe on the hospitality bar.

"Easy, tiger," Stacia said and giggled. "You don't have to do all of this. I can have some of the high school interns that come in tomorrow help. You've outdone yourself as it is."

She disappeared into the kitchen to fill the cream pitcher and hollered, "Where did you learn all that, by the way? You're fantastic! Have you ever thought about decorating professionally?"

She came back into the breakfast room.

"Not really," Harper said. "I picked it up here and there from a friend who decorated my home as well as helped me put on various events."

She added cream to her coffee and nibbled on a cookie from Stace's latest batch.

"I'll finish up a few things tonight, but there'll be plenty for your interns to do tomorrow with the wreaths, greenery and garland. I'll leave them instructions."

Stacia leaned across the table and gave her a huge hug.

"You saved my ass. Remind me to give you a discount on your stay next month."

"I could probably use that."

"Yeah, I thought so. You figured out yet how you're going to handle that situation?"

"Nope. Still thinking about it."

Harper tapped her finger on the glass tabletop, hoping Stace would change the subject. Thankfully, her cell phone rang. She looked at the display and cursed under her breath.

"Speaking of the asshole…"

"Want me to wait in the kitchen?"

"No, you're fine. This won't take long."

Harper answered Jake's call.

"Hello?" She practically screamed into the phone. "What? I can't hear you?"

Stace laughed out loud.

"Hello? Jake?"

Harper was cracking herself up too, while silently praising the strength Stace's strong cocktails had given her. She covered the phone with her hand until she could compose herself.

"I'm sorry, baby, I can't hear you. What? I'm in the Hollywood Hills on my way to a party. You're cutting out. What?"

By now, neither she nor Stacia could hold it much longer. Stace was doubled over in her chair, holding her stomach.

"Hey, I gotta go. I'll call you later. Bye for now."

Click.

"Damn that felt good!" Harper tossed the phone onto the table. "I'll figure out how to handle the money later. I just wanted to blow him off for once."

"You go, sister. For that brilliant effort, I'm going to fix you another drink. You're killing me."

Stacia went to the bar in the great room to make Harper another Black Russian.

"Wish I felt better about it," Harper said, taking the glass Stace offered. "I have a hard time messing with someone like that. I'm used to just telling it like it is, no pretense, no games. Take it or leave it."

"It's the whole fight fire with fire, I think, my friend. And that guy's nothin' but fire. I'm giving you an extra star on the chart for a fantastic performance."

Stacia gave her another hug.

"In that case, I'll have to put it back on the frig. I took it to my room last night so I could add another page."

Giving Harper the thumbs up sign, Stace wiped her hands on her apron then retied it tighter around her waist.

"Guess I'd better clean up the kitchen and get out of here. Thanks again for rescuing Christmas at the inn. You really did an incredible job. Robert has nothing over you."

"Glad to help."

And she was too. She was thrilled by Stacia's compliments, and she was also stuck on what her friend had said about turning her talents into a paying gig. The same idea had occurred to her that afternoon while directing the whole process. She was good at this. No, she was great. If she were in Briar Creek, she might consider helping Reggie on a regular basis. But, in LA, she wasn't sure how she could use her talent.

Decorators were relatively easy to come by here and possessed devout clientele. With no professional credentials, she wasn't sure how easy it would be to hook up with one. To start with, she could ask Robert for some names. And maybe she would. The work itself was so satisfying.

She felt good. Damn good. She'd found one of her grooves. When decorating, she was more than comfortable. She was in her element. This afternoon, she'd discovered a part of herself she'd never nurtured just for the sake of pampering her muses.

She glanced down at her watch and couldn't believe it was almost eight o'clock. The day had flown by since she'd first watched Robert's workers fight the evergreen beast in the hallway.

She walked over to the inn's iPod deck and queued up Amy Grant one more time. She dimmed the lights in the great room and curled up on the couch in front of the fireplace.

She stared at the flames and the beautiful river rock mantel, thinking of the two lone stockings that would have been hanging on each side had she been in Briar Creek.

CHAPTER TWELVE
DON'T WAIT FOR TOMORROW

Grant swirled his gin and tonic around the circumference of a Waterford glass, never taking his eyes off the Christmas tree.

Pink shafts glowed throughout the great room from the multitude of twinkling lights on the thick branches. Reggie had created a masterpiece that Bergdorf's would be proud to display in one of their famous holiday windows.

Taking a swig of his drink, Grant struggled to overcome the overwhelming feeling of emptiness that bounced off the walls of the room. Alone in the midst of so much space, he felt small. Regardless of how much he drank or how high he set the thermostat, the cold despair inside his body wouldn't give way to cozy and contented warmth.

He moved from the oversized suede sofa facing the tree to the leather wing-back chair in front of the fireplace. His father often sought refuge in this chair, in front of this same mantel, years before when Grant was a small boy. The chair and heat from the fire provided his father with the comfort and solace that his family would have been glad to give him, if he'd only let them.

Grant placed his feet on the ottoman and wrapped himself in the throw that his mother had made in one of her knitting clubs.

How had his life come to this? How could a man of his wealth and power have no one to come home to?

Hearing Jeffrey clear his throat, he immediately straightened from his slouched position. He jumped from his thoughts and half out of the well-worn leather cushions. "What the…"

"Sorry, sir."

Jeffrey set a silver tray with a crystal decanter of gin and miniature bottles of tonic water onto the end table next to Grant's chair. "I didn't mean to frighten you."

"Well, you sure as hell did. What did you need, Jeffrey?"

Grant's indignation thundered across the room. He never allowed people to see him pout.

"I'm about to go to my quarters for the evening and wanted to make sure you didn't need anything else."

Jeffrey took Grant's empty glass from his hand, filled it, and returned it to him.

"I'm sorry, Jeffrey. I'm really sorry." Grant shook off his foul demeanor and hung his head in shame. "Thank you. That was very kind of you. You startled me, that's all."

"Sorry, Mr. C. It won't happen again."

Jeffrey turned to leave the room without so much as looking at Grant.

"Jeffrey, um…" Grant fumbled with his glass, making a show of inspecting the cuts of the fine crystal. "You are welcome to have a drink with me, if you'd like. I see you've brought plenty to share."

Jeffrey walked back toward him. "And why would I want to do that? I'd be consorting with the enemy."

"Okay. I deserve that. Even more reason for us to have a discussion."

Grant removed his mother's blanket from his lap and attempted to fold it.

Jeffrey sighed, took the throw from him, re-folded it along its well-preserved creases and placed it onto the back of the chair. He stepped back, eyeballed the position of the throw and straightened it until it suited him.

"I trust this won't take long," he said, sitting on the edge of the velvet chaise on the opposite side of the mantel. "I have plans tonight. So please be brief."

"Very well," Grant said and cleared his throat. "I thought it would benefit both of us if we could call a truce."

"I was unaware of the war, sir."

Grant admired the way Jeffrey refused to cower to him and knew he more than deserved his disrespectful tone.

"It's never been of your doing, Jeffrey. I'm the one that's the asshole."

"Excuse me?"

Jeffrey's normally suave, totally in control posture stiffened, signaling Grant that he was on the right course.

"You heard me. Don't push it. I'm not going to repeat myself."

Grant figured he'd better hurry up and get this out before he lost his nerve or ran out of gin ammunition.

"I've been wrong to not treat you with respect. You have always worked hard here at the estate, and I do appreciate what you do."

"Thank you, Mr. C," Jeffrey said, a hesitant smile replacing his annoyed smirk.

"With Harper away, I wanted you to know that. I'm sure she told you often, but I know I never have." Grant loosened his tie from around his neck, making a mental note to quit wearing them at home. "That's all. Have a great evening. And why don't you take the day off tomorrow? I'll be okay here."

Jeffrey stood to go.

"Thank you, Mr. C, but I promised Reggie I'd help him finish the estate decorating tomorrow, so I'll be here at my normal time."

He reached out his hand and shook Grant's firmly, making good on their truce.

Grant returned the sentiment with a nod of appreciation and relief.

"And please quit calling me 'Mr. C.' Grant is fine."

"Not sure about that one, Mr. C." Jeffrey walked off the battlefield toward the doors of the great room with his head held high. "It rather fits you. I'll work on it though. Good night, Gr-a-nt. See? Told you it would sound strange. See you in the morning, Mr. C."

"Good night, Jeffrey."

Grant reached for his blanket, trying to settle back into his pity stupor. But before he could slouch back down in his chair, Jeffrey summonsed him just before sliding shut the last pocket door to the room.

"Mr. C, for what it's worth," he hemmed-hawed, looking toward the floor for help, "I hope you can get Mrs. C to come home."

"Me too, Jeffrey, me too."

And he'd do everything he could to make it happen.

Once Jeffrey had left, Grant looked back at the fire. The burnt orange flames popped and crackled, sending sparks hissing into the black iron screen fronting the blaze. The night he'd found Harper's note, his heart had exploded with the same intensity.

He was like the cold ash forsaken in a morning hearth. Without her love, the few embers left in his soul were almost extinguished.

If he weren't careful, his legacy would be that of his father's—an urn of ashes spread over the pastures of the estate—devoid of spirit because the person whose bones had been reduced to cinders had been cold and callous for as long as his wife and son could remember.

He took his cell phone out of his pocket. Pressing Speed Dial One, he anxiously waited till Reggie's voice recording rattled out the welcome greeting for the HOW 2LUV twenty-four-hour service.

Following the greeting, a youthful, high-pitched female answered, "Chick Tricks, Inc. How may I help you?"

"Yes, I, um, need to know which of the books in the 101 kit I am to read first," Grant said, shifting his weight in the chair.

After listening to her answer, he disconnected the call and reached into the drawer of the end table. Pulling out the book that the operator had suggested, he took a long pull of his drink. He opened the cover and began to explore the languages of love.

• • •

Grant awoke to a hand shaking his shoulder. Too groggy from the alcohol and too deep inside himself from a fitful night of disturbing dreams, he fought against the need to open his eyes.

"No, Harper, I don't want to go for a jog. I'll wait for my alarm."

The hand persisted.

"Please, let me sleep."

He tried to push the hand away, but couldn't.

"Mr. C, wake up. It's morning. My God, your neck is going to be all out of whack."

A cold chill surged over him as the blanket was pulled from his lap.

"What? Huh? Where am I?"

Grant opened his eyes and tried to shield them from the winter morning glare streaming through the windows of the great room. He tried to focus on Jeffrey, who in a maddening blur, rushed to the pantry behind the bar and hurried back with a dustpan and broom.

Shit. It was bad enough that Jeffrey had seen Reggie give him the Chick Tricks 101 kit. He didn't want him seeing that he was actually using it. He hadn't reached the chapter yet discussing how he was to come to terms with denial.

Jeffrey bent down and began picking up the largest chunks of broken glass.

"Here, let me help you with that. I'm the one who dropped my glass."

As Grant leaned over and pulled the book out of the puddle of gin and shards of shattered crystal, he felt his face grow warm. And it wasn't from the sudden gravity change.

"I must have fallen asleep."

"No problem, Mr. C. Why don't you just go on upstairs and relax. I'll put some coffee on and leave a carafe in your study."

Jeffrey swept up the last pieces of broken glass.

"That would be great. Thanks."

Glad to evade Jeffrey questioning his reading material, Grant practically ran out of the room, the dripping book tucked under his arm.

"I haven't set out your clothes for the day yet," Jeffrey hollered after him.

"No problem. I can find something," Grant yelled back, already at the base of the stairs.

He could have sworn he heard Jeffrey mutter "I doubt it," but he wanted to get out of speaking distance too damn badly to know for sure.

He took a long, blistering hot shower, trying to wash away the uneasiness left from his dreams. He'd thought his past was behind him, and he didn't appreciate the unpleasant reminders.

Like his dreams, where he relived countless birthdays without his father—starting with his sixth—he now faced a life ahead of empty days without Harper.

The double vanity he toweled off in front of served him another cruel reminder. Guess he didn't need two sinks anymore.

Searching through his wardrobe closet, he was aghast at the number of suits, shirts and ties arranged by season around the racks in the walk-in. He couldn't possibly wear all of these. Didn't he own anything else?

He opened one of the cedar-lined drawers of the closet's center island. Rummaging through a pile of cashmere sweaters, he slammed the drawer and opened the next. Sweaters were better than suits, but surely he had more casual attire somewhere.

Harper always wore those matching velour warm-up suits, so more than likely she'd bought him something of that nature as well. It wasn't as if he didn't relax too…well…sometimes.

The next drawer down revealed several pair of corduroy slacks, and white T-shirts filled the one below that. Closer, but still not what he had in mind. Jesus. Did he have anything to lounge around in besides his boxer shorts?

He scanned the shoe racks. If he had tennis shoes, he had to have something casual to wear with them, right? Bingo. Two, never-worn pairs of Nikes peeked out from the far corner of the rack. Okay. That was a start. He'd keep scrounging because there had to be athletic clothes somewhere.

He rounded the corner of the island and searched the drawers on the other side. He found where his socks and underwear were kept. Good to know, in case Jeffrey took him up soon on a day off.

When Harper had been home, she'd always laid out his clothes each morning on the top of the island, down to the belt, tie, socks, shoes and cuff links. When she left, Jeffrey had begrudgingly taken over.

Grant slid open the last drawer, half expecting to find a dastardly selection of tie tacks and pocket squares. Speaking of which, where were those kept? He'd have to ask Jeffrey.

Finally finding a single black jogging suit, he smiled. The smile quickly became a grimace as he pushed aside the cedar mothballs lining the drawer. Harper and Jeffrey had probably figured it would be Hell frozen in an ice age before this particular drawer was ever opened and its contents worn. Well, he'd show them.

Not only was he going to wear this puppy, but he made a mental note to check with Jeffrey about ordering him a few more. He'd definitely need some additional clothing along these lines for LA. From what he'd read in the style manual included in Reggie's Chick Trick Inc.'s kit, the casual look was in on the West Coast.

He pulled on the pants and tied the drawstrings. Not bad. Comfortable, actually. Not sure what to wear under the jacket, he opted for one of his white t-shirts. Maybe he'd better check with Reggie on that.

And as far as the shoes, he shoved his feet into the pliable leather and wiggled his toes in their new surroundings. Rocking back on his feet, he was quite pleased with the padded comfort, much better than his wing tips. Although he loved the feeling of power polished and buffed into those Johnston and Murphys.

He took a look in the dressing mirror that stood in the back right corner of his closet. With a big sigh of 'Here goes nothing,' he stepped out of the closet, out of his room, and down the hall to his office, followed only by the annoying squeak of his never-broken-in tennis shoes against the tile floors. His Johnston & Murphys sure as hell didn't make that obnoxious sound.

Grateful for the warm coffee Jeffrey had delivered to his study as promised, he settled into his office chair and flipped through yesterday's mail. Nothing out of the ordinary awaited him.

He slit open the envelope of the official invitation to the Chair-ity Ball that the Cantwell Group sponsored each year, as if he needed a reminder of the date. Harper, as well as his office secretary, always put it on his calendar before any other event or meeting of the year.

As his signature event, it was a must-attend. Even though his presence was a requirement, he'd always enjoyed the evening tremendously because of the hard work and genius of Harper and her crew. She never failed to give the community the premier event of the year, or to raise obscene amounts of money for the Briar Creek Arts Festival.

Glancing at the theme of this year's gala, he learned it was Mai Tai Madness. He twirled the small cocktail umbrella he'd pulled out of the envelope between his fingers. He'd bet a load that the umbrella in the invitations was Harper's idea.

He made sure the date was in his calendar. Sure enough, it was. All he had to do was make it through that evening, without Harper by his side, and then he'd be on a plane the following week to see her.

He flipped through the rest of the mail. Discarding most of it into the circular file under his desk, he pulled one of his bank statements from the pile as well as Harper's. He slit them open, then stopped to pour another cup of coffee.

Since age six, he'd gone through his statements every month, line by line. Until he was eighteen, his father had also reviewed them. It was one of the musts of being raised a Cantwell. You always signed every check and knew about every item on your statement, whether debit or deposit.

No one was ever allowed to do it for you. Those were the rules that, according to his father, had made, maintained and grown the Cantwell fortune for three generations.

Grant took out his ruler, the same ruler his father had given him for his sixth birthday present, and went through his accounts, item by item. No surprises. His Quickbooks program showed the same amounts and transactions as the bank's records.

Looking at the balance, Grant made a note on his phone to transfer a large amount to his savings and an additional amount to a couple of his money market funds, another of his father's lessons being that the majority of your excess should be saved and put into places with opportunity for future growth.

According to Grant Cantwell II, few things in life were worth spending money on. It should be saved or placed in financial vehicles designed to increase in value. Grant Cantwell III agreed, for the most part.

Taking Harper's statement out of its envelope, Grant paused briefly before unfolding each of the sheets and putting them in sequential order. Before aligning his ruler with the first entry, he laughed out loud. So much for his father's philosophy. When Grant had married Harper, he'd learned a whole new set of financial rules.

She'd come from nothing. Her father worked in a local factory as a fork truck operator, and her mother was a stay-at-home mom. Even though Harper was an only child, money was always tight.

Despite their financial situation, Grant had loved and admired her parents from the moment he met them until their death two years previously. What they didn't have to offer in terms of dollars, they more than made up for in the love and care they had shown Harper and him.

When he'd first met Harper, Grant was amazed and humbled by the concern she showed toward people less fortunate than her. Without a dollar she could easily spare, she never hesitated to give away what she had.

On several occasions in high school, he'd watched her donate to various causes and then skip lunch to go to the library. One day, when he'd caught up with her on the way home after school, she told him she always gave away her lunch money because she wasn't hungry. But he suspected differently. Once he'd started dating her and witnessed her appetite first hand, he knew better.

Sliding the ruler down the first couple of pages, he was surprised to find that she really hadn't been spending much money on anything in California. Other than the ungodly price the inn charged her weekly, it appeared that she rarely ate out, drank a little at a place called The K.O.W., and made weekly trips to Whole Foods Market. Bloomingdales only appeared a few times, as well as a handful of Beverly Hills boutiques.

Adding up the total fees charged by the inn, he thought he might say something to her about her lodging expenses. Not that the amount of money mattered, but it could be better spent by buying a place, if that's where she wanted to live. He preferred to own property, not help others make money off of theirs.

Although he hoped to bring her back to Briar Creek, if she chose to stay in Playa, he'd rather buy the entire inn outright than continue to pay their outrageous rates. Hell, if that was the average price, he'd go ahead and look into buying other rental properties there.

Turning to the last page of the statement, he picked up his coffee cup to finish off the small dab left. He didn't like the milky sweet syrup lingering in the bottom, but refused to waste anything.

After reading the second to last entry on the statement, he dropped his cup. It crashed against the desk, splitting into two chunks, on its way to the floor, soaking his pants before smashing into smithereens.

"What in God's name?!" He screamed out loud into the silent space of his study. "One point five million dollars?!"

He pressed his finger hard against the ruler and then slid it down under the name of the payee.

"Jake Benton? Who the hell is Jake Benton?"

As he pushed the intercom, his hands trembled.

"Jeffrey, could you come up here a moment please?"

His voice rose a full octave higher than normal, but he didn't care.

"Sure, Mr. C."

"It's Grant, dammit I said to call me Grant."

"Uh oh, Mr. C," Jeffrey blurted into the intercom. "Be right up."

Grant wiped at the wet coffee on his pants with a crumpled piece of paper he'd pulled out of his wastebasket. Carefully picking up the largest pieces of the annihilated mug, he threw them into the trash along with the coffee-soaked paper wad.

The intercom snapped back to life.

"I'm coming too," Reggie's smoky-rich voice drifted through the speaker.

Grant rolled his eyes, too pissed to care if all the fruits in his house showed up in his study. He had more pressing issues at hand. Denial was no longer a viable option.

While he waited for Jeffrey and Reggie, he did a Google search on Jake Benton. Instantly, he found Jake's website. So much for needing the fruits' help solving the riddle.

Jake Benton was a Sapphire. A fucking Sapphire. That explained how Harper knew him. But she knew him enough to give him a million and a half dollars? That was another issue entirely.

When Jeffrey and Reggie knocked on his study door, Grant called them in. He motioned for them to be seated in the chairs across from his desk. They both sat, Jeffrey looking like he was appearing before the Spanish Inquisition, and Reggie too busy on his cell phone to give a damn.

"Yes, Harper." Reggie winked at Grant and pointed at his phone. "Everything is coming along splendidly for the ball. I wish you were here too. Sure thing, sweetie. I can't wait to see the pictures. Gotta run, darling. I'll call you later."

Reggie tossed one hand into the air, making anxious gestures, as if his manic motion was speeding up his conversation. "Okay, smooches to you too. Ciao."

He tucked the phone into his shirt pocket.

"What can we do for you?" Jeffrey spoke up first.

Grant rocked back and forth in his chair in smooth, calculated movements, like he did when trying to posture against a defiant client. "Tell me what you know about Jake Benton."

He watched the two exchange concerned looks and figured out rather quickly that they knew something he'd find useful.

"So how's Chick Tricks 101 coming along?" Reggie asked in a decidedly poor attempt at changing the subject.

Okay. Fine. Grant would play along for a while. "Why do you ask?"

"I'm asking, my friend, because you'd better be one quick study if Jake's already far enough into the picture to have your panties in a twist like this."

Reggie made the 'That's the truth, girlfriend' body toss that Grant now knew meant serious business in the gay world.

"The question should be," Jeffrey said while holding up his hand to Reggie, signaling him to stop speaking, "Why are you asking us about Jake?"

"Judging by her bank account withdrawals, it seems that Harper knows him rather well. I want to know from the two of you what I can do about it."

Grant gave up rocking in his chair. The gliding motion no longer gave him the powerful sensation it did in his boardroom. Who was he kidding? On this front, he couldn't posture for position. He didn't know his ass from...well, his ass...about what to do now.

He collapsed his head onto his desk. When he lifted it, Jeffrey and Reggie jumped up, ran around to his chair and embraced him.

"Oh, for Christ's sake, sit down. I don't need a hug."

They continued with their bear hugs. Grant obviously hadn't made a dent in their misplaced affection.

"I need advice on how to handle this. How to handle her, him, and the rest of my fucked up world."

Jeffrey and Reggie returned to their chairs, appearing mildly offended by his rejection of their compassion.

"Mr. C, I know Harper has a certain fondness for Mr. Benton, but I don't think you've totally lost yet. If that helps," Jeffrey said.

Grant raked his fingers through his hair and moved forward in his chair, trying to find a dry part of his pants to sit on.

"I can't wait for three more weeks to go out there, can I?"

"Well," Reggie piped in, crossing one leg over the other and dramatically kicking it out and in as if he were a Rockette.

"Harper did just tell me on the phone that Hollywood is on tour for the month, so I would think if you could go now…"

Grant stood up and paced the floor behind his desk, his wet pants forcing his boxers to further lodge themselves in a most undesirable spot.

"How soon can you have me ready?"

"Depends on how much you can learn and how quickly. Nice pants by the way, but you really need to go with a different T-shirt. The glare off that white is giving me a Jurassic-size headache."

Reggie pulled a crumpled piece of paper from the pocket of his velour smoking jacket. "I can rearrange my schedule over the next couple of days."

"Okay. Do that."

Grant scrambled for his iPhone on the opposite end of his desk and started tapping app after app.

"Jeffrey, I'll need you to do some serious shopping for me. I have nothing but suits and matching ties to wear, and I'm not going to LA like that. Apparently, I don't even have appropriate T-shirts."

He mocked Reggie, who wasn't about to change his assessment.

"Well, you don't. White is so out for basic tees."

"Gotcha covered, Mr. C."

Jeffrey took out the notebook that he always carried with him and made some notes.

"In the mean time, I'll get a hold of my secretary today and clear my schedule through the holidays." Grant tapped his screen until he wondered if the device would explode.

Reggie stood and turned to leave but crept back to the corner of Grant's desk.

"I hate to ruin this plan, but what will you do about Mai Tai Madness?"

"Shit." Grant pounded his fists against his desk. Looking first at Jeffrey and then Reggie, with an almost painful hesitation, followed by a quiet resolve, he stated in barely more than a whisper, "I'd be most appreciative if the two of you would be my representatives at this year's event. I'll be happy to pay you. Name the price."

Jeffrey looked at Reggie.

Grant could hardly force himself to wait out their answers. Madness party or not, he'd be the one going mad if he didn't try everything he could to get Harper back. And with Mr. Sapphire interrupting his plan, he had to come up with a Plan B.

"Mr. C, we'd be honored to represent you. No payment is necessary. Haven't you learned yet that everything isn't about money? Just give it your all and bring Harper home."

Jeffrey left the room with his list in hand, but then stepped back in and said, "I'll need to measure you. I'll go get my tape and be right back."

Reggie took a tissue from his pocket and dabbed at his eyes.

"Okay, kiddo, give me a few minutes to direct my staff on how to finish the estate for the holidays, and then we'll begin your love training."

"What should I do while you're doing that?" Grant was a nervous wreck, something he had no idea how to handle.

"Well, go blow dry those pants for starters. You've got to be all bunched up down there!"

Reggie shooed him away as if he were a pesky fly.

"Okay, good idea. I just have one thing to finish here, and then I'll go do that."

Grant punched a few numbers into his laptop and maneuvered his hands across the built-in mouse pad. A few clicks, and a transfer from his account to Harper's was complete. That should tide her over until he got there.

He got up from his desk, trying to casually maneuver his pants out of a certain crack. Finally foregoing finesse, he yanked them free.

Leaving his office, he headed for the master bath to find a hairdryer, his shoes squeaking the entire way.

CHAPTER THIRTEEN
MUSE THERAPY

After tackling the inn's Christmas tree, Harper slept better than she had in weeks. She leaned up on her elbows, enough to see the clock on her nightstand, and was thrilled to discover it was only six A.M.

The inn's Sunday crew would have the quiche and strudel that Stacia had prepared last night out of the frig and into the oven. The thought of opening her door to smell the kitchen in all its glory had more than visions of sugarplums dancing in her head.

For the first time in weeks, she had plenty of time to have a cup of coffee, get dressed, and make it to breakfast. It was just what she needed to celebrate her slumberous victory.

She'd attributed her fitful nights to her rough adjustment to Jake's lifestyle. Years on the road entertaining until ten P.M., followed by after-parties and receptions, meant he was up until the wee hours of the morning, then in a hotel bed or on a plane sleeping the day away. Wee hours of the morning had yet to appeal to Harper.

Breakfast was now a luxury. Lunch was normally brunch, consisting of whatever leftovers Stacia and company had waiting for her sleep-deprived arrival into the kitchen. She snacked late afternoon/early evening, compliments of the inn's daily wine and cheese reception. Dinner was anytime after nine, usually around eleven, whenever Jake would finally show up, after another unexpected encounter with some long-lost friend who had a project going that he was dying to be part of.

Harper stretched her sore limbs, which ached from bending and twisting in odd positions to accommodate the evergreen monster. The thought occurred to her that she could relate to Jake's artistic passion—not in the musical sense—but she'd had a creative moment last night, where nothing could have come between her and her tree.

Grant had never understood or appreciated her need for artistic expression. Hell, until last night, she didn't understand or appreciate how deep her desire ran for artistic outlets.

Dragging herself out of bed, but with a slight spring in her drag, she thanked the powers that be for last night's creative bliss.

Maybe it wasn't Jake's nightmarish schedule that was totally to blame for her physical exhaustion. Perhaps her pent-up creative juices had been too busy trying to get out to allow her body to rest. Holed up in the inn, she'd become a frustrated artist—a wonderful addition to her status as a rejected lover, times two.

About to dump a scoop of coffee into her coffeemaker, Harper's room phone rang, startling her and causing her to empty half the remaining grounds onto the floor of her kitchenette.

She picked up the receiver, unable to decipher, without her glasses, who would be calling this early in the morning. She was confident it wasn't Jake.

"Hello, doll," a voice croaked in a barely audible whisper. "Can you hear me? It's Robert."

"Robert? That's you? You sound awful."

"Tell me about it." He struggled to complete a full sentence, pausing to breathe as if it were a conscious exercise instead of an involuntary requirement of life. "I've got mono."

"Mono? Stace told me it was just the flu."

Guilt overcame her for relishing yesterday's opportunity to cover for him at the inn. She had no idea his illness was this serious. "How are you going to get through the holidays?"

"Well...," Robert stammered, struggling to speak at all, "Stace told me how fabulous the inn looks. Here I thought you were just my favorite customer and friend. So anyway, I was hoping that...maybe...you could fill in for me."

Harper's spirit soared with the positive rush flowing through her. What a fantastic opportunity. But brain waves of reasonableness cautioned her. She was way out of her league decorating Hollywood for the holidays.

"Oh, Robert, I couldn't possibly. It's one thing to decorate a tree. But spreading the ho-ho-ho for your customers in Tinsel Town is another thing entirely. I do charity events in Music City, not celebrity fetes on the red carpet."

"Well, girlfriend, from what I've heard, you've got the talent."

Two labored puffs later, he finished the clincher of his persuasive effort, "So here's your chance to go for the gusto. See whatcha got."

"Gusto? Robert, after they finish with me, your clients will be kicking your ass with gusto."

Could she even consider doing this? Her body screamed "yes." But was she totally nuts?

"Listen, doll, I'll pay you whatever you demand…just do this…for me. Please. Can't you tell I'm desperate?"

"Of course I know you're desperate or you wouldn't have called me." Harper paced the floor, twisting the phone cord so tight around her wrist that her skin turned bluish red. "Okay, I'll do it."

That was her creative spirit talking on its own behalf, not her brain.

"Fabulous. Okay…you'll start tomorrow and work at least…until after New Year's," he said, then groaned.

"Till after New Year's?" Thinking it would be a week or so, not six or more, Harper panicked. "I can't work till New Year's. I've got company coming in three weeks. Robert…"

"I'll see if I can come up…with someone else to help you…by then," he said, fewer and fewer words making it out between each deep breath.

He sounded so miserable that she thought he was about to cry.

"Okay. Sounds like you need to rest for a while," she said, taking a damp towel to the spilled grounds.

She punched the on switch to start the caffeine flowing, glad for the inn's bold brews. "Check in with me tomorrow, if you can, so we can discuss the events you have scheduled. I'll do my best."

"Thank you, Harper. Thank you so much. My staff will open the shop tomorrow at seven…so anytime after that is fine for you…to go in." Reduced to a faint murmur, he faded almost out of Harper's range. "I'll have them make you a key."

"Okay, Robert. Get some rest. Talk to you tomorrow."

Hanging up the phone, Harper rubbed out the stabs of fear piercing her forehead. Suddenly the idea of creatively exploring her talents ceased to energize her. Instead, it terrified her.

This was so not what she'd envisioned, but what the hell. She'd either drive herself nuts waiting out the three weeks until Grant arrived or have a little fun while sprucing up homes for the holidays in the Hollywood Hills.

Certain that any therapist would recommend the latter, she tried to drown her anxiety with her first sip of hot coffee. Having forgotten a substantial portion of the grounds were in her wastebasket instead of in the automatic drip basket, she gagged and spit the barely brown murk into the sink.

Her calendar app called back to active duty, she typed in the names of a few of the regional lifestyle magazines she'd found in the inn's lobby. She'd need to purchase her own copies to deface as she studied up on the West Coast's seasonal vibes.

She had the pulse of a Tennessee Christmas, but this side of the country was all new to her. How to decorate the playgrounds of Hollywood's elite would have quite a different feel from the abandoned ballrooms and upper middle class galas of the Tennessee Hills.

She'd also need the files she'd meticulously kept on the events she'd planned and produced back home. She made a note to call Reggie so he could gather them from her study and overnight a package to her. She hoped he also had time to toss out his thoughts on Hollywood holidays.

Her stomach growled loudly. She tossed her phone onto the small desk in her room and made a mental note to see if Stace could hook her up with a larger work station, then headed for the shower.

Thankfully, she'd gotten up and at 'em in time for breakfast. She needed the extra sustenance, especially the temporary sanity Stace's spinach and feta quiche offered.

Once in the dining room, she nearly swallowed her breakfast whole. She didn't have time, like usual, to examine the unique birds living in the wetlands on the other side of the inn's windows. While going over the list she'd made of the items left to complete the inn's holiday décor, she devoured every bite of quiche, Stace's specialty. The high school help would be arriving within the hour, and she wanted to have every task outlined in full detail for them.

Since it was Stace's day off, Harper hadn't planned on being gone from the inn, in case the students needed help. But with her new job dangling over her like mistletoe with a sign reading "kick my ass" instead of "kiss me," she wouldn't have time to hang around for any design emergencies.

Following a quick trip into Marina del Rey for a power run to the Barnes & Noble magazine rack, she'd be locked in her room, digesting thousands of pages of glossy print, looking for what makes the holidays sparkle in Tinsel Town.

By the time she hit the back door of The Bloom Factory tomorrow morning, she'd have a list of basic must-have supplies to check against Robert's inventory and, if necessary, an order ready to be placed.

Hopefully Robert would fess up his sources so she would know how to quickly get her hands on the bare essentials for a fairly reasonable price. But on such short notice, they might be shit out of luck getting anything remotely cost-effective.

Checking off the final project for the interns, she left their instructions in the Sunday staff's in-basket on the counter inside the kitchen door. In stark contrast to the pile of mail waiting for Stace's return on Monday, the single envelope in the slot neatly labeled with Harper's room number could have easily gone unnoticed. Turning it over, her eyes caught the familiar logo of Briar Creek Savings Bank. She froze.

Her bank statement. Perfect.

In the rush of her decorating frenzy, she'd temporarily forgotten about her financial nightmare. If she'd received her statement clear in California, Grant would have already received his copy as well. As she slit open the envelope with her fingers, her hands quivered.

Papercut. Dammit. She stuck her finger in her mouth, trying to squelch the nasty sting.

She flipped through the pages of her statement until she reached the last one, hoping to find that Jake's withdrawal hadn't made this statement's cycle. But there it was. She winced. Fuck.

There was no way in hell Grant wouldn't have already seen the transaction. He, like his Grinch of a father, would have already marked the item as unaccounted for. Hell, the size of it could cause a cardiac infarction.

Actually, she was surprised he hadn't called yet. It wouldn't be long, though. Maybe she should call him first. Probably not a bad approach. She'd call him this afternoon and prepare him. Evidently he hadn't opened it yet, or else he would have been her wake up call.

To give Grant credit, unlike his father, he was generous with his money. She just wished he were as generous with his heart.

On her way back to her room, she shoved the statement back into the envelope, making a mental note to stop at an ATM in the marina to check on her current balance. And somewhere in her schedule this afternoon she was going to pencil in ripping Jake's ass. He may be able to piss with her, since she hadn't found a way to stand up to him yet, but he wasn't going to mess with Grant. Grant worked way too hard to be used by someone like Jake, who obviously had no regard for anyone but himself.

The more Harper thought about it, the angrier she became.

She smacked the envelope against the palm of her hand, studying the bank's logo as tears swelled in her eyes. The design was a small circle, including the outline of a family—a father, mother, one boy, and one girl—all holding hands. The irony sank in.

The bank, with Grant as chairman of the board, promoted itself as a family institution. The Cantwells, once under the heavy hand of Grant's father, couldn't even be called a family, if that term was defined by the love shown among its members.

Grant had never been shown love. He'd only seen it in action when he met her family. Even then, he never participated emotionally. And Harper had never forced him to because she saw how uncomfortable it made him.

He tried to show he cared by opening up his wallet. He'd even provided well for her parents after her father retired. And when they fell ill, first her mother and then her father soon after, Grant had made sure they received the best care possible.

Harper would never forget his valiant efforts to ease their pain, and hers, during their health's slow deterioration.

She'd hoped, with time, he'd learn how to give love with more than his wallet. She'd hoped he'd learn it was okay to express his feelings in ways that didn't fall under the jurisdiction of the Federal Reserve. But she'd never been unable to reach him.

Maybe it was her. Maybe she alone couldn't repair his heart. Maybe it had been stomped too deep inside him to be resurrected. Or maybe, and this is the thought that punched a hole through her gut, maybe she wasn't the person to reach it.

Throwing the envelope into her desk drawer, she shoved the drawer shut, making a loud bang that echoed off the walls of her room.

Harper didn't have time any more for this introspective, depressive bullshit. She had to find and heal her own wounds. And Grant would have to do the same, if he wanted to. If he didn't, that wasn't her problem. It was his.

She had enough problems of her own. Today. This week. And for the next three to six weeks. Ho-freakin-ho.

Her responsibility to dress Hollywood for the holidays excited her more than any project she'd ever committed to. But at the same time, her darkest fears had been awakened. What if she failed? Having her marriage at its end was enough disappointment for the year. Failing this creative venture would send her to Sunnydale in a sleigh drawn by eight reindeer.

What a jolly attitude she had. She made another mental note—this one, to find the spirit of the season. She couldn't very well be spreading holiday cheer feeling like the broken babe left in Toyland.

• • •

As she punched in her password at the automatic teller, the midmorning sea air swept through her ponytail, almost dislodging her ball cap. Not brave enough to read the information on the screen, she pulled out the paper receipt as it slid out from the designated slot. She took a deep breath before turning it over to read the available balance. Seeing the figure in print, her heart caught in her throat.

How could that be? Where had all that cash come from since the last statement date? The numbers shown made it appear as if Jake's debit had never happened.

She had to get a hold of Grant today. It wasn't his job to fix her mistakes. She should have opened her own bank account when she'd left Briar Creek. But when it came to money, she'd always trusted Grant and still did. He made excellent financial decisions. She obviously didn't. Thank God the banks would reopen the next day, and she could do whatever she had to do to get Jake off of her account.

She tucked the receipt inside her billfold and pulled out the list of resources she needed from the bookstore. Even though her balance was fine, she crossed off a couple of the magazines on the list. Frugality never killed anyone she knew of, except Grant's father. And he, more or less, was the architect of his own demise, the Grinch who'd never come down from his green mountain to discover the heart of Whoville.

After several hours of clipping and cutting images from the periodicals, Harper taped and tacked them onto her bulletin board. At her request, housekeeping had replaced the watercolor seascape on her wall with a large cork-board. Perfect for collaging. She'd always liked Reggie's technique of collaging to help visualize the look and mood of a design.

Keeping her collage on the wall in front of her desk should help focus and create just the looks she envisioned for Hollywood Christmases. From the seasonal pictures she pasted, she also made her list of most wanted accessories to get the process started. Next, she would top off that list with any ideas she found on Pinterest, her favorite online scrapbooking site.

A dull ache crept across her lower back. She was so engrossed in her work that, she had no idea how long she'd been at it. Leaning back in her chair, she stretched and attempted to find relief. Time for a break.

She reached for her cell phone. She pressed through her recently dialed numbers until Jake's name popped up. Maybe she could harness the creative energy from her mind for her tongue and give him the thrashing he deserved.

She dialed his number, tapping her glue stick against the corner of her desk while the line rang. Whoever said patience was a virtue was full of shit. It was complete agony. One more ring, and his voice mail would pick up.

Listening to his overly theatrical message—once thinking it was so professional, now convinced it was simply another sign of his over-inflated egotistical bullshit—she resigned herself to the fact that she'd probably be leaving a short and very direct message.

"Call me when you get this. We need to talk."

She didn't have a wager for her star chart on this one. She wrote a note on her schedule to call him back if she hadn't heard from him by tomorrow evening. She'd never followed up with the unanswered messages she left him before, but she wasn't about to let this one go ignored.

She dialed Reggie's number, only to get his voice mail as well. She left a message asking him to send her event files.

On a roll, she called Grant's private line, ready to leave him a message. Completely startled when he answered, she forced herself to speak.

CHAPTER FOURTEEN
IT'S YOUR CALL

"Grant?" Harper sank into her desk chair, her knees turning to sugar-free Jello.

"Speaking."

He was seldom contrite with her, unless money was the issue, so she no longer wondered whether or not he'd reviewed her statement.

She couldn't drag this out. And she couldn't squelch the nerves eating at her stomach either. Talking to Grant about money never caused her anything but indigestion. He'd always given her so much that, she could never bring herself to ask for more.

The familiar tightening of her body was an unpleasant reminder of her life in Briar Creek, when the only reason Grant would converse with her was in regard to some monetary expenditure he didn't approve of. But this time, she truly had screwed up, and she owed him an explanation.

"I got my bank statement today," she said.

"Wish I could say I hadn't, but that's not the case," he said.

His voice sounded hollow, as if he were in a submarine, meaning he'd probably put her on speaker-phone.

Odd, she thought. He never uses that feature. He detests it, feeling as she did, that it's an insult to the person on the other end of the line. If someone wasn't worthy of their full, undivided attention, they didn't take the call to begin with. She swore, though, that she could hear other people in the background whispering to him.

"Grant, is now a good time to talk about this?"

Papers shuffled and something fell to the floor with a loud thud.

"I'm not sure there's really a better one. Wouldn't you agree?" Despite his gruff tone, he seemed distracted.

"Am I on speaker phone?"

"As a matter of fact you are. Sorry. I'm in the middle of a project right now that can't wait, so we're going to have to have this conversation while I continue working, or not have it at all. Your pick."

His nonchalance caught Harper off balance, twisting her heart that much tighter. "Okay. I'm sorry if I'm interrupting you, but I didn't want to put this issue off."

"Sounds reasonable."

A voice she easily identified as Jeffrey's instructed Grant to stand still and look straight ahead.

"You're going to have to speak louder, or I won't be able to hear you…ouch!"

What in the hell was going on? He not only had her on speaker, but Jeffrey was in earshot of every word.

"Grant, I'd really like to talk to you privately. It won't take long." Harper stood up from her chair and paced the room.

Speaking louder and more directly into her receiver as Grant had asked her to do, she said, "Hello, Jeffrey. No offense to you, my friend."

"No problem, Harper. I miss you. You should see what Mr. C, I mean Grant, has done with the estate for the Christmas…"

He stopped mid-sentence, then continued. "Talk to you soon."

She heard more items being shuffled around the room.

"I'll be back in a few minutes with some tea," Jeffrey said.

"I miss you too, Jeffrey," Harper said, trying to catch him before he left.

Jeffrey called Grant by his first name? And Grant had the estate decorated? Suddenly life as Harper knew it at the estate had vanished.

"He's gone now, so let's get this over with. I've got things to do." Grant must have picked up the receiver because the echo was gone.

"Yes, of course. About Jake's withdrawal…"

Harper leaned her forehead against the wall for support. She contemplated beating it a few times against the drywall, but didn't imagine that would help her thought process.

"I want you to know that I knew nothing about, nor did I approve of, what he did. I simply…"

"Harper, what you do with the money I give you is your business," Grant said, then stopped and sighed as if he were struggling to decide what to say next. "It always has been. And I'm not going to change that now. However, I don't think it's very smart on your part to relinquish your authority over your account to someone else. My father…"

"I'm well aware of what your father would say, Grant. Let's not bring him into this."

It pissed her off that Grant could never talk about money without mentioning that tight ass's two cents' worth.

"You're right. I'm sorry for that."

Up until this point, he'd maintained the curt bravado she'd expected and deserved, but suddenly he sounded defeated. Maybe it was the mention of his father—never a pleasant topic.

"No, you're the one who's right, Grant. I called to apologize and let you know that I've already called the bank and left a message for them to remove Jake from the account first thing tomorrow morning."

Harper threw herself back onto her bed and stared at the ceiling, hoping Grant hadn't lost all faith in her.

"I won't let this happen again," she said and meant it.

"That's probably a good idea. Anyway, I replaced the funds in your account yesterday."

"Grant, you didn't need to do that."

So that's why her balance was no longer affected by Jake's slippery fingers. She knew better than to hope that he'd come to his senses and returned her money.

Grant had more than eased her burden when he had no reason to help her. She didn't deserve his kindness.

"I could have managed fine until next month. You don't need to cover for my stupidity."

"Just do us both a favor and make sure the bastard doesn't do it again." Jake hesitated briefly before continuing, "Do you need help handling him?"

"No!" Harper shouted into the phone before she could stop herself.

Knowing he'd taken a direct hit to his eardrum, she softened her voice, "No, I need to do this myself. I'm really sorry, Grant."

"Well, I hate to cut this short, but I've got to get back to business. If you change your mind, call me." A brisk bravado tempered his response once more. "On second thought, email or text me because I'll be unavailable to talk for a couple of days and then away…on business… starting Wednesday."

"Okay. But don't worry. I can deal with Jake on my own."

Harper hoped she sounded more convincing than she felt.

"Okay. If that's what you want," he said, his voice muffled, as if his hand were partially covering the receiver. "Let me know if things don't work out like you think, and…you need my help."

Where had this Grant Cantwell been when she was sharing a home with him? Perhaps he cared more than he'd ever chosen to let on.

She heard the clank of a silver tray being placed on his desk. Jeffrey must be back with tea. Odd that he was so involved with Grant's project. Grant liked to work alone. Not to mention, he normally couldn't stand to be in Jeffrey's presence. He avoided him like he did anything remotely embodying kindness.

"I've got to go. Good luck with Jake." Grant interrupted Harper's jumbled thoughts.

"Thank you. And thank you for your kindness."

She wasn't sure how he'd respond to that. Come to think of it, he probably wouldn't respond at all.

"You're welcome. See you soon."

"You're welcome."? That's it? No hem-hawing. Just a sincere "You're welcome"? What the hell was going on with him?

Harper reached for her jogging shoes. If she didn't purge some of the mass confusion filtering through her body, she'd go crazy.

She stretched like she always did before a run, but she was wound too tight to feel anything close to warmed up and ready to go. She repeated her routine.

How was she supposed to find herself when everything once a constant in her life was in a state of upheaval?

She stepped out the front door of the inn and hit the pavement. Watching the sun—a fireball of red—slowly descending in the early evening sky, she kept a steady pace and ran toward the beach.

With sweat pouring over her shoulders and down her chest, she stepped off the jogging path, her feet meeting the heavy resistance of the deep sand. The salt of her sweat combined with the salt of the sea, forcing a healthy escape of her inner demons.

Her chest muscles tightened, but not from the tension of her ragged breath, rather from her shredded soul. Fighting her way through the sand toward the sprays of surf rolling in, she slowed her pace. The vast unknowns of the ocean pulled on her like the strong currents taking the tides back out to sea.

She lifted her face to the sun as it hovered low on the Pacific's horizon. Its majestic intensity competed with the desperation threatening to overwhelm her.

She dropped to her knees on the final swell of sand free of the ocean's foaming froth. Her soul cried out with the screeching gulls, who were probably pissed because she was interrupting their dinner dance. Judging by the smell of fish and kelp that never seemed to leave this stretch of beach, she seriously doubted she'd caused them to miss their meals.

Wiping the sea's gritty residue from her skin, she hugged her knees up close to her chest. As the sun slowly fell into the Pacific, a cold breeze blew over the beach. Caught in its path, she shivered.

The birds continued to cry out in a state of constant torment. They soared around her, providing sharp contrasts to the streaks of yellow and purple smoke feathered across the sky in the sun's wake.

Help me, she prayed to anyone up there who might be listening, hoping they could hear her above the damn birds.

Wiping a drop of sweat from her brow bone, just before it tumbled into her eye, Harper winced as an arch of red light surrounding the drowning sun almost blinded her. A young couples' laughter got her attention as they playfully pushed each other into the path of the tides.

The man backed up and motioned for the woman to pose as he adjusted the camera hanging over his shoulder for one last shot of the day—no doubt a moment that would be perfectly captured in their family scrapbook.

The woman cupped her hands, making it look as if she were holding the sun in her hands, the glow of the crimson ball surrounded by the dark outline of human hands.

With the hiss and thunder of the tide pounding in her ears, Harper watched as the final piece of the sun sank beneath the woman's hands and under the water's surface. One incredible moment indelibly etched into Harper's mind forever.

Her prayers had been answered. She'd left Grant behind to face an uncertain world, not knowing what she'd find. But it wasn't about waiting to see what she'd find, it was about going after whatever it was she wanted. It was about making life happen in the direction she chose to travel, not waiting on a personal travel guide.

It was her turn to hold the world and its sun in her hands. All she had to do was reach for it and hold on.

She pushed herself up, dusted the sand off of her jogging pants, and turned back toward the inn. She had her own horizon to find, her own world to embrace. The difference was that this time she was on her own, for the first time in her life, without a keeper.

CHAPTER FIFTEEN
LIFE BLOOMS

Harper's hands shook as she unlocked the back door of The Bloom Factory. She had taken a huge leap agreeing to run this place for Robert. Her jumpiness was more than the fear of failure. It was in part from recognizing the possibilities ahead of her.

Wanting to arrive well ahead of Robert's staff, she had called him the night before and asked him to have someone bring her a key. She had the key, but she had to quit shaking long enough to fit the damn thing into the lock.

Succeeding at last, she pushed open the door, trying to balance her collage, tote bag, and the mug of coffee that Stacia had sent with her. Turning on the lights in the back office, she rushed toward Robert's desk, dumped her bag on the floor and collapsed into his chair. She glanced at her watch. She had exactly an hour and a half to get her crap together in order to convince the staff she knew what she was doing.

In front of her, in the center of his desk, just as he had promised, was his event calendar. Ready to face the music, she turned back the cover and flipped through the pages until she landed on the day at hand.

At least nothing of outlandish proportions was listed for her first day or the rest of the week, but turning to the December month-at-a-glance, her heart dropped. Nothing but a sea of red and green ink. Once she could focus, she counted no less than two major events each day in addition to the call-in orders that were the other mainstay of Robert's business. Thank God Robert had hired an additional person to man the phones.

Diving into shallow water posed a grave danger, so where did diving in way too deep figure in to her life expectancy? Robert's schedule made her former life as a philanthropic queen look rather mundane. This was nuts. No wonder he had mono.

She reached for the file cabinet next to the desk. Pulling out the top drawer, she found the files containing his notes on each of the events scheduled. Her overfilled tote bag of inspiration was nothing compared to the hullabaloo of ideas that Robert had shoved into each event's folder.

She'd always considered herself lucky that she had the organizational skills to go along with her creative flare. Working with event planners and decorators, she'd learned that her strengths were a rare combination.

Even Reggie, when it came to his planning notes, was one mass of crumpled coffee and food-stained papers. As she thumbed through Robert's files, she learned that he wasn't much better. Although his scattered notes didn't have leftover food on them, they consisted of multitudes of torn pieces of paper with scribbles covering every inch.

She took pride in the fact that anyone could open one of her files and go from A-to-Z to execute an event just as she had done before them. Every name, phone number, quantity and design how-to was accounted for in her records. Nothing was left to guesstimate, which was probably the reason she and Reggie had been so good together. She was the method to his madness.

She shut the file drawer, hoping when she reopened it the contents would have magically organized themselves. No such luck.

Heading for the stock room, she figured she'd better get started by checking for the bare basics she'd need to begin preparations. Passing through the shop's front retail space, she was momentarily spellbound by the holiday wonderland Robert had created.

For a minute, with such a potent reminder of the magic Reggie commandeered back at the estate, her heart sank. She wished she could see it in person. Pictures didn't do justice for this kind of genius. Gently rubbing at the tiny tight knots in her chest, she took a deep breath and pushed on.

Not bothering to ruin the magical scene with shop lighting, Harper basked in the softness of the tiny bulbs twinkling from the twenty-plus themed trees Robert had designed. Each had its own dominant color element—from her favorite pinks to winter white and the iciest of blues. Amidst all of the decadent sparkle, she was at home.

Robert had gone from Victorian Christmas pasts to the modern slink and sizzle of Tinsel Town and everything in between. Each tree was fabulous in its own right. And she especially got a kick out of the brilliant upside down trees he'd hung from the ceiling.

How she could keep the talent of The Bloom Factory at its present height was beyond her wildest imagination. Good thing she wasn't able to sleep much. It would require as many waking hours as she could muster to fulfill the shop's seasonal calendar and all of the unknown orders.

Harper's head ached from the pressure of the job ahead, but at the same time, a fantastic energy warmed her soul. Ideas were already starting to flutter in front of her eyes and formulate into cohesive units for the first two events on Robert's list—a couple of open houses in the Hollywood Hills.

She had to get this right, not just for Robert, but for herself.

She ground up the last of the coffee beans she found in the tiny kitchenette to make a fresh pot and let the gingerbread and spice allure of the Christmas blend permeate her mind. She turned on the candle warmers displayed in the gift section and cranked up the classical Christmas tunes he'd left in the CD changer.

Thank God she was singing to and enjoying a rousing rendition of "Jingle Bell Rock" when she entered the storage room. When she saw the hazard zone that awaited her, her short-lived inner peace and confidence were knocked off their pedestal. How Robert ever found anything in this hellhole was a mystery.

Well, that was going to have to be the first job of the day for at least two of his staff. She could not work in this mess.

There was no way she could even tell what was where or if it even existed. Hell, all she knew was that she had piles of partially used spools of ribbon and hundreds of boxes of decorative accessories.

The shelving units were overloaded with strands of pearls, ceramic cherubs, partially finished topiaries, wreaths of every size and material, tube after tube of glitter and sequins and dozens of tubs of decorative floral picks and ornaments. Trees, Santa statues and grapevine reindeer stood in precariously balanced heaps all across the floor, in no particular order. Empty boxes of previously used materials had simply been thrown on top of the stacks instead of being broken down and recycled.

Harper had exactly one week before the first event to make some kind of workable atmosphere out of this decoupage of disaster. Hopefully, she could convince Robert's staff that this environment was not conducive to their ultimate productivity or her sanity.

She went back to his desk to redo the task list she'd previously made out for the day. Forget diving into the first project, she'd have to clean up this creative ground zero before she'd even know what she had to work with.

She turned on the computers, flipped on the rest of the light switches to their humming and buzzing phosphorescent glory, and grabbed a tablet to begin jotting down the messages that had been left the night before on Robert's answering machine.

Eight recordings later, hearing the voice of the ninth caller, her pen fell to the floor. She hit the replay button, certain she was just imagining what she'd heard. But she wasn't.

Jake really must think that he could schmooze the world.

Harper hit the rewind and play button one last time.

"This is Jake Benton, you might know me from The Sapphires. Anyway, I'm in a bit of a jam with my, um, girlfriend."

He cleared his throat then continued, "I need an obscenely expensive arrangement sent to The Inn first thing Monday morning, in care of Harper Cantwell. And I mean first thing."

Harper cringed, brushing her hands over her arms to squelch the multiplying chills.

"I mean it. Go over the top bold. Cost is no issue. In fact, if this isn't Robert listening to my order, ask him what to do. He knows what Harper likes."

A paging system calling for him to report to the green room sounded in the background.

"Sign the card 'Luv ya. Miss ya. Will call later today. Jake."

He left his payment information, which luckily wasn't the Visa she'd had issued to him as an automatic debit from her account.

"I'll call back tomorrow to confirm your receipt of my order."

Harper absent-mindedly recorded the information he wanted on the card like she'd done for every other order and then scratched through it.

She threw her pen across the room and pounded her fists against the wood desktop. She ripped the sheet from the order tablet and wadded it up, scrunching it into a tight ball before slam-dunking it into the trash can. One less order to deal with.

Just what she needed, flowers to cover up the money he'd taken without her consent.

His idea of thoughtfulness and hers were obviously miles apart. He claimed he loved her and wanted more out of their relationship. Harper had a feeling it wasn't more of her that he wanted, but rather more of what she could provide him—out of her billfold.

Grant would never use her or play her like Jake did. Maybe getting no attention was better than getting the wrong kind.

When the backdoor swung open, and Robert's first couple of staffers stepped inside, Harper was saved from further heartache. After the necessary introductions, she sent them to the storage room to give it the attention it desperately needed. She handed the next person who came in the orders she'd taken from the overnight service, minus Jake's.

She headed to the front of the store and turned the sign on the door from 'Closed' to 'Open', then, following a fresh fill of coffee, she returned to her desk and tore into Robert's first event file. Deciding she'd better take a crash course on each of the events scheduled before ordering supplies, she settled in for a long, tedious day.

• • •

Harper rubbed her eyes and forced herself to review the folder for the final holiday event to be catered by The Bloom Factory. So much for making any New Year's Eve plans, she thought. According to Robert's records, she would be decorating for a party in Beverly Hills for a film producer and no less than two hundred of his closest associates.

She'd sent the staff home hours ago. The clock in the display in the storefront window chimed eleven. The previous two nights she hadn't made it back to the inn before one A.M. Judging by the mess of notes she still had to make some sort of sense of, scattered throughout the pile of photos in the last job folder, it would be three A.M. tonight.

Her supply order would finally be ready to be placed by tomorrow. And everything she'd need, other than the fresh flowers, which would be brought in daily as needed, should arrive at the shop on Saturday. That would give her a couple of days to do the set-outs and schedules for each job before the first event a week from tonight.

She picked up the phone and dialed Szechuan Palace for a carry-out order. In her case, it would be a carry home order. Since the restaurant was located next door to the inn, it had become her second kitchen. Nothing like a little moo shu pork and barbecued pork slices for a bedtime snack. All she had to do was say her name and what time she'd be there, and the cooks would fix her up.

She had enough chaos in her life, so she never changed her dinner order. At this point, after going on seven months in Playa, she'd throw the Palace owners into a frenzy without her weekly contribution to their budget.

Last night, beyond exhausted from the thirty-five hours she'd worked in two days, she'd barely made it the two blocks between the shop and the inn. Forgetting to stop and pick up her food, they'd delivered it.

Tonight, with only enough energy to pull open Szechaun's large red doors, she paid for her brown bag meal, walked across the parking lot the restaurant shared with the inn, and buzzed the night manager to let her in, too tired to dig out her keys from the depths of her tote.

Dragging her weary body to the elevator, she pushed the lobby button on the control panel and leaned against the back wall as the elevator door shut and the cab rose. She closed her eyes, willing herself not to fall asleep standing up.

When the doors opened, she caught sight of herself in the hallway mirror and gaped at her reflection. Not pretty. She hitched the fallen strap of her bag onto her shoulder, adjusting its weight to more easily accommodate her aching body.

Just as she rounded the corner, passing the kitchen and coming upon the breakfast room, she gasped, dropping the Szechuan sack to the floor.

Her heart leapt to her throat and lodged itself firmly in place. She opened her mouth to say his name, but only she could hear her faint whisper.

"Grant."

CHAPTER SIXTEEN
KNIGHT IN SHINING EVERGREEN

Grant hoped the look on his face didn't mirror the horror in hers. Was he that scary? Not the effect he'd hoped for.

But for the first few moments he saw her, he was helpless to control anything. He simply stared, not able to take his eyes away from hers. After missing her beyond all comprehension, and fearing he'd never get a chance to face her, here he stood, in front of the woman he couldn't bear to lose again.

But she wasn't the picture perfect woman he remembered. She looked as if she hadn't slept in days—like the weight of the world filled her spirit and her tote bag.

"Here, let me help you." He bent down and picked up the sack oozing with grease. Since when did she eat such unhealthy food?

Placing it on one of the glass-topped bistro tables, he reached for her tote. While she stood stiff as a statue, he tentatively slid the strap from her shoulder and lifted the bag off her arm. Jesus, it was heavy. Setting it on the floor, he braced it against the table leg so the contents wouldn't spill out.

"Thank you," she whispered, still daze-like.

She swallowed a couple of times and ran her fingers through her hair, no longer neatly swept up, but rather wild with stray wisps falling around her face. She straightened her soil-stained shirt and brushed at her wrinkled slacks.

"What are you doing here?" she asked.

She didn't sound angry at his early arrival, just surprised. He hoped that was a good sign.

"I was worried about you and had some cancellations in my schedule. So I decided to take December off."

The look of mass confusion registering across her face made him doubt his plan as if seeing her again after so much time wasn't hard enough. He moved around her to the antique buffet to pour himself a glass of ice water.

Taking the pitcher into his hands, he tried to steady his nerves, but they got the best of him, resulting in the pitcher's spout clinking against the glass. "Would you like some water?"

"No. No thank you. I think I'll fix myself a real drink."

Harper rubbed her neck, moving it at peculiar angles as if trying to relieve a catch.

What Grant wouldn't give to rub away her pain.

He wasn't used to seeing her so down. If he discovered that her weariness had anything to do with Jake, he'd have words with that asshole, even though he'd promised Harper that he'd let her handle him.

She opened a cabinet in the bottom of the buffet and pulled out a bottle of Crown and a can of diet soda. She held up both. "Care to join me?"

"Sure," he said, taking two glasses from the rack on the buffet and setting them down in front of her.

She twisted the lid off the bottle and popped open the soda can, pouring way more than a shot of whiskey over the ice in each glass then adding a splash of soda. After a quick stir, she passed him his drink and took a substantial swig of her own.

She pulled the white cartons from the sack.

"There's plenty to share. If you like, I can make you a plate."

"Sounds good. I haven't had anything since before my flight."

He busied himself with the drinks, not able to look at her. It hurt him too much to see her so worn down.

"Let me get a couple of plates from the kitchen. We can eat out on the deck if you'd like. I could use the fresh air."

Wadding up the sack, she tossed it into the trash and disappeared around the corner.

Fresh air sounded great to him.

He walked across the breakfast room, through the open French doors into the great room. Taking a quick survey of the room on his way to the patio doors, he was temporarily stunned by the gigantic Christmas tree filling the corner of the room.

The designer had spared no expense. It was every bit as magnificent as the tree Reggie had created back home. Grant never thought he'd find a decorator to rival his talent, but he had.

Seeing Harper enter the room, their plates heaped high with something that looked wonderful, he turned to her.

"Harper, this tree is fantastic! I never thought I'd say this, but whoever decorated this beast could give Reggie a run for his money."

A sudden spark took over her Harper. Even the lifeless pallor of her cheeks gave way to a blushed bit of color. She smiled back at him but didn't say anything right away. She sat one of the plates down on the coffee table between two oversized white sofas and walked over to the fireplace. Lifting the end of the greenery covering the mantle, she pulled out a cord and plugged it into the wall, illuminating hundreds of miniature white lights nestled amongst the boughs of fresh pine.

"Someone must have forgotten to plug in this strand. I'll have to check my master list."

"Wait a minute. You did this?" Grant asked.

Harper looked down at her feet.

"I helped a little bit."

Grant opened the door to the deck, trying to balance the two drinks in one hand. "That's why everything looks so perfectly coordinated. I'd recognize your handiwork anywhere."

"You would?"

The shock in her voice troubled him, but he kept himself in check. That's what his Chick Trick Kit advised him to do when it appeared he was way out of his realm of credibility.

"Our house looks much like this," Grant said.

He flinched, not from the chilly ocean breeze catching him as he stepped out into the night air, but rather from mentioning the home they once shared. It would probably be prudent to change the subject before his emotions got the best of him. "Wow. There's a strong breeze tonight."

"Always is," Harper said.

She followed him out the door to one of the cocktail tables, so small and artsy it could barely accommodate them.

"We're so close to the water here. We feel it every night. Actually, it gets pretty gusty during the day too."

"What's the area we're looking at? It looks kind of like a wetland from what I can make out in the moonlight." Grant seated himself on one of the bistro set's matching iron chairs. Settling back into the cool cushions, he breathed in the damp sea air. It had been a long time since he'd been on beachfront property.

Hell, he couldn't remember the last time he'd taken a vacation. And he'd certainly never taken a month-long hiatus.

"The Ballona Freshwater Marsh."

Harper pulled her chair up next to his and had barely sat down before she dug into her plate, foregoing the manners she used to insist on in both public and private settings. She must be famished, Grant thought.

Between bites of the best barbecued pork slices he had ever eaten, Harper filled him in on the marsh, sometimes talking with her mouth full, which was a pleasant surprise. He liked it when her passion took over her formalities.

"It's to be about fifty-one acres when it's done and will have many native birds, trees, and shrubs and grasses. I guess it helps filter out pollutants before they reach the Pacific as well as provides a wonderful wildlife habitat."

She shoveled another forkful of shredded pork something-or-other into her mouth.

"You can take tours from dawn until dusk. It's pretty interesting. You should take one while you're here. You'll see snowy egrets, great blue herons, Pacific tree frogs, and California bluebells."

"How much did the project cost?"

Grant cringed as soon as the words were out of his mouth. That was the old Grant. The new one wasn't supposed to be worried about the financial aspects of everything.

Harper didn't seem to be put off by his question, though, and answered it between bites of pork.

"About 18 mil just to construct. I think some conservancy group pays for its maintenance."

They sat in silence for a few moments, both concentrating on devouring their food. He'd forgotten how hungry he was and made a mental note to find out if any of the restaurants in Briar Creek could make something like this. It was delicious.

He looked out over the marsh as the full, gray-white moon reflected off the patches of water dotting the landscape. The wind whistled as it whipped through the grasses and thick brush, the rustled strands composing their own symphony. It was kind of an eerie sound, more symbolic of Halloween than the Christmas season.

But in a strange way, the restlessness that thrashed in the beachside wilderness was reminiscent of the tidal waves roaring inside him. Being in Harper's presence again, sharing this close space with her, stirred all of Grant's feelings into hyper-drive. She moved him like no other woman ever had or could.

How he'd fucked things up so badly between them was inexcusable. He only hoped he'd learned enough to make them right.

He pulled his pants leg away from his shins, not sure if the heat that had come over him was from the hot sauce he'd dumped on his dinner by accident or from being so nervous. Seeing her again had also woken up his hibernating libido. He suddenly needed a substantial cooling off. Thank God for the strong breeze.

"Your cargo pants look nice on you, by the way."

Harper looked him up and down, a skeptical smile forming across her lips as she wiped away leftover barbecue sauce from the side of her mouth. "So do the Skechers."

"Still takes some getting used to. But they're both fairly comfortable."

Grant adjusted his jacket so his gunmetal gray tee, with all of its obnoxious screen print symbols, could be better seen.

Couldn't the designer have picked one motif instead of multitudes for such a small space? The clustered look made him motion sick when he looked at it for too long.

"Jeffrey says this look is much better suited for out here."

"He's right."

Harper covered her mouth with her hand. For a moment, Grant thought she was going to laugh, but she didn't.

"You look great," she said.

Thanks, boys, he silently said to Jeffrey and Reggie. Delighted Harper had noticed, he tried to stay cool.

"Thanks."

"Wish I could say the same on my own behalf. I'm afraid you caught me a little worn out."

Grant fumbled with his napkin, totally unsure how to say what he wanted to without offending her. He wanted to get to the bottom of her apparent physical depletion.

Looking into her eyes, he tried to gather his vocabulary into coherent sentiments. Gosh he hoped he didn't ruin what he thought he'd gained this evening.

"You still look great, Harper, but I did notice you seem a bit tired. Anything I can do to help?"

Grant folded and re-folded his napkin, trying to press out the creases he'd made when he'd twisted it all to hell minutes before.

The surprise on her face hurt him. Had it been so long since he'd ask her about her needs that she didn't think he cared? It was more than obvious she didn't know how to accept his sincerity and concern. He made a note to check with The Boys about improving on that skill.

"You certainly can't help with my predicament. Unless you have some deeply repressed floral design and event planning talent."

Harper finished off the last bite on her plate and pushed it, with its squeaky-clean surface, onto the table behind them.

"So, I was right. You did much more than just help a little bit around here. You're the one who decorated the inn for the holidays."

Grant's heart danced with pride because he'd noticed her talent. That had to help his cause.

"Yes, I did the decorating," Harper said and smiled at him. "And thank you for noticing. But I'm afraid my handiwork has gotten me way more than I can handle."

"What do you mean?"

He thought she loved to decorate. She was always sprucing up something.

"Well, my friend Robert, who owns one of the premiere design and event planning companies in LA, came down with mono and has to rest at home for the next six weeks. For some unknown reason, I agreed to take over for him for the holidays."

"Wow! Can you do that? Do you know what you're doing?" Ouch. That's not what he meant. God, he was an idiot. Harper more than knew what she was doing, but having to do it by herself was another issue.

He saw the hurt on her face and reached for her arm. He touched her gently, fearing she might slap him away like a pesky mosquito, which he definitely deserved. "I didn't mean that like it sounded. I know you have the talent and know-how. I'm just concerned that it's too big of a job for one person."

Harper let out a deep sigh and relaxed under his touch.

"Yeah, I'm worried about that too. Robert has a great staff, but way too few of them. And he didn't build into his estimates the means to hire more. I've just got to work with what I have. It's tough, but I can do it."

"Harper, you look exhausted."

Grant removed his hand from her arm before she could feel him tremble.

"I wish I could help you. But I'm afraid that's not my area of expertise. You know me. I'd be more of a hindrance."

"I know. But thanks for your concern."

With a strong, salty-scented gust of wind, her hair blew off her face. The moonlight illuminated her tired eyes, but there was a spark Grant hadn't seen for ages.

"Any time."

Now what should he say? Dammit, even though his three-day Chick Tricks Inc. crash course had taught him some things well, seeing her near tears and stressed to the max was not in the lesson plans he'd covered so far. He'd never seen her like this. Worse yet, if she ever had been this upset, he'd never noticed.

He'd have to discuss the situation with Reggie and Jeffrey tomorrow when he gave them an update. He looked at his watch. Hell, he'd be talking to them today, not tomorrow. It was damn near two A.M. He couldn't remember the last time he'd seen that time of the morning without it being related to his work.

"Do you always work this late?" he asked her.

He got no response. She was staring out into the mist settling over the wetlands and didn't seem to have heard him. He touched her hand and felt her jump before she turned to him with tears rolling down her cheeks.

"Harper! What is it? What's wrong, honey?" Grant caught a few of her tears with his thumb as they trickled down the side of her cheek. "Hey there. Don't cry. I'm right here."

He hadn't seen her cry since her parents had died, and even then, he didn't think she knew that he'd seen her break down. He'd thought she needed time alone, so he'd stayed outside their bedroom door, sleeping on the hallway floor, so he'd be able to hear her if she called for him. But she hadn't reached out to him. 'Course, he probably would have blundered the opportunity to help her anyway. He just wasn't good at this sort of thing. Even as a student of Chick Tricks 101, he still didn't have a clue what to do other than what he was doing now…holding her hand.

Harper held onto his fingers tight and then massaged them with her own.

"I'm sorry, Grant. I'm just a mess tonight. You caught me at my worst. I'm sure I'll be fine after some sleep."

"What can I do?" He squeezed her hand and wiped away another tear.

"Just you being here is sort of a nice thing." She took a tissue out of her pocket and wiped her running nose. "I wasn't expecting you and really don't know what to say to you. But it's nice."

"Well, that makes me feel good…I think," he said and laughed.

Reggie had instructed him that when he didn't know what to do, he should shut up, smile or laugh. So he laughed, again.

Harper chuckled with him between tears and sniffles, so it must have worked. Her crying was really yanking on his heart-strings though. If he didn't do something, he'd be in need of a tissue too.

"How about I walk you to your room, and we'll call it a night?"

"Okay. Let me clean this mess up."

She slid off her chair and moved it out of the way so she could reach the table.

It was just like her to have to finish tidying up before taking care of herself.

"No, I'll come back down and do it. If you can tell me what exactly I should do," he said sheepishly while opening the door to the great room and following her inside.

Without warning, Harper stopped and turned to him. He bumped up against her, his eyes meeting hers for the briefest of moments.

She backed away then, putting much-needed space between them.

"I can't tell you how much you being here tonight has meant to me. You've become quite a good listener." She squeezed his hand. "Thank you, Grant. Just put the dishes in the kitchen sink. The girls will wash them in the morning."

"No problem," Grant said, his voice barely audible as they left the great room.

Actually, after her unexpected touch, he pushed himself to great lengths to speak period.

She led him toward the guest suites.

"Will you be having breakfast before you go to the shop? I could meet you…"

He shoved his hands deep into his pockets. Try to be smooth, dumb ass, he coached himself.

"Breakfast doesn't start here until around six. I try to be at the shop by then so I have an hour or so to prepare before the staff comes in."

The clock in the hallway chimed on the half hour. Two thirty. He shouldn't have kept her up so late. She had to be up again in two and a half hours. No wonder she looked like a zombie.

"I could bring you something. Just tell me what, where and when."

Although being her mealtime delivery boy wasn't how he'd expected to spend his time with her, now that he knew her work situation, he'd do anything to make it easier for her. He didn't have other plans anyway. She was his plan.

"Okay. How about breakfast at the shop? It's just two blocks down from here, toward the beach. You'll see it. There's a big Bloom Factory sign out front. Say around ten?"

She rubbed her red eyes and yawned.

They arrived at her room at the end of the hall. Room 101. Grant recognized the number from her correspondence to his attorney. She reached in her pant's pocket.

"Shit. My keys must be in my bag. I must have left the damn thing in the breakfast room."

"I'll get 'em. Just sit here on this chair, and I'll bring it to you."

Harper sank into the soft cushions without a fight. "That'd be great."

Surprised she didn't fuss about his getting something for her, he hurried back to the breakfast room and retrieved her tote from under the table. When he returned, she was asleep, half hanging over the arm of the chair.

Grant lightly tapped her arm and called her name, but she was out.

This was not exactly how he hoped to get into her room, but he couldn't very well leave her on a chair in the middle of the hallway.

He put her tote over his shoulder and leaned over to pick her up. The overloaded bag swung forward and nearly clipped her forehead. If it had made contact, it would have knocked her out for good.

He dug the key out of the side pocket and tossed the bag aside. Tote bags were such a pain in the ass. Harper needed a tablet to put all this information in. Why she was so resistant to new technology he'd never understand.

He'd go buy her one tomorrow. No. No, he wouldn't. Reggie would have heart failure if the first thing his prized student did was buy something for the woman of his dreams. He was supposed to be talking and listening to her, not courting her with his wallet. Jesus. This was all so foreign to him.

Trying to move quietly so as not to wake her, Grant used her keys to unlock her room. Then he picked her up and carried her to her door. Using his shoulder, he pushed open the door and moved along the wall, feeling for a light switch while trying not to drop her.

Turning on the first one he found, he tried to focus on the surroundings, but the only thing he could see was the larger-than-life evergreen forest that covered almost the entire cedar chest at the end of her bed. The damn thing had to be at least three feet tall with massive boughs poking out in every direction from its large clay pot.

After placing Harper on her bed, Grant removed her shoes from her feet and tucked her under the turned-down comforter.

He saw a card sticking out from the left side of the forest and debated for at least half a second before carefully tilting it out just enough so that he could read it.

Jake. What a jack-ass. Didn't he know that flowers didn't make up for disappointing a woman?

At least Grant could say that he'd already learned that lesson.

He looked back at Harper, securely stowed away in dreamland, hoping her visions were more pleasant than his had been lately.

He took a pen and paper from her nightstand and carefully lowered himself onto the edge of her bed so as not to disturb her.

As he scribbled down his thoughts, the heady fragrance of Jake's bouquet was almost more than he could stomach. Leaving his note on Harper's nightstand, Grant couldn't resist moving a lock of hair from her forehead and tucking it behind her ear. She stirred but didn't open her eyes. God, she was beautiful when she slept.

Planting a kiss on her sun-bronzed cheek, he left her room knowing he'd never be able to live again without her.

But how could he show her his love when she'd rejected the only ways he knew how to give it to her? Chick Tricks Inc. insisted that he rely on his heart to find his answers. But he'd closed those channels when he was a young boy. To be the man he wanted to be, and the man Harper deserved, he had to find a way to open them.

Stepping back onto the moonlit deck to clean up their late night dinner table, the marsh's rustling reeds whispered to him that if he didn't figure it out soon, he'd lose the woman he'd love forever.

CHAPTER SEVENTEEN
THORNS AND ROSES

Harper's alarm clock buzzed. She punched the snooze button, cursing under her breath that there was no way in hell it could already be five A.M. She opened one eye enough to check the time. Unfortunately, the ugly red glare of a large, squared-off digital five, followed by two ominous zeros, proved her wrong.

She rolled over to face the day, confused because the natural light that usually welcomed the early morning was gone. What had happened to her room with a view? And damn if it didn't smell like a pine forest in here.

Reaching up, she flipped on the lamp on her bedside table.

Turning back toward where the window was, she couldn't see past a gigantic mound of poinsettias, Christmas roses, mistletoe, holly berries, silver and gold-dipped pinecones and evergreens. The boughs were so huge they took over the end of her bed. Talk about over the top. The freaking thing must have cost a fortune.

Oh, Grant. Who else would go to this much expense to impress her?

She picked up his handwritten note, not lost on her that it was the first time he'd ever left her a note with a gift. But would he ever learn that buying her things wasn't the answer she was looking for?

And it wasn't like he needed to explain the flowers. They certainly made their own statement.

She unfolded the small torn-off piece of the inn's notepad, laughing at how uncomfortable Grant must have been without his monogrammed, family-crested stationary. And God forbid he'd had to use a cheap Bic instead of his Mont Blanc.

> Thanks for sharing your dinner with me.
> See you at ten.

Grant

P.S. The forest at the end of your bed is not from me. Totally not my style.

Between the sleepy confusion caused by just two hours of sleep and the way-too-fragrant blooms, Harper practically tripped over her feet making her way to the end of her bed. She ripped the card from the holder buried among the branches.

Jake. What an asshole. How did he get that order through without her knowing it? If he thought for a minute he'd made up for his actions, he had another think coming.

She read the message on the card. Her stomach muscles clenched. It was virtually identical to the one he'd left on the shop's answering machine.

She opened her desk drawer and pulled out the itinerary he'd given her of his tour. Following the list partway down the page, she found the name of his hotel and jotted down the number. She'd wait till she got to the shop so he'd be nice and awake to better comprehend her ass chewing.

She dug through the shelves in her closet until she found something comfortable to wear. No time for high fashion these days, not to mention she'd pretty much ruined all three of the outfits she'd worn this week. Between runaway glue guns and tree sap, she'd have to squeeze some time in over the weekend to shop for clothes to get her through her tenure at The Bloom Factory.

Picking black cotton drawstring pants and a baby pink hooded jacket, she grabbed a towel set from the linen closet and hustled to the shower. If she wanted to complete the items on her list before her staff arrived, and give Jake a wake-up call he'd not soon forget, she couldn't arrive at the shop much past six.

The hot water drained instead of rejuvenated her spirits. She cranked up the cold faucet and rolled her shoulders first backward and then slowly to the front as the water cascaded down her back. She rotated the nozzle to the massage setting and let the heavy, pointed pressure pound her into reality.

Grant must have been real enthused over Jake's flowers. Not that he had a right to say anything, but his response was most intriguing. So what exactly was his style? Tiffany's for sure and sometimes

Louis Vuitton or diamonds. Flowers, though, had never been high on his gift list.

Grant had given her a lot of make-up gifts over the years, but he'd never taken advantage of her like Jake had done. He'd expected a lot of her during their marriage, but never without asking first. And she hadn't really minded helping him. Probably, now that she thought about it, because he always seemed genuinely appreciative.

It was the pain she'd endured from his never expressing more than that, never coming one step closer to showing an intimate connection with her. He always stayed at least an arm's length away, usually much more. She wanted his heart, not his approval.

The thought of his arm touching hers last night when she'd unwittingly broken down in front of him made her shiver now, like it did then. During their marriage, he'd never reached for her like that, even when she needed him to. Even when her parents died, he'd stayed away, leaving her alone in their bedroom to deal with her devastation and grief.

His touch last night had felt both gentle and genuine. His hands had trembled, but the warmth radiating from them had touched her deeply.

Her pleasant feelings about his early arrival also surprised her. Not too long ago, she'd moved across the country to get away from him, even wondering if that might be too close. Now, seven months later, she was at peace with his being right next to her. Not just at peace, but almost comfortable with his presence.

She rubbed water out of her eyes as she finished rinsing the shampoo from her hair. The spirited smell of rosemary mint didn't rejuvenate her or clear her mind, despite the promise on the bottle. If they made a shampoo that truly delivered both of those needs, she'd buy them out of stock.

Maybe it was just her overwhelming exhaustion, and the mental strength she lacked because of her workload, that prevented her from pushing Grant away. But whatever the reason, for now, she was willing to let him into her life.

There wasn't anything wrong with two people in the process of divorcing becoming friends, right? Although she didn't know of any couples who had done that, she was sure there were a few. She'd have to Google it—next year, when she had time to look up anything other than design and catering suppliers.

She towel-dried her hair and quickly dressed. She'd stood in the shower much longer than she'd planned. The Bloom Factory needed her, and she needed to bury her anger and confusion in greenery, lights and bows.

Slipping on her Steve Madden bowling shoes, she laughed, remembering Grant's new style. He looked cute. A little uncomfortable, but cute. She wasn't sure about the wild T-shirt, but he seemed proud of it. She was more than curious about what he'd show up in today.

Emptying her tote, she sorted through the monstrosity of information buried in there, setting aside the folders she no longer needed and packing the new files of ideas she'd been working on any spare minute she found. While walking home the previous night, she'd noticed the damn bag seemed to be getting heavier. But she'd attributed the extra weight to her exhaustion.

Picking it up this morning, she knew better. Maybe they made another size bigger. She added that to her list for weekend shopping.

Pulling the bag onto her shoulder, it settled into its well-indented slot. She grabbed her cell phone and keys, took her pink Coach baseball cap from the rack, placed it on her head, and headed out the door.

She stopped in the kitchen to say good morning to Stacia, but she wasn't there, although she'd left a steaming paper cup of coffee on the counter for her, along with a note telling her to have a great day.

According to her note, she'd gone to show a new guest to her suite. She also mentioned that if Harper could get away early from the shop, maybe they could go to the K.O.W. the following night to hang with Stokey while he bartended, hinting that it would be quite all right if she brought Grant along.

How long had Stacia known Grant was on his way? Harper intended to find out.

She just might invite Grant to join them at the K.O.W. It would be nice to introduce him to her friends and get their take on him.

She pushed the down arrow on the elevator and waited while it made its way to the lobby.

Tomorrow was Friday. She couldn't believe she'd been working at the shop for almost a week. And even more nauseating was the fact that her first events were less than a week away.

As she walked to the shop, she took tiny sips of the hot coffee Stacia had graciously made for her, waiting for it to cool off so she could gulp it down for a much-needed jolt of energy. The sea gulls were waking up with her and heading out toward the beach for their morning meals.

She loved early mornings in Playa. The sleepy beach town haze took its time slowly burning away, leaving behind sunshine and smiles to spare.

People did tend to be happy here. Harper wasn't sure if it was the abundance of good weather and warm beaches or the general laidback atmosphere. It definitely wasn't the Pacific's water temperature, which was freezing no matter what time of year.

She wondered how Grant would take to Playa's laissez-faire mood. Relaxation was not his forte. She seriously doubted he'd know what to do with himself.

To be fair, the lifestyle was an adjustment to her too. But compared to the fish-out-of-water that she'd been, Grant was a migrating great blue whale.

The fact he'd taken a month off still hadn't sunk in. He worked so hard and more than deserved the time away, but Harper was worried because he didn't know how to function in a non-business setting.

She almost wished she hadn't given in and promised Robert she'd work the whole six weeks. When he'd called her back, unable to find someone to cover the last couple weeks of his absence, two weeks beyond the four she'd originally promised him, she'd seriously hesitated. But her creative drive pushed her to stick it out, especially since one of the projects she was most excited about wasn't until New Year's Eve. She didn't want to plan the event, see the designs through to fruition, and then not be there for the final results.

At least she'd also have something to do, somewhere to go, to kick off the New Year.

Grant would have to fend for himself during the days and evenings that she had events to attend to. He wasn't her responsibility anymore anyway. She wasn't sure why she'd even thought about how he'd manage without her help. She must be delusional from the lack of sleep.

Unlocking the back door of the shop, Harper set down her bag next to her desk. She went to the front of the store and turned on the electric candle warmers. She pulled two vanilla gingerbread candles from the shelf and placed them on the burners. When the fresh pine from the trees displayed in The Bloom Factory's front window mixed with the aromas from the candles, it would remind her of this time of year at the estate.

She dumped out the cold coffee left in the pot from the night before and made a fresh one. Cranking the stereo system with her favorite seasonal melodies, she checked the morning work orders.

Being in the shop first thing in the morning was wonderful. There was something about being here alone that, surrounded by the creative possibilities the place offered and knowing all of it was at her disposal, really pumped her up. She felt more alive than she ever remembered.

The shop provided the creative freedom she needed. She thrived on the thrill she felt with every new piece she designed, and she got supreme satisfaction out of watching the staff create the ideas she sketched on paper. Going forward, if she could keep her creative juices flowing as smoothly as she had the last few days, she'd be able to successfully carry out Robert's holiday schedule.

When she threw the main switch, the fluorescent lights hummed to life. She pulled the completed orders off of the pin holder and started entering them into the computer to figure yesterday's take. After entering the first several receipts, she stopped short. A single piece had gone for almost five hundred dollars?

She looked at the name on the order. Figures. That's how much Jake had paid for her order. It was by far the most expensive one of the day, probably of the week.

Her temper boiled, and the angry heat of her burnt pride flashed hot against her skin.

She stomped toward the back room and dug her cell phone out of her bag along with the piece of paper listing Jake's hotel information. As an indignant rage clouded her vision, she could hardly read the numbers. She sank down into the depths of Robert's chair, wishing it would swallow her, but not until she'd told off the gigolo.

She jabbed at the numbers on her phone. Rocking back and forth in her chair, she prayed the steady motion would give her the strength and upward hand it seemed to give Grant when she saw him rock the same way in a meeting.

Jake's never-ending thrill ride was about to lose her as a passenger. She was sick and tired of the ups, downs, and spirals he constantly threw at her.

"Copacabana, may I help you?"

"Jake Benton's room, please."

Harper tapped her fingers against the desk, noticing how badly she needed a manicure.

After a brief moment of silence, the operator returned. "I'm sorry, Ma'am, but Mr. Benton has asked not to be disturbed."

"Oh, trust me, dear," Harper said, purring like a large cat about to take down its prey. "He'll take my call. Tell him it's Harper."

"Well…okay…" The hotel operator hesitated a moment longer. "I'll try. Hold please, while I ring his room again."

"Thank you, sweetie. I'm not going anywhere."

The shop's front door chimes sounded. Good. She was hoping some of the staff would come in a little early. She'd scheduled more to be done than they could possibly do during their regular hours. She counted her blessings that they were so dedicated to their jobs.

"Hey, baby," Jake said and yawned. "This must mean you got my flowers."

Judging by the clinks and clambers of the receiver, he was trying to schmooze her even before the damn phone settled against his ear. He followed the honey with a long sigh and half grunt-half whimper. As if she gave a damn that she'd awoken him.

"Yes, Jake, I got the flowers. I'm thanking myself as we speak."

She took a short, puffy breath and tried to calm down.

"If my adding machine is accurate, the amount you owe me totals $1.5 million dollars. Is that the figure you have?"

"Hey, you," he said, his schmoozy tone on its highest setting. "What's the matter? You gave me authorization to use the account. Baby, as soon as I get back, we've got filming to start. There's so much equipment to buy and…"

"Jake, you don't even have a script ready yet. Do you? Fuck buying equipment. All you need is your laptop."

Harper didn't even wait for his answer. She had to get the rest of this out while her finesse was still lost at sea.

"Do you not recall that we agreed to discuss any expenditure before my money was used?"

"No, baby, I just assumed you'd be okay with it. What time is it anyway?"

He still wasn't taking her seriously. But after she told him he'd been cut-off, he would. Till then, she decided to have some fun at his expense.

"It's about six A.M. here in Playa, probably nine on the East Coast. I'm at work, Jake, trying to catch up on a few projects before my staff gets here."

That got his attention.

"What do you mean you're at work? Since when do you have a job?"

Panic took hold of his voice. Good, Harper thought. Maybe he was getting the hint that his money train was about to derail.

"Since your actions made the extra cash necessary."

She gave him just enough time to take a breath before hitting him again. "Between Grant being here for the next month and my hours at The Bloom Factory, I wanted to let you know I'll be hard to reach for the next couple of weeks."

"Whoa, wait a minute, what's Grant doing there?" Jake stuttered, awake enough now to sit up and take stock of the shake-up in his world. "Hey, listen, baby, I'm sorry if I upset you. You know how much you mean to me. I'd never take advantage of you or hurt you."

Harper was silent. Jake needed to sweat.

"You don't know what it's like to grow up without love. I thought I could survive without it. But then I met you, baby. And my world changed. Not because of your money, but because of you."

His tone had changed from suave confidence, to panic, to sickening sweet nothings.

"I need you, Harper. I want to come home and be with you. Try to build my life, with you in it."

"You just don't get it, Jake. I gave up on the one man I thought I'd love forever because he couldn't make me a priority in his life."

Harper wiped the tears from the corners of her eyes before they fell onto her sketches and ruined them. That was twice in less than twelve hours that she'd been in tears. Utterly ridiculous. She didn't have time for emotional turmoil.

"Figure out what you want, Mr. Sapphire. And if it's me, you'd better work like hell to prove it because I'm too busy, too tired, and too disillusioned to believe a damn thing you tell me."

Before hanging up, she had one more thing to say. Make it two.

"And by the way, your access to my account has been canceled."

She rushed to finish the conversation because she had way too much work to do to give this much more of her energy.

"You can also stick the $500 flowers up your ass. You gained absolutely no ground with those, Schmooze Boy. When you want to make up with me, do it on your dime, not mine."

She disconnected the call while he was fumbling for what to say next. Tossing the cell into her bag, she let out a long overdue exhale. Finally sticking it to him felt fantastic, but the triumph didn't completely mask her disappointment in him. She'd believed his care for her was deeper than her pockets.

But even if she was right, and he did care, he was too much for her to handle right now. She was having a difficult time taking care of herself, another person she didn't know very well anymore. She didn't have the time or energy to suffer at the hands of Jake's recklessness.

Hearing someone step into the back room, she turned around. There stood Grant, awkwardly balancing two hot cups of coffee with a sack full of take-out cartons.

Oh, God. Please don't tell her it was Grant who'd caused the front door chimes to ring when she'd first called Jake. That would mean he'd heard her entire conversation.

He smiled at her, in the awkward way someone does when they've interrupted what should have remained a private moment.

He walked into the office, still smiling, until he caught his flip-flops on the raised metal door frame, nearly falling flat.

At least she could count on him to make her laugh when she had no other reason to.

CHAPTER EIGHTEEN
MISTLETOE MAGIC

Goddamn shoes. Flip-flops suck. In the short distance from the inn to the corner bistro and back to Harper's shop, Grant must have tripped five times. But he wasn't about to give up on them. Of all the new apparel must-haves Reggie and Jeffrey had insisted upon for his trip, these were the clinchers. The style manuals confirmed their opinions. He had to adjust. But it would be nice if he didn't break a bone in the process.

"Hi," she said.

Her face was flushed.

"Nice flip-flops."

"Very funny. Hope Robert paid his liability insurance." Grant looked down at his feet, suddenly glad for the diversion his clumsiness had created. "I'll get used to them. The damn things just don't have any support."

Luckily, he'd been blessed with good balance, so he'd managed to keep the coffees and take-out containers intact when he stumbled into her office. He finished the treacherous journey to the edge of her desk and set the items on the corner. Pulling over a nearby chair, he took a seat before setting up their impromptu meal.

Leave it to him to make his grand entrance with a comedic stumble and incredibly bad timing. But if it eased her tension to laugh at him, he'd keep showing up and making an ass of himself.

He'd love to take care of Jake for her, but he respected her for wanting to do it on her own. That said, she definitely needed help caring for herself, something he'd never shy away from again.

"Sorry if I interrupted you. I know I'm really early, but I thought maybe you could use some breakfast."

He removed one of the Styrofoam cartons from the plastic bag, pleased with himself for remembering she liked bacon, sausage and cheese in her omelet. Hopefully, she hadn't changed that preference.

He set her order in front of her. "Here you go."

He wished she'd say something, besides commenting on his shoes. "I think this is how you like your omelets."

She smiled as she took a large bite. "You thought right."

She swallowed another forkful.

Her appetite these days was something else, Grant thought. Wasn't anybody seeing to it that she ate during this stressful time? He'd just have to do it himself. Conveniently, it gave him a good reason to see her.

Waving her fork in the air, she swallowed a bite, leaving her with less than half of her meal to finish.

"Thank you for bringing this. And sorry you had to hear all that stuff with Jake. But at least you know I'm dealing with him."

"You did great."

He added raw sugar and cream to his coffee and stirred, taking his frustration with Jake out on the stir stick, almost ending up with a latte instead of the bold roast of the day. "How'd he take it?"

She washed down her omelet with a substantial gulp of coffee. "Actually, for the first time since I've known him, he was fairly speechless."

"Probably a good sign."

Grant couldn't have cared less about the money Jake had taken. His only concern was the possibility that Jake would take his wife. Grant wasn't going to give Jake a chance to make up the ground he'd lost.

Even though Grant wasn't sure he could handle Harper's answer, he had to ask: "So how are you going to handle it if he puts the full court press on you to make up for his asinine actions?"

He fidgeted with the bent stir stick while she took her time answering him.

"Well…"

She pulled the stick out of his coffee and put it in her mouth, chewing on the end of it after already mutilating hers.

"I don't think I'll have to worry about it, really. He's too stuck on himself to worry about me."

"I hope you're right."

Jesus. He hoped she was.

He'd just have to occupy most of her free time, what little of it there was, in order to further hamper Jake's efforts to make amends.

"So how long will he be gone?" he asked.

"Till the day before Christmas. He'll arrive at LAX sometime early Christmas Eve. I'm not sure when I have to be there to pick him up."

She threw the mangled stick into the empty carryout sack.

Looks like he had about three weeks to win her back.

Perhaps it was best to change the subject.

"So, what would you recommend I do on my first official day of vacation?"

"The jetty and beach would be my first choice," she said while looking him over. "But I'd make sure to use strong sunscreen."

He laughed.

"What? C'mon. You don't think my white legs and arms can take the rays?"

He knew the cargo shorts and strategically disheveled designer tee was a bad call. His executive tan was scary at best.

"I'm not just worried about your legs and arms. Try your face, your ears, your nose, your lips, and that little bald spot on the top of your head."

Harper had that "trust-me-on-this" look that effectively warded off his willingness to challenge her concerns. She looked down at her empty breakfast carton, tearing the edges of the cardboard.

Her uneasiness regarding her concern for his well-being was evident, but he let her advice comfort him. How could he have failed to notice how caring she was toward him?

She was one terrific woman. He'd been a lucky man. But even his father would admit that a man can't count on luck because it always runs out. Instead, he had taught his son to go after what he wanted, rather than wait for it to come to him.

But his father failed to teach him what he needed most, probably because he'd never realized it himself. Grant wasn't about to make that mistake twice. He just hoped he wasn't too late.

When he snapped back into their conversation, Harper was looking right at him.

"And God help you if you take your shirt off. You'll be a fried lobster. When you get back to the inn, ask Stacia for a high spf lotion. She'll fix you up."

"Oh yeah. That's what I was going to ask you about."

Grant busied himself picking up Harper's empty breakfast tray and his untouched one while he ventured into uncertain territory.

"I met Stacia this morning at the office when I was making arrangements for my business mail."

He could tell by Harper's immediate joy that the woman meant a lot to her.

"She's a great person. You'll like her."

"Yeah, she seems terrific."

When Harper talked about someone she loved, an indescribable glow surrounded her, another thing he loved about her. He wished she lit up like that when she talked about him. He was going to try like hell to make that happen.

Finished with the clean-up, he sat back down. He turned his legs away from the window, no sense blinding her with the glare.

He pulled out his Armani sunglasses, stylishly hooked onto his T-shirt pocket, just like Reggie had shown him to do. He opened and then folded them, before sliding them back onto his pocket, trying to find something to occupy his time while he found a way to ask her what he needed to.

"I'm supposed to get back to Stacia after I talk to you."

"About what?"

Harper seemed confused as she shuffled through the folders on her desk, organizing them into various piles.

Grant had the feeling they'd been set-up. But he didn't mind a bit, especially if that meant Stacia was on his side. He'd take all the help he could get. Besides, one of his tactics was winning over Harper's friends. According to Chick Tricks Inc., that was always a plus.

"She said something about you guys going to some local bar, the King of…Tuna, some kind of fish."

Harper's laughter was a good thing, Grant supposed. At least it beat the flashes of anger she'd displayed during her conversation with Jake.

"She said I'd be more than welcome to tag along. If it's okay with you, of course."

Her laughter stopped, replaced by an awkward silence. He didn't like how she fidgeted in her seat and prepared himself for his first taste of rejection. First day. First rejection. Perfect way to report his progress to his coaches. That would earn him a big 'F'.

"Uhmmm, I guess it would be okay."

The relieved look in his eyes must have been evident. Getting real with his feelings was supposed to be his goal, and real was what she was getting. He couldn't have hidden his fear no matter how hard he tried. The distance and uncertainty between them was killing him.

"Sure, what the hell. Tag along. It's just us girls and Stokey, the best bartender in town."

An ornery grin replaced Harper's original cynical look.

"I should probably warn you though that Stokey is gay. Gayer than gay. I know how you feel…"

"Oh, that's fine. Really. It is. Reggie and Jeffrey have been schooling me on this stuff, and…"

Heat rushed Grant's skin.

He didn't want her knowing about the Chick Tricks Inc. thing, but he was finding it hard not to bring The Boys into his conversations. They had made such a positive impression on him. Because of their friendship, his life views had changed. Even though he hadn't completely embraced their philosophies or lifestyle, he was more open to them than before.

"That's something I'd like to talk to you about, GC3."

She hadn't called him that for ages. He used to find it mildly irritating, as if he were some big, dumb Texas oilman, but it did have a rather endearing ring. And it was definitely less stuffy than Grant Cantwell III.

The fact that she hadn't called him by that name for a while must have resonated with her too. She had a puzzled look on her face as if she were trying to decide if she should use an endearment from their past.

Maybe he could get through to her. Maybe he still had a shot at bringing her home. At least she'd hate him less than she must have when she left the estate two hundred eighteen days ago.

"Okay. Talk to me."

He had to be careful what he revealed about what Reggie referred to as his "emotional development blueprints." Even though he was doing his best to feign indifference, Grant knew what Harper was more than likely curious about.

"Why are you so chummy with Jeffrey now? And Reggie, of all people. Jeffrey I kind of get. He's never treated you with anything but kindness and respect. Respect you didn't deserve for the disdain you showed him. I suppose since I left, he's your only ally."

That hurt. But as much as he wasn't proud to admit it, she was accurate as hell.

She tapped her fingers on the desk, like he'd seen her do when she was contemplating something.

"Reggie though. That relationship floors the hell out of me. I never, ever, would have put you two on the same team. Now that is a conversation that after a few drinks tomorrow night, I'll be most interested in entertaining."

Best to leave this one alone until he'd had a few drinks too.

Harper got up from her chair and grabbed a clipboard.

Damn. He knew she had to get busy, but he didn't want to leave her.

Like a good sport, he took her cue.

"Hey, look, I know you have a lot to do, so I'll get out of here."

He got up and returned the chair to where he'd found it.

"Hope you enjoyed breakfast. You really do need to take care of yourself, Harper." He motioned to the shop surrounding them, "Especially if you plan to get through all this.

Call me if, you know, you need anything today. I'll bring you lunch, dinner, whatever you need."

Grant turned and walked to the door. He stopped under the arch, trying to think of something else to offer her that didn't cost much money. Reggie had advised him not to appear desperate to please her. But how was he supposed to act when his wife was waiting to sign him off if he couldn't change her mind? This speaking from the heart approach was hell. Why couldn't he just fall at her feet? With the damn flip-flops, it would be easy to do.

Before he could think of anything else, she spun him around to face her, leaned into him, and kissed him on the lips.

Startled beyond reality, he stiffened like a boogie board, or whatever the hell they called those small surfboard-like death rides.

Her lips were sweet from the cream in her coffee and mixed with the salt from her omelet. The touch of her skin to his filled him with a wonderful, almost intoxicating, warmth.

Struggling to find his voice, he finally managed to say, "What was that for? It was only an omelet and some coffee. How 'bout I bring you a steak and a bottle of wine for dinner?"

She backed away from him, her face as red and heated as his.

"Mistletoe," she whispered and pointed up. "You're standing under the mistletoe."

"Oh. Right."

Screw the sunscreen. He wasn't washing his lips for the rest of the day.

He turned to leave, but caught his flip-flop on the raised tile in the entryway of the shop. Stumbling forward, he tried to turn and wave goodbye to her.

He laughed, and she laughed with him—a good sign, according to The Boys.

• • •

Four hours later, the sun took its throne high in the western sky and bore down hard on Grant's chest. He tried to push himself out of the confines of the beach chair the inn had provided him. The boldly striped, metal-framed contraption was the most awkward, uncomfortable piece of shit he'd ever lain on.

Looking around Playa's beachfront, he noticed most of the other patrons reclining in the same sort of seats, with one caveat. They seemed to be relaxing in theirs, while he struggled to find any such position.

They also had umbrellas hoisted in the sand, which kind of defeated the purpose of enjoying the sun, didn't it?

He intended to enjoy the fresh air and temper down the glare radiating off his neon white body. He was determined to experience the beach like he'd never been given the opportunity to do as a child, so he kept trying to reach something close to comfort.

His father disliked only one other thing as much as debt, and that was sunshine. He avoided it at all costs, without so much as ever explaining to Grant why. But his father's hang-up meant Grant spent vacations in the artificial light of institutions like the Smithsonian and The Louvre instead of on the beaches of the world.

His body was starting to feel a little tight, almost crisp. He repositioned himself on the fully extended seat, this time on his stomach. He was probably just stiff from fighting the beach chair from hell.

And even if it were the early stages of sunburn, he'd come here to break through his personal barriers, and that's what he was going to do. Unlike his father's pictures of vacation—standing next to the iron bull on Wall Street or a Warhol in the Guggenheim—Grant's photo would be on one of these goddamn chairs, sipping a Corona.

But he wished the squawking birds would go away. They smelled. Or if it wasn't them, something sure as hell did. Maybe it was fish. Dead fish. Is that what smog smelled like?

Then again, he hadn't been too impressed with the cleanliness of the water along the jetty. Maybe the floating trash was the culprit.

The strong sea breeze blew over him, chilling his hot skin. He was almost cold. Maybe he'd try out the water. With the sun blazing away for the last few hours, it was probably like bathwater by now.

He stood up and tried to brush the sand off of his body. Thank God he'd quit applying the sunscreen Stacia had sent with him. He'd managed to wipe most of it off with his towel. The damn sand stuck to it, leaving a grisly film all over him that itched like hell. Without the thick lotion covering him, the sand simply fell away when he walked down to the water's edge.

Never one to ease into anything, he went for the gusto. Running out following the out-breaking tide, Grant took a nice shallow dive into the Pacific.

He shivered and sputtered his way from the cold shallow depths to the sun-dappled surface of the water and then back to the beach. His teeth chattered with such force that he worried his laminate veneers would crack under the pressure.

What the hell good was the sun? No wonder no one else was in the water except a few morons surfing. And they had wetsuits on, now that he looked.

What could Harper have thought he would find so wonderful about spending his first day here? He hadn't relaxed a damn bit.

He'd spent the last few hours bored out of his mind. He'd planned on bringing his laptop, but then decided against it, once Stacia told him that the heat and sand wasn't good for it.

Now, his skin felt strangely tight, as if with his every move it was stretching beyond its normal capacity. It couldn't be sunburn. With the breeze, it wasn't hot enough. Besides, the clouds hadn't lifted from the sky until around noon. How could he get sun-burned without any sun?

He should have brought a book along. Everyone else seemed to be reading, if they weren't sleeping. Maybe he'd try that next time. He'd have to ask Harper what book would be good to start with because he hadn't read for pleasure in years. If the Tennessee Land Title Association or Board of Realtors' logos weren't on the cover, chances were he hadn't heard of or seen it.

To think people worked hard a good portion of each year to sit on a beach for a week or two. He couldn't do it. No way. Not in this chair anyway, and definitely not by himself.

When Harper was with him, though, even if it was someplace he didn't particularly care to be, she made it tolerable, if not downright enjoyable. She could always find something for him to notice that he would otherwise miss. And she always offered an offbeat, artistic way of looking at the world, compared to his black and white, all-business perspective.

Maybe he could get her to come back to the beach with him to explain what exactly she found so terrific about it, being as he'd missed the point completely.

Ironic that he'd spent the better part of their marriage missing the point. The wisdom in Reggie's Finding Your Emotions Starter Kit was beginning to soak in. Grant was done letting his business compete with his affection for Harper. Hell, it wasn't even a competition. Till now, she'd never stood a chance.

He'd been drowning in an emotional swamp, much larger than the Ballona Freshwater Marsh. With Reggie and Jeffrey's help, he'd identified his issues. Now he just had to change how those issues controlled his behavior. He had to beat his emotional insecurities.

He could sure talk the psychobabble talk, but could he walk the walk in front of her heart? He shook his head thinking about how dumb he'd really been. For the first time, he wondered how his mother had ever lived with his father. At least she'd had a son to fill her time. Harper had no one.

All of this deep thinking was starting to make him sleepy. A nap sounded nice. The time change must be hitting him. He didn't realize the three-hour difference between Tennessee and California would be so disorienting. Actually, he hadn't even felt it until now. He was getting very drowsy.

He dried off with his beach towel, careful not to wipe the rough cotton too quickly across his tender skin. They must not use much laundry softener at the inn because it felt like sandpaper scraping against his stomach.

He reclined the chair all the way back and fixed the towel over its entirety. That he could take a midday nap amazed him. He might get accustomed to this. He yawned. Stretched. Ouch. That hurt. And drifted off to sleep.

• • •

Crashing tides woke Grant. His throat felt parched. He reached for his water bottle. Drinking down what was left, he sat up and almost cried out in agony. He examined his body.

Bacon. He looked and felt like one of those pre-cooked strips, right out of the microwave. At least he didn't have the Cantwell white legs anymore. But was brick red any more attractive? Maybe he was taking this disavowal of his father's ways a little to the extreme.

Grant took his time gathering his sun and surf paraphernalia. Even if he was in a hurry, he wasn't in any condition to hustle. Not sure he'd be using the equipment again anytime soon, he carefully packed it in the bag the inn had provided.

Every move he made was a painful. Every step a challenge. Christ. Even his feet were burned—on both the top and bottom. Glad he only had to slide his feet into the flip-flops, he gingerly made his way off the beach and back toward the shop.

He wanted to swing in and see how Harper's day was going before he returned to the inn. Good thing it was on the way. He couldn't have withstood much of a detour.

CHAPTER NINETEEN
SUNBURN IN THE CITY

Saying Harper had a cow when she saw Grant was an understatement. She immediately ordered him to the inn and called Stacia to make arrangements for his care until she could leave the shop. She promised him she'd be there to take over as soon as she gave her staff directions to finish out the day's designs and event preparations.

Great. Now he'd screwed up her career goals as well as her personal life.

As Grant lay on his bed, looking around his suite, he'd never seen so many aloe plants in all his life. But he had to admit that when Harper broke open the leaves and laid them on his ripened skin, it felt good. Damn good.

When she lifted the leaves away every half hour or so, they looked like steamed vegetables, but they sure did the trick. Grant was starting to feel much better, and the pain was dwindling.

"What time is it?" he asked from underneath a sticky strip of steamed green. "I'm so sorry…"

"It's 10 P.M., and would you please find something else to say besides you're sorry. I've heard that same phrase for the last three hours."

Harper lifted the latest aloe strip from his lips and applied another cold, gel-like piece.

He was such a moron. Sun poisoning was one hell of a way to score points and precious time with her.

"Do you think I'll be able to make it to the K.O.W. tomorrow night? I was really looking forward to that."

Grant tried to move his arms, but if he did, he'd mess up the juicy layers Harper had just put there.

"If you're not in the hospital by then."

"I am not going to the hospital."

"You are if I say you are."

He couldn't get over Harper's new, sassy attitude. He'd first heard it in her tone with Jake, and now she was giving him the raspberries. He liked it and could definitely get used to her feistiness.

She picked up a glass of water and offered him a drink.

He nodded as best he could, welcoming any cold liquid he could get. She removed the aloe strips from his lips and tilted a glass so he could sip through the straw. The cold fluid felt good as it slid down his dry throat. He took another draw with much more force than the first.

"Easy there, cowboy. You probably shouldn't shock your system anymore than it already has been."

She took away the glass and set it down on the bedside table.

"I hope I didn't screw up your work schedule this evening," he said, trying to ease his body up at a better angle to see her.

Every inch of his skin that moved against the sheets ignited a small fire.

"You didn't. I really needed to take a night off anyway."

Harper hadn't moved from the chair next to him for hours, at least not during the thirty or so times he'd checked.

As he hesitantly pushed himself up closer to the headboard, he noticed she'd changed into pajamas. Her perfectly rounded, bra-less breasts were outlined beneath soft pink cotton. Pink really was her color.

Color was no longer a problem for him. And fortunately, Reggie and Jeffrey thought he looked great in red.

This certainly wasn't how he'd imagined spending an evening with her, but he couldn't afford to be choosy. He'd take any time he could get, even when he felt and looked like the newest arrival in Hell.

Pulling the aloe strips away from his face, Harper interrupted his perfect view of her breasts.

"Just for the record, I saw you looking."

Since she'd never notice his face reddening with embarrassment, Grant didn't attempt to make it look like he was a damn bit upset about getting caught.

"Sorry."

"I'm not," she said. "Actually, I'm rather impressed you even noticed. You never used to."

She picked up the files she'd been working on and turned her back to him, walking across the room to put them on her desk.

Was that a thong she was wearing under her pajama bottoms? Christ. Since when did she wear thongs? As she walked away, Grant thought her rear end looked smaller, more defined, more toned. Thank god, she hadn't lost her perfect curves. He was rather fond of those.

Whatever she was doing to stay fit—in spite of her poor diet—was more than agreeing with her, and her new look definitely agreed with him. She looked great. Except for the fatigue, she had a lean spunk he hadn't seen in her since high school. Had he robbed her of that too?

She turned back around and returned to his bed, holding up a couple of DVDs.

"I thought maybe we could watch a movie."

"Sure."

He couldn't believe how she was willing to take care of him, even though he'd never been there for her.

She pulled off the Fendi ball cap he'd gotten her on some business trip and ran her fingers through her hair.

He noticed how much longer it had gotten, and the beautiful sun-kissed streaks that ran through it. The indents from the cap gave her a wonderfully disheveled, but completely loveable, look.

"I'm afraid you're out of luck on choosing what we watch. Since you screwed up the night, you're stuck watching what I want to." She flipped through the stack of cases in her hands.

"Fine with me. And more than fair."

She helped him sit up a little further, fluffing a couple of pillows so he could lean comfortably against the headboard.

"So what are we watching?" he asked.

Not too long ago he would have dreaded her answer. Come to think of it, her answer wouldn't have been necessary because he wouldn't have been watching a movie with her at all. Proud of his change, he waited for the verdict.

"We'll start with Notting Hill."

She removed the DVD from its cover and placed it in the player.

"You haven't seen that yet?" Grant asked.

If Reggie knew what he was talking about, Grant had a hard time believing any woman hadn't seen that film. And the guy had certainly done well for his student so far.

"Of course I've seen it. But the real issue is that I get the feeling you have too. Care to explain that?"

Harper plopped down on the chair beside his bed, folding her legs up underneath her and tucking a small decorator pillow behind the small of her back.

Oh, boy. Time to dodge a big bullet.

"Well…I have seen it."

Grant groaned a little, hoping she'd think he was in pain and would focus on that instead of his recently acquired film savvy.

"When did you see it? That's not your type of movie."

So much for his discomfort, she was on him like she meant business.

"I don't know when I saw it. A couple of weeks ago, I suppose."

Couple of weeks, his ass. Try within the last three days. But he wasn't going to admit that.

"Something's been going on with you, GC3. I can't put my finger on it yet. But I'll figure it out."

Harper picked up the control to get the film started and struggled to try to get comfortable in the chair. First trying the cushions on one side, she then shifted them to the other.

"There's plenty of room on the bed, you know. If you want to sit up here…with me."

If Grant could get on his knees and beg, he would.

Harper thought about it. "If I do, no funny stuff."

"Do I look like I'm capable of trying any funny stuff? Even if I wanted to?"

Grant held his arms straight out from his sides with the grace of an armored knight, the steam rising off of him from the aloe leaves still stuck there.

"I don't think I could put my arms around you if I tried."

Harper laughed and then covered her smile with her hands.

He wasn't sure why she'd stopped herself. His condition was as funny as it was pathetic.

"Okay, I'll be right over."

She disappeared into the kitchen, coming back with more water and a bowl of green, snow pea-looking things.

"What the hell are those?"

"Edamame...the most wonderful alternative to chips and popcorn I've come across." She crawled up on his bed and settled in, placing the bowl in the middle of her lap. She popped small beans from the pods and devoured them. "When you feel better, remind me, and I'll fix you some."

She hit the play button and pulled a couple of tissues from the box on his nightstand.

Grant felt her head land on his shoulder two-thirds of the way into the movie, at one of his favorite parts. If the pressure against his skin didn't sting so damn badly, he'd have felt even more blessed. But he wasn't about to lift her off of him, no matter how much his raw, sun-burned shoulder begged for relief.

He looked down at her sleeping on him and knew she was where he always wanted her to be. He tried to pull the aloe out from under her cheek, but it was stuck, and he didn't want to wake her.

"Hey, Harper." He softly called her name. "It's late. We should probably..."

He didn't want her angry with him or thinking he took advantage of her by letting her sleep in his bed.

Without even opening her eyes, she whispered into his ear, "I could show you the bookstore set at Universal Studios, if you'd like, sometime. It's not far from here."

"That'd be great. I'd like that."

Grant repositioned her on his shoulder so she wouldn't have a kink in her neck. He took the unused tissues out of her hand so he'd have them for the end of the movie.

He didn't used to believe in Hollywood's happily-ever-afters. But maybe they were possible.

CHAPTER TWENTY
FRIENDS IN NEW PLACES

Harper completed her work orders with a new-found confidence. Pushing moss and holly sprigs into Styrofoam forms, she worked her magic like a pro. A spirited zing she hadn't had for weeks surged through her. She recognized the creative passion energizing her but was stymied by an unidentified motivator driving her even harder.

Despite riding high on positive energy, she chastised herself for sleeping with Grant. Oh, for gods' and goddesses' sake. She couldn't define resting her head on his shoulder as sleeping with him. What was wrong with her? Not to mention his shoulder was covered with aloe vera plants, which pretty much ruined the mood.

She had to admit though that she'd taken extreme pleasure in watching chick flicks with Grant—more pleasure than he'd evoked within her for years. He may have thought she was asleep the entire time he'd held her, but she wasn't. And he'd never been so attentive.

She rotated the form of the moss and holly deer so she could continue packing material into the foam on the other side. She smiled, amazed how brilliant her work was turning out despite her personal upheaval. She was on a roll, if only she could keep herself on the track.

Unready to acknowledge that the source of her renewed energy could be Grant, Harper stuffed a large hunk of moss in the depression of the deer's rump.

For the last ten years, he'd made her feel like a female Atlas, responsible for holding up the world of Cantwell Realty so everyone could admire its good will. He had been a constant drag on her system, not a sustaining life force. Now it was as though something had changed, something deep inside him. Even though Harper didn't completely understand it, she liked the soothing influence he now had on her. He offered a constant in her turbulent world, an axis around which she could safely turn. Besides, it felt nice to cuddle up next to him. For the first time since she'd slept at the inn, she woke up feeling well rested.

But why hadn't he ever allowed her to rest on his shoulder before? Why hadn't he been the soft place for her to fall? She'd so wanted to share her vulnerabilities, secrets and needs.

Instead, he'd been a man who kept to his side of the bed. An invisible fortress had risen between them.

Harper dispensed a stringy wad of glue from her glue gun under a large bunch of mistletoe and secured it, like a crown, to the top of the deer's head. Perfect. Now that her prototype was complete, she'd let the staffers make the others they needed for one of the events.

Glancing back down at her layout, envisioning the continuity of her design, she was pleased. Fifty more holly and moss-covered deer would perfectly coordinate with the thirty grapevine versions she and her help had covered in white lights the previous day and make wonderful centerpieces for the Bed and Breakfast Association's Holiday Gala.

As soon as the guests turned off Sunset Strip, wound their way through the gated communities of Beverly Hills and hit the driveway of the hostess's home, they could follow the lighted deer with red, frosted glass noses, all the way to the front door.

The hostess said she'd been gushing to her friends all week about Harper's concept. And after checking to make sure that no other party for the season would be using Harper's theme, she'd approved the idea.

After instructing her crew on how to finish the deer, Harper checked her watch. She couldn't believe how the day had flown by. She'd promised Stace she'd quit no later than seven, which left her with only a half hour to spare.

Checking her list, she didn't see anything she could start in the little time she had remaining. The rest of the items would have to wait until morning.

Pleased she'd managed to save an outfit from ruin for the first time since she'd started at the shop, she triumphantly hung her smock on a hook.

She grabbed her bag, stuffing the file she'd need to review for tomorrow's projects into the deep-pocketed middle section, and reached for her sunglasses on the shelf above her desk.

Catching a glimpse of herself in the antique mirror mounted on the wall, she set aside her bag and tried to make a stylish mess out of her unmanageable upsweep. My God. She could see her roots...every last one of them. Reggie would have refused to be seen with her in public.

Before the parties started the middle of next week, she was going to have to take a day for herself to shop and find a salon. She was nowhere near presentable, and she refused to appear at the events looking like an artful disaster. Part of her style as an event planner was that, during the event itself, none of the patrons would be able to distinguish her from the other guests. She always dressed as if she were on the guest list and mingled with the crowd. That way, she got very honest opinions regarding what people liked and didn't like about what she'd come up with.

She always looked calm and together during her events, never leaving any doubt that she was in control and more than capable of pulling everything off without a hitch.

After the stress and strains of getting these parties off the planning pages and onto the red carpets, Harper was in no form to party with the It Crowd of Hollywood.

Her personal style sense for each event was probably the only thing she'd taught Reggie. He'd begrudgingly adopted her approach, although he pouted every chance he got over his preference for scene-stealing drama.

Walking back to the inn, she rearranged her schedule in her mind. Even though she had To Do Lists already lined up for every day for the rest of the month, tomorrow, the last Saturday before the parties began, offered her the best chance to squeeze in time for herself. All of the boutiques and salons were open during the weekend, so she could hit them all in one day.

By the time she pressed the buzzer for the inn's gate attendant, she'd made her decision. She'd open the shop in the morning, as she always did, get the staff started on each of the items she had on her list, and then leave them to their creative genius.

Since she couldn't physically attend every event, she had to be able to trust them on their own. Why not give them a test before the madness began?

Passing the kitchen on her way to her room, she was disappointed to discover that Stace was already gone. She was anxious to see how Grant had done all day recovering from his burns. Stace had promised to keep an eye on him and report in, but she hadn't called. Grant's sunburn was serious, and whether she should be or not, Harper was worried.

Thrilled to be back at the inn at a decent time, she unloaded her bag onto the desk in her room and started to undress, thinking a long, hot shower would relax and rejuvenate her for a much needed night out.

As hesitant as she was that Grant was going along, she was curious to see how he'd react to her new friends and the K.O.W.

• • •

Grant reached for the brass nautical-inspired door handle of the K.O.W. To pull himself together, he took a consciously controlled breath, just like Reggie had instructed. Before hurtling himself into an environment foreign to his virtually non-existent social skills, he sucked in another jagged breath, nearly choking on the rush of air.

He had no choice. Either he opened the damn door and faced his fears, or he signed on the dotted divorce line and lost Harper forever. He threw back the door and crossed the threshold into the unknown.

Immediately, the strong stench of stale smoke and spilt beer hit him. He hated that smell. There was something to be said for drinking from Waterford glasses in the comfort of his smoke-free great room.

He searched through the thick haze, trying to find Harper. It didn't take him long in the small room. What a seedy establishment. He would never have chosen this type of atmosphere for her. What could she possibly find attractive at the K.O.W.?

She hadn't noticed him arrive, which was just as well. He needed all the extra seconds he could steal to figure out what to say when he got to her.

Reggie had taught him a couple of good lines for this sort of moment, but he'd be damned if he could remember a single one. Shit. He had about fifty feet to come up with something.

As he walked across the wooden floor and closed the gap between them, his adrenaline surged.

Passing by the old mahogany bar, he had to give credit where it was do. It was pretty nice, obviously well taken care of too. The padded railings added a nice touch.

Just as he was about to pull out the barstool next to hers, she turned toward him. A look of confusion crossed her face, and Grant thought for sure he'd blown it on his choice of attire, even though he'd agonized over it for hours.

His decision had ended up being fairly simple, considering everything but the premium designer tee and cargo shorts he'd chosen rubbed against his sunburn to the point that he couldn't function. And thank God for the flip-flops. He couldn't imagine putting anything more confining on his feet.

"You look fantastic," Harper said and hopped down from her stool.

She gave him a quick kiss on the cheek, pulled out the stool next to hers and motioned for him to sit.

"Thanks. It's the only thing that I could manage with the burn."

Grant normally didn't allow women to pull chairs out for him, but he appreciated her taking charge. He was nothing but a tongue-tied testosterone disaster.

He took his place next to her.

"You look terrific yourself."

So much for fancy lines, he thought, deciding to just stick with the truth.

And boy did she ever look terrific. She'd never worn anything like this at home. It was some sort of short and ruffled, Little House on the Prairie skirt, although the fancy beadwork covering it had Harper written all over it. The cowboy boots were an interesting choice too. According to Reggie's manuals, they were much more than just a Music City staple. They were now popular on the West Coast too. The tight revealing cut of her tee was definitely not Briar Creek style though. It was different, but nice.

"Well. What'll it be to start the night?" Harper pointed toward the taps and well-stocked liquor shelves behind the bar. "Gin and tonic?"

"Sure." Grant hoped the place poured strong because he needed to relax. Otherwise, he'd never make it through this.

The bartender—a dashing chap with a bit of a British accent, who reminded Grant of Simon Cowell, and who seemed to know all of the patrons on a first name basis as well as what they liked to drink—came toward them.

"Grant, I'd like to introduce you to the best bartender in L.A., who also happens to be my dear friend, Stokey Abrams. Stokey, this…is Grant," Harper said.

Feeling as if Stokey may know more about him than Grant was comfortable acknowledging, he extended his hand and firmly shook Stokey's.

"Firm, power grip you got there," Grant said.

Stokey smiled and ever so hesitantly pulled back his hand. "Glad to finally meet you."

Trying to ease the tension, even if it was only in his mind, Grant responded, "The pleasure is mine."

Stokey nodded, winked at Harper and then squeezed her hands between his. "Your usual, sweetie? And how about for your husband?"

Stokey's face turned flaming red. "I mean Grant. What can I get you, Grant?"

Stokey turned back to Harper and threw up his hands, mouthing "sorry" as if Grant wasn't sitting right there.

Evidently she wasn't comfortable still claiming him as her spouse. That set him back.

"I'll have a gin and tonic. And I would imagine Harper's usual would be Crown and Diet?"

Grant looked at Harper for confirmation.

She smiled. "Right you are."

"Great. Thanks, Stokey. And could you just start a tab for us?"

"Will do."

That brought a big smile to Stokey's lips, as if no one usually paid for her drinks or knew her preference for top-shelf whiskey.

Hell, the way Harper looked these days, Grant couldn't figure out how she kept any man away from her. They should be lined up waiting to pay her bar tab.

Stokey winked at Harper again.

Did she have any friends who weren't overtly gay? Other than Stacia? Oh, and Jake definitely wasn't, although Grant sure as hell wished he were.

"You okay?" Harper asked, leaning into him. "Stokey wasn't trying to stir things up."

"Sure, I know. And we are still married." Grant tried to brush off Stokey's remark. "It's no big deal. I just hope you didn't tell him what a complete ass I was."

Harper giggled. "At least you're not in denial."

"You're right. I suppose it's much healthier now that I'm out of that stage," he said and fiddled with the video machine attached to the bar top next to him.

For fifty cents he could undress the playgirls grinning at him from the screen, one piece of clothing at a time. Not like it would take long with the skimpy outfits they were wearing.

"Need to borrow a couple of quarters?" Harper asked, turning the napkin Stokey had placed in front of her so that the picture was facing her.

She was just as anal as he was where organization was concerned. No way could either one of them let that damn thing face the wrong direction. At least they still agreed on something.

"No thanks. I haven't sunk quite that low yet. But I appreciate your thinking of me."

Grant nodded a polite thank you to Stokey when he set another drink in front of him.

"So why did you marry me?" Harper asked the question as if it held no more significance than a basic conversation opener.

Nothing like going for the kill early. After Grant swallowed what was left of his gin and tonic, since the first gulp was now in his nose, he turned to her. She deserved an answer—an honest answer. He only hoped his truth was enough to satisfy her.

"Because, even though I never showed you, I love you more than anything."

"Oh."

That shut her up for the time being.

"So who's all coming tonight?" Grant asked, anything to change the subject.

"Well, just Stace, her sister, and Stokey's life partner Glen."

She leaned in to him again and whispered, "Will you be all right with Stokey and Glen? They're pretty out there with their relationship, but they're great guys."

"Yeah, sure, whatever. It doesn't bother me."

"Since when?" Harper played with the straw in her drink like she did when she was fishing for information.

"Since you left me at the estate with only Jeffrey and Reggie for company."

Grant couldn't help but be tickled by the oops look in her eyes. "Yeah. Thanks for that."

Little did she know that if it weren't for both of those men, he wouldn't be with her now.

"Speaking of which, do you think they're…you know…what did you just call it…life partners?" he asked.

"Jeffrey? With Reggie?" It was Harper's turn to suck alcohol up her nose.

Grant certainly didn't think it was an illogical thought. "Yes. I don't have any other gay friends that are of our mutual acquaintance."

"Good point. But no, I don't think they're together. At least they weren't when I left. But what I'm more interested in is that you just referred to them as your friends," Harper said, looking Grant square in the eyes. "Did I hear that correctly?"

"Guess so."

Damn he had to be more careful about disclosing his relationship with them. He still wasn't ready to dive into the whole Chick Tricks Inc. story. As far as that went, he was still in denial.

"Grant Cantwell III, I can't put my finger on it yet, but something is up with you. I swear I'm going to get to the bottom of it."

Harper motioned for Stokey to hit her again.

"To recap, you watch chick flicks…pretty regularly it seems. You're dressing fashionably. You've brought me meals, knowing exactly what I like. And now you're bonding with homosexuals." Harper blew Stokey a kiss, after he gave her another drink. "Do you understand why I'm a little perplexed? Your father would be rolling over in his grave."

"Let's leave my father out of this, shall we?"

All he needed was to once more compare his failings to those of his father's. After his Chick Tricks reading, Grant was more than well-versed on his shortcomings.

"Okay. Okay. Sorry if it bothers you."

She flipped back her hair, which, to his surprise, appeared to be overdue for color. He couldn't remember the last time she'd let that kind of thing go, further proof she'd been working way too hard.

"I have a favor to ask you," she said.

She seemed to be struggling with what to say next.

"Sure. What is it?"

She never asked him to do anything. Hell, she never asked anyone to help her. He never could figure out how one person could take responsibility for so much without asking for assistance.

"I need to go shopping tomorrow," she said and ran her hands through her hair.

"If it's money...just name the amount," Grant said, unable to imagine how else he could help her with her shopping.

She sighed with a resignation in her body that he wasn't proud to have caused.

"It's not the money, Grant. I'm not going to make it quite that easy on you."

"Then what do you need? I'm confused."

"Yeah, you would be," she said, taking a long sip of her drink. "I'd like for you to go with me. I could use the company."

Grant downed a quick shot of gin.

"You want me to go with you? Okay...but I'm not sure that I'll be the kind of company you're looking for. Are you sure you wouldn't rather have Stokey, Glen, or someone like that along?"

He thought of the hell he'd gone through every day since he started dressing himself, mentally flipping through the pages of the style manual Reggie had made him memorize. "Since you left, I can barely dress myself. And you want my advice on what to buy?"

"No, I don't want your advice, although you haven't done too bad for yourself."

At least his efforts at that hadn't been wasted.

"I just want you to be there—you know, just to have someone to talk to."

"As you know, I'm not real good at that either."

~ 181 ~

Grant hadn't learned enough from Reggie yet to provide meaningful conversation at the K.O.W., let alone an entire day's worth without people, cigarettes and beer to distract her.

"I'm giving you a chance to redeem yourself."

Harper took the straw out of her glass and chewed on it.

"Okay. Thanks for the opportunity. I'll try and see if I can manage to not screw it up."

"Fair enough."

Grant settled into the back of his leather padded stool, not sure if it was the gin, his sunburn, Harper, or her offer that had warmed him. But he felt very lucky that Reginald Greene had clapped and snapped him this far.

He ordered another round of drinks and decided to just let loose for once, not sure how that really felt or what the result would be.

CHAPTER TWENTY-ONE
IT'S IN THE BAG

The next morning, Harper waited patiently in the Hummer for Grant to join her. He was never late. She picked up her cell and speed dialed Stace's phone at the inn's reception desk.

"Have you seen him yet?" She tapped her chipped fingernails on the steering wheel. "He's never late. Never."

"Well, we did have quite a bit to drink last night. Do you remember that?" Stace ventured a guess. "'Cause I do…sort of. Does he handle his liquor well?"

Harper hadn't thought of that.

"Good question. Can't say that I've ever gone out drinking with him. Would you call up to his room and make sure he's okay and tell him that I'm waiting?"

"What do you mean will I call him? You call him. He's your husband," Stace said defiantly, then laughed her ass off.

"You're real funny. Fine. I'll call him. Put me through to his room, please. If you can stop laughing that long."

Who cared if Stace had a point? What was she supposed to say to him?

Thankfully, she didn't have to worry about it because just as the line to his room starting ringing, a very bedraggled Grant stepped out the door to the garage. When the light of day hit his eyes, he flinched. He looked awful.

Unable to stifle a giggle, Harper honked the Hummer's horn. Grant jumped straight up, almost cracking his head on one of the low beams of the garage. GC3 had a hangover. This was going to be interesting.

She rolled down the window and hollered out at him, "Hey, handsome, need a ride?"

Grant did his best to grin and shuffled to the vehicle.

"Am I paying to rent this beast?"

"No, it's Jake's. I'm borrowing it while he's gone."

She unlocked the doors, wondering if she should have borrowed Stace's car instead of making Grant ride in Jake's. But why not burn Jake's gas? He'd given her his gas card so he could earn points, and she was more than willing to rack 'em up for him.

"Jump in. We've got a lot to do today."

"Great. I have to pretend that I'm that gigolo loser for the day. Talk about pimp my ride."

Harper couldn't hold back. "Very good, sweetie. I'm impressed with that cultural reference. And since when are you in the know about pimping rides?"

"I've been working on my cultural awareness. That's all you need to know for now." Grant reached for the seatbelt and wrapped it around him as if his life depended on it.

"What? You don't think I can drive this thing?" Harper had never told him that from the driver's seat she couldn't see where the hood ended or the tailgate began. But she knew for certain there'd be no parallel parking to blow her cover. She was a risk-taker, but not a dumb one.

"It is a tad bit bigger than your roadster."

Grant tugged on his seatbelt, as if testing it for resistance.

"Don't worry, when I'm driving this thing, I envision it as my little Bond mobile. Works every time."

"Let's hope so. But I wouldn't try to parallel park if I were you."

"Hadn't planned on it."

As if parking in LA was easy period. It didn't matter what Harper was driving. It was an acquired skill she had yet to master.

She slipped the gearshift into drive and headed for Santa Monica.

Grant didn't say much on the way, except for insisting they stop at the nearest Starbucks. Two bold brews later and they were once again headed for the first item on her agenda—her favorite nail salon for a manicure and pedicure.

After telling Grant her intentions, he acted uncomfortable but not in the least bit put off. Brownie points for that.

"What should I do while you're in there?" he asked.

"Why don't you join me?"

"You want me to get a manicure and pedicure?"

"Well, I can't think of any other way you'd be participating at a nail salon, can you?"

"Men do that sort of thing?"

"They do on this side of the continent. Want to try it?"

"Sure. What the hell." He turned to face her. "If you tell anyone at home I'm doing this…"

"What?" she asked and giggled. "You think your reputation as a super mogul will be ruined?"

"Something like that."

"Okay. I'll just tell them about the movies you're watching and leave out the part about the mani-pedi. Does that make you feel better?"

Harper couldn't resist teasing him. He was taking it so well that it was too rare of an opportunity to pass up.

"Thanks for your help," Grant said, then rolled his eyes and turned his head toward the window.

But not before Harper caught his amused grin.

"Any time."

She parked the truck in the widest spot she could find, several spaces from any other vehicle in the salon's lot. She gathered her large, hot pink sequined sack purse from behind her seat.

Nothing cheered her up like getting a mani-pedi. And this place was great. Walk-ins were welcome, and they had her in and out of there in half an hour. After the amazing massages they gave, her arms and legs felt ten pounds lighter. She'd give anything to have one of these salons in Briar Creek.

Grant had a near death grip on the door handle, probably thinking he wouldn't be anywhere near cheered up after the experience.

Harper tried to ease his mind. "You'll love this."

"Can't wait. I still can't believe you talked me into this."

"Actually, I can't either. Either you're softening up in your old age, or you're way too hung over to care."

"I'm supposed to be along today to redeem myself, remember? I'm hoping this helps my cause."

"You'll definitely earn a few points for this. Not immunity from the tribal council, but there'll be a small reward."

"There will be? I can't wait."

As they made their way to the salon's entrance, Grant took his dark sunglasses from the top of his head and lowered them over his eyes.

"Don't worry, no one will recognize you. But how Hollywood."

Harper pushed her own glasses onto the top of her head.

Once they'd signed in, the receptionist, who barely spoke English, and two technicians, who spoke absolutely no English, directed them to a wall filled with shelves stocked with every color of nail polish Harper could ever want.

Grant looked at her with the most horrific expression of total shock and disbelief. "What did he, or she, whichever it was, mean that we had to pick a color? If you think for one minute…"

"Relax. I'm going French today, and you'll just tell them natural."

"How can I tell them anything? None of them speak English."

Harper kissed him on the cheek and told him in a low hushed voice, "Just do what I do."

She patted his arm. "Trust me. You'll love this."

Seeing the technicians beckon them to their stations, Harper grabbed Grant's hand and led him deep into the heart of his never-never land. It's a good thing she'd decided long ago to never say never. The new GC3 was shocking the hell out of her.

She watched Grant as he carefully studied each move the technician made. Knowing his feet were sensitive, not to mention sunburned, she hoped he could make it through and enjoy some part of the experience.

She removed her flip-flops and rolled up her pant legs, telling him to do the same. Then she sat in the thick leather padded massage chair, directing him into a similar chair next to hers. She showed him how to work the controls on the chair and set hers to a low, gentle vibration.

He seemed to like the chair. Well, he did until the technician tapped his feet, inviting him to soak them in the hot, aromatic, bubbling water. At that point, he was itching to bail. She figured he probably would have if he could have figured out how to jump out of the chair without slipping and falling on his ass.

Deciding she'd better give him comfort and encouragement, she patted his hand when her technician was finished massaging and prepping the hand closest to his. And then did so again once that hand was polished. Grant's tension gradually eased until he almost looked like he was relaxing.

She wasn't used to seeing him not in control of a situation and was touched by his willingness to experience something so far out of his comfort zone.

For the first time, she realized that conversation wasn't what she'd needed most from him. What she'd wanted was a human connection. Oddly enough, she felt more of a bond with him sitting here in a manicure salon than she ever had in their twelve years of marriage.

He still needed her, like he did back then, but in a different, more viable way than she was accustomed to. He didn't need her to make him or the Cantwell Group look good. He needed her as a partner in life, someone to share new experiences with.

Leaving the salon a half hour later, she swore he walked lighter on his feet.

Sometime during their marriage, he'd lost that carefree spirit. She had a feeling his father had stuffed it away in a drawer, perhaps with his son's graduation cap and gown, forcing Grant to look upon his future with the seriousness and respectability that all Cantwell men were required to bare.

Grant had never told her anything like that. And he probably never would. He never talked to her about his feelings or opinions unless the topic had a NYSE ticker symbol. If it wasn't quantified by the number of shares or price per share, it wasn't worthy of discussion.

Speaking of which, he hadn't so much as mentioned Wall Street since he'd arrived in Playa. He hadn't been buried in newspapers when she'd seen him either. And where was his best friend, Mr. Tablet?

"That wasn't so bad," Grant said, opening the Hummer's door for her and placing her purse onto the floorboard of the backseat. "The massage was pretty great actually. Where to next? Great bag, by the way."

Harper stopped before clicking her seatbelt in place.

"Great bag? You know, you're scaring me a little."

"You used to complain because I never noticed those kinds of things. Sorry. Guess I'm trying a little too hard."

She saw the hurt and fear in his eyes, and she couldn't deny how much it meant to her to see how far he was willing to go to make her happy. Not wanting to shut him down or stifle his change, she tried to lighten the mood.

"Well, you don't have to worry about our next stop. I'm not requesting that you get a cut, color and style too, although I might sign you up for a body wax."

"A what?"

"Just kidding."

She started the truck and headed for Beverly Hills.

• • •

Harper's day with Grant stacked up one surprise after another. She'd gotten the biggest kick out of all of his over-the-top, pop culture references. If she didn't know better, she'd have sworn he'd been watching nothing but E! News since she'd been gone. That or he'd borrowed some of Reggie's repertoire. Knowing there wasn't any way on earth he'd spent that much quality time with her most flagrant and in-the-know friend, she chalked it up to his getting way too much sun.

Having him around for the day was more of a boon to her exhausted spirit than she could ever have imagined possible. He'd talked to her and listened to her more than he ever had during their marriage. Although she still wasn't sure why she'd invited him, she was awfully glad that she was relying on her impulses rather than continuously trying to rationalize everything she did.

Grant even asked her opinion on things—everyday things, not philanthropic bullshit, business or politics. Nothing they covered would have made it to press in The Wall Street Journal. Hell, most of it would have appeared only in the Lifestyle sections or Dear Heloise.

The oddest of all was that Grant didn't buy her a damn thing, or even offer to. Not that she wasn't using his cards for her purchases, but he himself gave her nothing but his heart and soul. The one thing he couldn't buy for her.

After dinner at her favorite café on the pier at Hermosa Beach, they indulged in the last item on her list for the day.

Sitting next to each other, huddled close for warmth on a blanket covering the chilly sand, they caught their first sunset together.

Just before the red ball fell into the Pacific, Harper took Grant's hands in hers.

"This is what life's all about, Grant. Not the Dow Jones average, but this—the fact you are sitting in one of the most beautiful places on earth to watch the sun set."

He nodded in agreement.

She caught the last of the fireball as it sank into the sea, and she saw it in the reflection of his eyes.

"It's beautiful. Unbelievable. But not as unbelievable as the day we've shared."

He looked at her with tears starting to fall down his face.

She wiped them away before they spilled onto his silk trousers and left a watermark.

They sat together in the new companionable silence they'd discovered, each in their own thoughts.

Harper asked the gods and goddesses above if she could love this changed man.

How could it be that one man in her life knew all the right words to her heart, but didn't believe in or act on them? And the one who wasn't adept at speaking them could show her, in his silence, how much he believed in their future, even though he didn't know how to say it.

She laid her head on his shoulder. If he only knew how much she'd missed having him as her rock.

She'd tried to explain it to him in the note she'd left him seven months ago, but she wasn't sure that a man like Grant could comprehend the lines she'd written, let alone what lay unsaid between them. But the man she was leaning against now would understand.

Grant had changed. And Harper liked what he'd become.

CHAPTER TWENTY-TWO
NOW OR NEVER

Four days later, Grant paced the main dining room of Bistro Sole, making sure everything had been done to his exact specifications. Thank God Glen managed the restaurant and had been able to arrange for Grant to rent it out for a couple of hours to create a special lunch date with Harper.

After their wonderful day together on Saturday, he'd thought he'd managed in some small, but hopefully significant ways, to earn a place back in her heart. But he'd hardly seen her since then. She'd been in event planning overdrive—party mode as he'd come to call it in Briar Creek.

He'd taken her breakfast and lunch each day at the shop, never staying longer than to set up her food, kiss her on the cheek, and leave her to her work. Although he'd waited in the inn's kitchen for her, making sure she had plenty to eat late in the evenings upon her return, she'd been so exhausted, he'd fed her and then tucked her into bed.

He knew what it was like to work on a deadline, self-imposed or otherwise, and respected her time, even though he wished he could spend more of it with her. But she'd always been supportive of him in that regard, so he owed her nothing less.

From what Stacia had told him as well as Harper's staff at the shop, the first large event had gone perfectly. As if he expected any less. Harper was an amazing event planner. He still regularly received compliments from colleagues for all of the festivities she'd turned into signature events for Briar Creek.

Grant knew her style well enough to know she'd never take the credit but pass it on to her staff instead. So he'd wanted to do something special for her to show her how proud he was of her accomplishments.

Without her knowledge, he'd had her Bloom Factory staff come in early today, before she arrived, and set up decorations in the bistro. He'd also had Jeffrey call Glen to take care of the menu to make sure it was something she loved.

Grant knew he had only an hour at most before she'd want to go back to the shop and finish out her day, and he wanted everything to be perfect for the sixty minutes he'd have with her.

Anxiously looking out the front window toward the shop, he waited to give the cue to Glen that she was on her way. After what seemed like an eternity, she walked out of the shop. Grant watched as she hit the pedestrian walk button.

"Here she comes," he yelled toward the kitchen where Glen and his staff waited.

He straightened the imaginary tie that hung from his linen palm tree-motif shirt, one of Harper's Saturday Bloomingdale's finds. Damn, he couldn't get used to not wearing one. He paced the floor, praying he wouldn't fuck this up.

If he didn't tell her he still loved her, he'd go crazy. Hell, he could barely be in the same room with her and keep his hands to himself. He couldn't live the rest of his life with his Wall Street Journal as his BFF, even though he'd been raised to think he could.

He hurried to the door, tripping over the entryway rug. One of these days he'd learn to walk in flip-flops, if he didn't break his neck first.

Opening the door without even taking time to say hello, Grant hustled her into the bistro, then closed and locked the door behind them.

"Ah hah. I've got you to myself for the next hour."

"That's a good thing, right? And hello, by the way."

She looked too worn out to even sound halfway adventuresome.

"I hope it's a good thing, sweetheart. You deserve a special treat. You've worked way too hard. But I've heard that your diligence and talent are more than paying off."

Hoisting his arm high into the air and snapping his fingers twice, Grant gave Glen the signal to get busy. It always worked for Reggie.

Pulling out a chair for Harper, he dodged her speculative look. She acted as if she wanted to say something, but then deciding against it, silently sank into the cushions.

"I've got a little surprise for you. I want you to feel how special you make your clients feel when you work for them."

Harper smiled, giving Grant the encouragement he needed to carry on with his plan.

"The bistro looks incredible, Grant."

Hearing her approval, he was pleased he'd decided to use her designs to give the room a seasonal boost.

"I'm glad you like it."

From where they sat, there wasn't one place within their view that didn't have a white-lit topiary covered with Christopher Radko-style ornaments. The brilliant colors of the ornaments reflected off of the tiny white bulbs, giving the room a child-like Christmas morning authenticity. Thanks to his father's bah humbug bullshit, Grant had missed out on scenes like this as a child, and he'd been too stupid and set in his ways to participate in them with Harper either.

Grant moved the oversized ornament he'd placed in the center of their table to the side. Knowing how much she loved Radkos, he'd chosen a jewel-toned Christmas tree that was new this year.

Glen served fresh pears and brie, followed by chicken cordon blue and a tremendous tiramisu for dessert. Even though Harper was too tired to eat much, Grant saw her eyes light up as each item was brought to their table.

"You've outdone yourself," she said, taking a final bite of the tiramisu.

She wiped her mouth with her napkin, then folded it and placed it on top of the table. "Thank you for a wonderful break, Grant."

"You're most welcome." He reached for her hand. "I'm so proud of you, Harper. And you are the one who's outdone herself. Your designs, your long hours to see them through to fruition, your wonderful way with your staff...you're brilliant at what you do. I hope you know that."

He kissed her fingers. "And I only wish I would have known how to tell you this all of those years when you'd done the same things for me for the Cantwell Group. Please know how much I appreciate and love the work that you do."

Grant saw tears come to the corners of Harper's eyes and felt them having their way with him too.

"How could I have been such a fool to lose you?"

Before he could think of a reasonable answer, someone knocked on the door to the restaurant. He'd made sure the CLOSED sign was hanging on the door when he'd locked them in. Couldn't people read?

"I'll get it."

From the sound of his voice, Glen was as irritated as Grant was.

As Grant struggled to figure out the best way to tell her the rest of his feelings, Glen brought an overnight parcel to their table.

"I'm sorry, Grant, Harper, but the driver had this express package for you, Harper. He didn't want to have to bring it back because he'd miss the guaranteed delivery time. So your staff told him you were here."

Before either of them could say a word, Glen set the package on the edge of the table and disappeared.

"Something you're expecting?"

Grant felt like a dark cloud had descended over the room.

"No." Harper turned the package around so she could read the return address. "It's from Jake."

Thus, the cloud. Sent from the Dark Knight himself, Grant thought.

"I can wait and open it later," Harper said, clearing the package from the table and placing it at her feet.

"No, go ahead. I'm dying over here to see what's in it."

At least if he saw what it contained, he'd know what he was dealing with. If she opened it now, he'd also be able to gauge her reaction to it.

Grant's throat had gone desert dry. He started to pick up his water glass, but quickly set it back down on the table. His hands were shaking too badly to make it to his mouth without dumping it down his shirt.

Harper carefully tore back the strip sealing the contents and pulled out a small box, professionally wrapped but not resembling anything that could be immediately identified.

Opening the paper with the precision with which she did everything, Grant came close to grabbing it and ripping the damn thing to shreds.

Finally, she pulled out a small CD case and a card.

She read the card silently to herself and then looked at Grant in hopeless confusion.

"What? What for Christ's sake does it say?" As much as he didn't want to know, he had to if he were to deal with the asshole.

"Apparently, while Jake's been on tour, he wrote me a song. This is the demo disc." As she placed the card and the disc back in the box, Harper's hands shook.

"How sweet," Grant said.

He knew he had every right to be hostile, but he planned to do his best to fight the dragon on the inside and not make Harper feel any worse. She was under enough stress. And if he'd ever bothered to communicate his love for her, they wouldn't be in this situation.

"There's more," she said, without looking at him.

"And that would be?"

"He invited me to spend Christmas with him in Catalina on his sailboat." Harper looked at Grant, her fears and frustrations coming out in a deluge of tears.

Damn him. Just as Grant had feared, the asshole was making another move. Well, tough shit. Grant had come too far to give up now.

"Well, having you crying by the end of the meal wasn't exactly what I had in mind." Not really what he'd wanted to say, but he couldn't think of anything else that didn't involve annihilating Jake in front of her.

"It's not you. It's not your problem at all, Grant. You…this lunch…in fact, your whole visit has been nothing but wonderful." Harper got up from her chair and reached for her bag, placing the package inside.

"No, this is my problem," Grant said, walking over to her and taking her into his arms. "If I hadn't been such an uncaring pig during our marriage, you wouldn't even be in this situation."

She melted against him, her body deflating into the soft fabric of his shirt. He pressed her head against his chest and held her, with no intention of letting go. Why hadn't he ever bothered to hold her like this before?

She sniffled and pulled away from him, wiping her nose and eyes with her hands until he handed her a napkin. She tugged at the clip holding her hair into place on top of her head and adjusted her fitted tee over the low-cut rise of her jeans.

Stomping one of her feet against the floor, as if proving to herself that she had the strength to hold onto her emotions, she said, "Grant, it was my fault too. I lost myself trying to make you happy and be the wife you needed me to be."

He started to speak, but she put her fingers on his lips to stop him.

She continued, "I've just about saved what was left of me, and I'm not about to let any man take it away from me again."

Grant wiped the last tear from her face and smoothed down a piece of flyaway hair.

"I'm sorry for the part I played."

"I know you are. And it means a great deal to me to hear you say so."

She stomped her foot again—her cowboy boot landing with a determined thwomp against the tiled floor—and pulled herself up straight and tall.

"Thanks for a great lunch. I've got to get back to the shop."

He ushered her to the door in silence. Opening it for her, he placed his hand on her shoulder. She turned back to him.

"Are you going to Catalina, then?" he asked.

He was surprised by the glimmer of confusion in her eyes.

"No, of course not. We've got plans, remember?"

Wishing she sounded a little more excited about it, but too overjoyed that she'd stuck with him rather than run off with Hollywood, Grant struggled to speak.

"I'm not so sure my plans compare to Catalina."

"Whatever you plan, it will be nice, I'm sure."

She kissed his cheek.

"Thanks again for lunch. See you at the inn later?"

Grant's mind was spinning out of control. The whole afternoon had taken a turn he wasn't expecting. He had nowhere close to enough savvy to deal with it.

"Grant?"

"Oh, yeah, sure, I'll catch up with you later."

He kissed her back, again on the cheek, tired of this particular gesture of friendship and determined to go for her lips soon. With

~ 195 ~

Jake back in hot pursuit and closing in, he couldn't afford not to go for it all.

He watched her cross the street to the shop.

He may have won this round, but Jake had to be stopped, for good. Grant may have been in the lead, but he wasn't willing to bank on winning yet.

He settled up with Glen, easing his friend's oversensitive mind that giving Harper the package was the right thing to do. It wasn't like she wouldn't have gotten it later anyway. And this way, Grant had been able to see her reaction.

He hurried back to the inn to call Reggie.

He had to figure out a way to put some extra zing into his holiday plans. He wanted to make Harper forget that she'd had another offer. How could he be so confident in his boardroom and such an idiot at the important parts of life?

His plan to tell her during lunch how much he still loved her had been shot all to hell. Now he had to figure out a way to work that conversation into their holiday festivities. At least he had the opportunity to do that. But whatever he did, he had to make sure he gave her a Christmas she'd never forget. A Christmas that would bring her home for good.

CHAPTER TWENTY-THREE
IT'S NEVER TOO LATE...OR IS IT?

Harper waited for Jake's voicemail to pick up but was surprised when he answered after two rings.

"Hey, baby. What's up?"

Not knowing what else to say, she decided to get straight to the reason for her call. "Thank you for the package."

"Thank you for inspiring me. Have you listened to it?"

"No, not yet. I won't have a chance until I get back to the inn later tonight."

Not exactly true, but close enough. She wasn't about to crank it up on the shop's sound system. She wasn't sure she wanted to hear it at all, let alone have to explain it to her staff's inquiring ears.

"Oh, well, let me know what you think then."

Harper couldn't miss the disappointment in his voice.

"So how about Catalina? Pretty terrific, huh?"

"Sounds nice, Jake."

Trying to focus on the layouts for the afternoon while she talked to him, Harper tapped her fingers on her workbench and took the pencil out of its place on top of her ear to scribble a few changes to her work orders.

"Hey, Baby. You okay? You sound kind of upset or something."

Jake had asked about her? He'd asked how she was feeling? The day was full of surprises, but this comment, in particular, really threw her for a whirl.

Listening was not one of Jake's fortes. In fact, she doubted it was something he could even participate in. For as long as she'd known him, it was always about him. Listen to me. Hear me roar. I'm so worthy. Stop what you're doing because I'm here and nothing else matters.

She couldn't remember one time when he'd asked her anything—anything unrelated to money.

"Harper? I'm worried about you. Can you hear me? Are you still there?"

"Yeah, sorry, I'm here. Just a little distracted. That's all."

She arranged the orders by the priority in which she wanted them filled and stood up from her chair. She needed to get a move on.

"Thinking about Catalina already?"

His voice was smooth, husky, and lyrical, almost as if he were singing her a Siren's lullaby. But it didn't have the effect on her that it used to. The ignition switch that used to jumpstart her body whenever she heard his voice was gone.

It would be nice if Catalina were all she had to think about today.

"You know, I'm sorry to have to go so soon, but I've got some stuff I need to finish here at work. I just wanted to say thank you for the CD."

She probably should have told him that she wasn't going to Catalina, but she had too much work to do and no time to argue with him. And he always put his needs first, so this time, she was putting herself first. He'd just have to wait to see if she bothered to show up for his proposed boat ride.

Balancing her cell on her shoulder as she carried the file full of work details to the front counter and handed it to her assistant, she caught a glimpse of Bistro Sole across the street.

"I'll talk to you soon."

"Hey, Harper, are you going to pick me up at the airport Christmas Eve?"

So that was the real reason he'd called. Oh, yeah, she'd called him. He had her so riled up and confused. Shit. She just couldn't deal with all of this right now. She had work to do.

"Sure, yeah, sorry. I really need to go. Thanks again. See you at the airport."

She disconnected their call, knowing it was going to be one long ride home from LAX and already dreading every minute. At least she'd tell him in person that she wasn't keeping the date, instead of leaving him hanging like he had her so many times.

As much as she wanted to stick it to him, it just wasn't in her to treat someone like that, even if he deserved it.

As the hot afternoon sun beat down on the bistro's tiled roof, the glare went straight to her heart. She loved him. It was that simple, yet that difficult. Not Jake, even though she did believe he could be more than just a gigolo.

She'd fallen in love with Grant, the recovering emotional Grinch. Or maybe it was more accurate to say she was still in love with him. She didn't just love him. She wanted him back. She may not have been able to figure out exactly why he'd changed or how he'd gone about it, but he had. And that's what mattered. She'd seen it when he looked at her that first night in the inn. And he'd proven it to her many times since. He'd gotten a mani-pedi, for cripe's sake.

Harper went back into her office and flung herself into her desk chair. Burying her head in her hands, she prayed that what she felt was real and right. And if it was, she prayed she'd find a way to tell him.

The more she pondered it, the less sense it made. Grant, her soon-to-be ex-husband, now had a hold on her heart that refused to let go. For twelve years she'd tried to connect with him, but he'd never let her get a damn bit close.

Just when she'd found the pieces of herself that she'd abandoned for him, he was opening up to her. Unfortunately, now she was too busy with her work to do anything about it. She sighed and rubbed away the knots in her stomach.

Maybe this was how Grant felt when his work consumed him. For the first time, she understood how hard it could be to balance a personal life with a professional one—not that she'd ever sacrifice those she loved for a job, but she did understand how it could happen.

At the brink of being overloaded by her work, she could forgive him for leaving her as his last priority while they'd been together. She couldn't forget it, but she could forgive it. Appreciating how far he'd come to put her first in his life, she was ready to see if they could make it work.

She tried to rub out the headache that was creeping into her temples. She had too much work to finish to focus on all of these new feelings at once. She had fifty Frostys that needed glitter baths and eyeballs, and a thousand sugar snowflakes to pick up in Beverly Hills at the confectionary artist's shop.

Frosty, snowflakes, and love. When she was in charge of making them all happen simultaneously, it didn't feel like a Winter Wonderland. But she hoped the end result would be magical.

If she even stood a chance at having time with Grant over the holidays, she had to find a way to work smarter. Working harder wasn't an option.

She popped a couple of ibuprofen out of the industrial-size bottle that Robert kept in his desk and washed them down with what was left of a bottle of water. Maybe if she took a break and got in her run now, instead of later, she'd soothe her spirits back into productive placement so she could finish the projects she had to knock out before calling it a day.

She changed into her running clothes, laced up her shoes, and hooked the armband of her iPod around its well-worn spot on her bicep. Lining the Velcro up with her tan lines, she secured it into position and hit the pavement.

She cranked the music up as loud as she could stand it, trying to drown out her throbbing thoughts. As soon as she reached the bridge leading to the jetty, her spirit found a glimpse of the calm that the view always brought her.

When her feet landed on the crushed asphalt of the jetty, she picked up her pace. Breathing in the salty air, she sprinted toward the end of the long strip reaching out into the Pacific.

Past the first bench. Then the second. And soon the third. She was half way to the fourth and final one before she could make out the identity of the person waving at her from the end of the path. Dropping her sunglasses below her eyes, she saw Grant sitting on top of the last group of rocks before the jetty ended and the open ocean began.

She reached the end of the path, right before the rocks jutted off into the Pacific, and motioned to him to give her a minute. She took her time, stretching her tense muscles from their fully contracted state back to a semi-relaxed but exhausted one. To slow her heart rate—as if that were possible with Grant right in front of her, she did her breathing exercises.

Using her arms to wipe away the sweat running down her forehead, she tried to catch the rest of it before it landed in her eyes.

Somewhat successful, she adjusted her sports bra, which always seemed to ride up toward her neck when she ran.

She didn't really like seeing people she knew when she was working out. If having to face Grant so soon after recognizing that she still had feelings for him was the gods' plan of attack, then she was obviously not praying for their mercy nearly hard enough.

Making an attempt to smile, trying to convey more confidence than she felt, she made her way up onto the rocks and took a seat next to him.

"Hey. What are you doing out here? Hope you wore sunscreen this time."

She worried about him re-burning the spots that were raw and peeling.

"As a matter of fact, I did. What are you doing jogging at this time of day? It's a little warm, isn't it? Is everything okay at the shop?"

Grant wasn't as worried about the shop as he was about Jake, but he didn't want to bring up his name. Dealing with his express delivery was enough for one day.

"Just a little stressed with all the work, that's all. Sometimes I like to run it off in the middle of the day. Makes me more productive."

Although Grant suspected that Jake had more to do with why she was running now than anything at the shop, he let her think he bought her explanation.

"Anything I can do to help? I'm not real good with a glue gun, but if you'd point me in the right direction, I've got some anxiety to work off too."

"I bet you do."

Harper brushed up against the side of his arm while she maneuvered herself on the rock next to his so she could see his face.

"Listen, I'm really sorry you had to see me get Jake's package today."

"Have you listened to his song yet?"

"Nope. I haven't had time."

That made him feel better. Surely, if she still cared for the gigolo, she would have listened to it as soon as she got back to the shop. Maybe he still had a chance.

As they sat in momentary silence, panic overtook him. Wonder if this was his last chance? Maybe Jake's song would reach her heart before he could. Maybe he didn't have time to wait the two and a half weeks until Christmas Eve. Maybe he should tell her something…anything…to tide her over.

He took her hands between his and gently rubbed them. The tension he felt running through them was more than he could bear. He had to tell her something to try and help ease her mind.

"Harper, I owe you an explanation for why I've always shut you out of my life." He pushed his thumbs into her palms, rubbing her skin with his.

"Grant, you don't owe me…"

"Yes, I do. I always used my father as the excuse for my behavior. But I should have seen from my mother's emotional suffering the result of his approach to life."

He had to make her see how wrong he'd been and how he'd make it right to her, if she'd give him one more chance.

"I think that's why she died so young, don't you?" Harper asked, caressing his hands with her own.

"I didn't, until recently. But yeah, I think it was more than her health that failed her. It was my father's emotional abandonment. And I wasn't any help. I lived every day to be like my father."

The guilt flowing out of Grant seemed to be lifting the iron weights that had sat unnoticed on his shoulders till now.

"I thought that if I could just close off the rest of the world and concentrate on building my net worth, he'd love me."

The heat of the afternoon sun beat down on him, but the heat of the pain rising inside of him was much, much hotter.

"Didn't work so well, huh?" Harper asked.

How she would even have the desire to listen to him when he'd always shut her out was beyond all logic. He didn't deserve to win her back, but he had to keep trying anyway. She deserved better, and he wanted to be that better for her.

"No, it sure didn't work. I lost you."

Grant lifted her face up to his and gently cupped both of his hands around her cheeks.

"I lost you once, Harper, but I swear to you, I'll never let you go again. I'll always be here for you, whether as your husband or not."

She started to speak, but he stopped her. He had to finish his thoughts. There was no calling Reggie to find the best words or the right way. If he was ever going to break through the wall he'd erected between them, Grant had to do this on his own, in his own way.

"I'll never abandon you again. Whether we share a life together or not, as husband and wife, I'll always be here for you. As your friend. Your confidant. Whatever you need me to be."

Like the seagulls that soared around them and out into the Pacific, Grant felt free—finally free—from the emotional bonds of being born a Cantwell. His body relaxed, all except for his heart.

"I do need you, Grant, even though I'm not sure how."

Harper searched his eyes for answers that he thought he could give her. But he kept them to himself, wanting her to answer them for herself.

Looking around them, he understood the magic of this place that until now had been lost on him. He understood the magic of her and the power she had over him. He'd never forgive himself for projecting his limits on her soul, forcing her to live in his emotional prison. All he could do was set her free, if that's what she wanted.

Before he lost his nerve, he leaned down, his lips brushing hers. And before he could convince himself not to, he kissed her with all the pent-up passion he'd felt for her since the first day they'd met.

When she kissed him back, he lost himself in her, throwing out the little shreds of insecurity still left inside him.

He sat there with her, hand-in-hand, facing the uncertain horizon, all the while thanking the powers that be that he'd been given the chance to open up to her.

He walked her back to the shop, neither one of them saying a word. But, in their silence, if his heart rate were any indication, their bodies were carrying on quite the conversation…a conversation that had taken way too long to happen.

Once back in his room, he called his attorney and made the arrangements for their divorce decree to be sent to the inn, following the holiday weekend.

CHAPTER TWENTY-FOUR
MY HEART IS TAKEN

Harper pulled up the Hummer outside of the baggage claim area at LAX. Not even thinking it possible that the place could be any more of a zoo than normal, she bulldozed her way to the front of the line. Jake had called and said he'd gotten his bags and would be waiting, so where the hell was he?

She didn't want to pick him up at all, but she needed to put an end not just to their date but to their relationship. The short ride back to Playa would give her more than enough time. If he'd just make it to the damn truck.

Knowing she couldn't leave the vehicle unattended without security teams rightfully coming after her with a vengeance, she searched the packed sidewalk to try to pick him out of the crowd.

Finally the tailgate popped open, and when she looked through the rearview mirror, she saw him toss his bag into the trunk. He ran around the side of the vehicle and threw open the passenger door.

"Hello, luv. Ho, ho, ho. I'm back."

He threw his arms open wide, leaned back and bellowed, "Merrrrry Christmas."

Santa Clause he wasn't. And his damn Hummer was sure a lot more awkward to drive than a sleigh. On Christmas Eve, she'd prefer to be at the whim of reindeer rather than L.A. traffic. As she cut off the car behind them and made a dash for the freeway, the driver honked and flipped the bird.

"Wow, Mrs. Claus, sure you don't want me to drive?" Jake put on his seatbelt for the first time she'd ever been aware of.

"I got it covered. So how was tour?"

Once they were on Sepulveda Boulevard, headed the seven miles to Playa, Harper settled down and backed her foot away from the gas.

Jake yawned. "Tour was tour. Too many shows, not enough travel time between, crazed fans. You know how it goes. Fun stuff when you're a rock star."

A rock star? She wouldn't call swooning to sixties and seventies ballads rock star status, although the Sapphires' three-part harmony was wonderful. No mosh pit had ever swelled up in front of any stage she'd seen him on yet. That pesky little "me me me" thing that drove her nuts had reared its ugly head after no more than fifteen minutes with him.

Harper took a quick peek in his direction, thrilled to see his eyes closed. She hoped he'd stay asleep so she could practice what she planned to tell him.

Yawning as he spoke, he popped awake long enough to ask, "So what'd you think of my song?"

She'd forgotten to call him after she'd listened to it.

"It was nice. Had a good sound."

He snored like a grizzly bear settling in for his winter nap.

So much for that conversation.

Although she'd liked the song and was touched by his efforts—it wasn't everyday that a man wrote a song for her—she doubted he could live up to the commitment he promised her in his lyrics.

A half hour later, pulling up in front of the inn, she gently shook his shoulder. "C'mon, Jake, wake up. We're at the inn, and you need to go home."

He rubbed his eyes and sat up from his slouched position. "Let's just sleep here tonight, baby. Can you just park the truck and wake me up when it's time to go upstairs?"

That would buy them both a whole thirty seconds, she thought.

This wasn't going to be any easier than she'd figured it would be. Maybe she should have just told him on the phone two weeks ago. Nope. She didn't operate like he did. She dealt with challenges head-on, not by voicemail or by failing to show. Okay. So she was doing it at the last minute, but he more than deserved that.

Not wanting whoever was in the inn's kitchen watching the monitor to see her arguing with him, Harper pulled the truck into the garage.

"Jake, wake up, I need to talk to you."

He reached his hand across the console dividing them and pressed his fingers softly between her legs.

She pushed his hand away.

"We can talk later. C'mon, luv, I've missed you so much. Let's go to your room. We'll talk in the morning."

He just wasn't getting it.

Before she could open the door, he rolled on top of her, kissing her with more heat and need than she'd ever experienced from him. But she couldn't let him continue.

"I'm sorry, Jake," she said, pulling away and reaching for her purse on the floorboard. "I can't do this."

That seemed to wake him up a bit. He opened his eyes wide, a look of mild shock registering in their dark depths before he dropped back into his seat.

"Well, okay, is everything all right?" Before he bothered to wait for her answer, he pulled a small Tiffany's box out of his coat pocket.

"Here, luv, open this." He wiggled his eyebrows, doing his best Groucho Marx impersonation. "Just the first of a few surprises to come this weekend."

"Jake, about this weekend..."

Harper tried to push the box back at him, but he only did the same to her.

"C'mon, baby, please open it. It took me hours of precious time to find just the right thing."

Releasing the large white bow, she opened the package, just so he'd quit whining, and took out the leather box tucked inside. Holding her breath, she cracked open the gilded front edge, revealing a stunning diamond necklace set in platinum in the form of a complete circle. His attempt to buy her affection only reaffirmed that he wasn't what she wanted. She'd never allow herself to be bought—and in Jake's case, sold out—again.

Jake snatched the box from her, and, before she could figure out how to refuse his gift, took the necklace and began placing it around her neck.

"Hold this a second, luv."

He placed her hands on the circular pendant, then swept her hair back away from her neck, re-clipping it much higher on her head, so he could fasten the necklace in place. After he closed the security clasp, he kissed her neck.

"It's beautiful, Jake."

But all she could think about while he put it on her was how she wished it were Grant doing the same because his affection came from his heart.

She had to stop this before it went any further.

"Jake, I really need to go."

Reaching her hands behind her neck to release the clasp, she said, "I can't accept this. And about the weekend…"

Evidently thinking that she must be adjusting the chain instead of taking it off—obviously not listening to her, as usual—he moved the pendant so it was centered in the hollow of her throat.

"I can't wait either. How about I pick you up around ten tomorrow morning, and we'll head out?"

"Jake! Listen to me, dammit! You picking me up won't be necessary." She saw her words once again go right over him. But finally, they circled back around and blind-sided him.

"What do you mean that won't be necessary?"

Harper didn't miss the edge in his voice.

"Jake, as much as I appreciate your thoughtfulness, I won't be spending the holidays with you." She took off the necklace and started putting it back in the box. "Grant is here, and I promised him we'd…"

"Wait a minute. You're turning me down to spend time with your ex-husband?" Jake slammed his hand against the steering wheel. "I can't believe this. Why didn't you tell me?"

She lowered her head. "He's not my ex yet, Jake. And by the time you sent me the invitation, I'd already accepted his. I probably should have told you on the phone, but I wanted to do it in person."

He shook his head. "Thanks. This way feels much better."

Dropping his head back onto his headrest, he sighed. "So he beat me to the punch this time. Okay, I'll play along. When can I see you again?"

Feeling bad for disappointing him, especially on Christmas Eve, knowing he had no one to celebrate the season with, she blurted out the first thing that popped into her head.

"Well, we're spending the holidays here at the inn. You're more than welcome to stop by tomorrow evening, if you'd like. Several people are coming over for cocktails and hor d'oeuvres around seven."

At least she hoped that was still Grant's plan. But she was sure Jake wouldn't take her up on the offer when he knew Grant would be there. And she felt good that she'd been kind and offered.

"I'll have to see. I may just go to Catalina anyway." He brushed his hands through his hair. "I could use the time away. I've got a lot of thinking to do and a couple of songs burning at me."

"Okay. Whatever you want." Harper opened the door and stepped out of the truck. "Merry Christmas, Jake. And thanks for thinking of me with the necklace. It really is beautiful."

She handed him back the box. "I just can't accept it. I'm sorry."

He leaned out the window and pulled her face toward him, kissing her with an almost desperate desire. "I love you, Harper Cantwell. Merry Christmas."

The look on his face told her he was just as surprised by his words as she was.

"I'm sorry, Jake. I can't say the same."

She turned away from the truck before she lost what little courage she had to walk away without telling him more.

She'd waited for him to say that for so long. But now that he had, it didn't mean what she'd thought it would, coming from him. He'd offered her too little, way too late.

• • •

Harper turned around in front of the mirror in her room. Even though it was almost seventy degrees tonight in Southern California, she'd chosen to dress for the evening as if she were back in Briar Creek. Christmas just didn't seem like Christmas in beachwear.

And nothing cheered her mood like pink. Perhaps it was its soft close-to-the-heart hue, but it brought out everything kind and warm in her world. And after ending it with Jake, she needed nothing but good thoughts.

Her lamb's skin pink leather jacket hugged her bare arms and rested against the perfectly matched silk tank she'd bought to go with it. Both looked stunning against her brushed wool crepe slacks in a tone only slightly variant to the other pieces. With pink suede, open-back pumps to match, she couldn't make herself to appear any happier. Hopefully being decked out in her favorite color would help compensate for the lousy day she'd had so far and calm her nerves for her evening with Grant.

Taking a couple of deep breaths to steady her restless soul, she squared her shoulders to her reflection and made up her mind to put Jake behind her for tonight and enjoy the time she had with Grant. He'd be returning to Briar Creek after the holidays, and as surprised as she was, she'd be sad to see him go.

Maybe she'd ask him to stay a bit longer. But after walking out on their marriage, how could she expect him to be open to her wanting more from their relationship? How could she ask him for a second chance?

She dropped her room key into her jacket pocket and closed the door behind her. Walking down the hall toward the kitchen and great room, she smelled something burning in the kitchen. Odd. Stace had the night off and, even if she didn't, nothing would be burning under her watch.

When she got to the kitchen, Grant greeted her, looking rather frazzled behind a dirty apron. He shrugged his shoulders and grinned, waving his hand around to clear the black smoke rolling out of the oven.

"I thought I had it all under control. I followed the damn directions just like Reggie told me." A look of complete horror found its way across his face, and his cheeks took on a much more intense shade of pink than her wardrobe.

"What do you mean like Reggie told you?"

Harper looked at the cookie tray Grant was fanning smoke off of and saw what remained of the yellow, camel-shaped spritz cookies Reggie fixed every Christmas Eve. The pan that was already on the cooling rack was supposed to be for the green wreathes, but they looked like they'd been through a forest fire.

"Well, I've asked Reggie…and Jeffrey…on a couple of occasions now to help me learn a few things."

Harper enjoyed his uneasiness way too much to stop questioning him, especially since it appeared that he might just spill the beans.

"What kind of things?"

"Oh, it's really no big deal."

Grant dropped the cookie tray onto the stove burners and threw his oven mitts into the sink.

"Yes, it is. And I'm not letting it go this time. I've told you ever since you've been here that I thought something was up with you. What's going on?"

Grant took off Stace's apron, which was way too small for him, and tossed it into the sink with the oven mitts. Once he had the silly thing off, Harper was pleased to see he'd also kept with their tradition and worn something like she'd have seen him in if they were home at the estate—corduroy slacks and a beautiful cashmere sweater. She was afraid he'd keep with his new sense of style and have some funky, elf-motif silk-screened tee with green and red flip-flops.

As much as she liked some of his new look, she missed the Grant she knew. Peeking at his feet underneath the kitchen worktable, she was thrilled to see a pair of his Cole Haan loafers had also made it back on his feet.

"You haven't answered my question." Harper sat down on a stool next to him, not about to get up until she got an answer.

He picked at his cookie catastrophe. "I've forgotten what it was."

"Nice try, Betty Crocker. So what all has Reggie been teaching you?"

Harper thought about eating one of his cookies to make him feel better, but she couldn't bring herself to do it. The camels looked hard enough to be mistaken for dog biscuits.

"You mean what he's tried to teach me?" Grant picked up one of the camels and threw it into the trash can. "Look at these pieces of shit."

"Let's not concentrate on your failures. How about some of your successes? For example, I have a feeling my favorite elf may have had something to do with your new wardrobe as well as your apparent love of chick flicks. Would that be a fair assumption?"

"Could be. But I've been sworn to secrecy…elf's code of honor."

Grant reached for a bottle of champagne chilling in an ice bucket and popped the cork, pouring them each a flute full.

"Wouldn't want to get you in trouble with the elves." Harper took a sip of the bubbling spirits and decided to let him off the hook for a while.

She'd learned enough to satisfy her curiosity. There was no way he would have ever thought of all this on his own. Reggie and Jeffrey were involved…that she was sure of.

"Shall we go in and sit by the fire?" Grant picked up the champagne bucket and gathered both of their glasses, leaving the kitchen fiasco behind for the comfort of the great room.

"Sure."

Harper found the air freshener that Stacia kept for culinary emergencies on the shelf under the work-table, sprayed it, and then followed him.

"You look beautiful tonight, by the way. Pink really is your color."

Grant's eyes followed the line of her body from head to toe with a need Harper had seen burning more tonight than at any time since he'd been here.

"Thank you for noticing."

"I've always noticed," he said, hanging his head, "I just never bothered to tell you."

He reminded her of a small boy, afraid to speak his opinion too loudly, in case someone would shout it down.

"I'm glad you decided to let me know."

His compliments warmed her more than the champagne and fire.

He set their glasses on the sofa table and took her hand, leading her to sit next to him on the couch in front of the roaring electric fire.

"Not like the heat producer at home, huh?"

"No, but it'll do. It's all in the atmosphere, you know," Harper said.

"Yeah, I guess it is. Sometimes. But only if you're sharing it with someone special." Grant put his arm around her and pulled her toward him, planting a kiss on her forehead.

She looked up into his eyes and was about to get lost in them until she heard a large commotion and lots of almost recognizable voices coming from the elevator opening in the hall. Before she could process the sounds, she turned toward the door to the room, finding all of her new friends fighting for the best position. Under the arched doorway stood Stace and her sister, Stokey and Glen, and poking his way slowly through the middle was Robert.

"Grant, you said they would all be here tomorrow…" Before she could get the rest of her thoughts out, they all came barreling into the room.

"Surprise!" Stokey shouted.

"Merry Christmas, my friend," Stace whispered as she hugged Harper close to her. "Your husband is a complete dream."

Glen came in carrying a tray full of cookies. Evidently, he'd been worried about Grant's Betty Crocker initiative.

Seeing Robert was a huge blessing. Harper hadn't even had time to talk to him since the parties had started, and she had so much to tell him. She hugged him to her. "Here, sit down, so you don't wear yourself out. I'm so happy to see you."

"No, no, girlfriend. You can't believe how glad I am to see all of you. Merry Christmas, my sweet angel."

He kissed both of her cheeks and then planted one firmly on her lips.

He must have felt her flinch.

"Don't worry. I'm not catching."

She wasn't disappointed at all that she wouldn't be alone with Grant for Christmas Eve. The fact that he'd thought to include her new friends was wonderful. She couldn't get over how he now thought and planned with his heart instead of his financial portfolios.

Grant disappeared into the kitchen and came out with two more bottles of champagne, followed by Stace who had a tray full of crystal flutes. After making the rounds and pouring each of them a glass, he lifted his high into the air.

Stacia took a spoon from the basket on the buffet and clinked the side of her glass to get everyone's attention.

"Thank you, Stacia," Grant said, looking around the room, making eye contact with everyone before settling his attention on Harper.

"Merry Christmas, Harper. I'm afraid I don't have anything else to give you tonight except all of our friendship and love. We just want you to know how much we all love you."

Tears filled her eyes, and she couldn't speak.

"Tonight, we're celebrating the season of giving by celebrating all that you've given to each of us with your never-ending kindness."

She couldn't take her eyes off his as he continued.

He shifted from one foot to the other before looking briefly down at his feet, then back at Harper with an earnestness she'd never seen in him before.

"Robert, I'll let you take over from here."

"Very well then, my new friend. Harper, I've come here tonight, not just as your friend, but as your business associate."

She cleared her head, not sure of the new direction of the conversation. Seeing Grant falter, she grew uneasy.

"You have stepped in for me at The Bloom Factory and taken the shop to new levels of success with your tireless dedication, work, management and design skills." He took a sip of champagne to wet his hoarse voice before continuing, "I don't even think my clients want me to come back."

Everyone laughed, even Grant, making Harper feel better. But the fear in his eyes still discomforted her. He didn't like what was coming next. She'd seen that look before when he wasn't pleased but was forced to make the best of a situation.

"I'm here tonight to offer you a full partnership in The Bloom Factory. I'd love to have you around, and so would the rest of Hollywood. You've found a new home with us."

Despite her friends all cheering for her and congratulating her, the room was a blur. It was as if she were appearing in slow motion on a movie screen. The camera-man catching the action focused his lens on her and Grant. They stood motionless, searching each other's eyes for what their future would hold.

Harper recovered enough to remember her manners.

"Thank you, Robert. Thank you all for being my home away from home and my creative life force. With each of you and because of you, I've been able to put my life back together."

She took a slow drink of her champagne to gather her thoughts.

"I appreciate your offer, Robert, and assure you I will give it the consideration it deserves, but not tonight. Tonight is about friendship. And for this special moment, I have Grant to thank, the man who has brought so much to my life, and truly reached my heart."

She raised her glass to him and gave him back her heart, making a silent vow to tell him he had it as soon as she could find the right time.

CHAPTER TWENTY-FIVE
THE GREATEST GIFT OF ALL

Harper woke up on Christmas morning to a soft knocking at her door. She'd slept clear through the night for the first time in weeks. She remembered that Grant had once again carried her to her room and tucked her into bed. Something about him being there when she conked out made her sleep well.

She stumbled her way to the door and opened it. She couldn't believe what she was seeing. Surely, she was still dreaming. There was Jeffrey holding a breakfast tray.

"Well are you going to let me in or make me stand here all morning, Mrs. C?"

"Jeffrey!"

Harper wrapped her arms around him, nearly causing him to drop the tray.

"Oh, I'm so glad to see you. But how? Who brought you?"

"Well, Southwest Airlines brought me, compliments of Mr. C." He blew past her with the tray, going straight to the kitchenette to finish preparing what he'd brought. "Get in that bed of yours so I can serve you like your husband asked me to."

"Grant did all this?"

Harper scrambled into bed like a child eager to hear what other surprises awaited her.

Jeffrey smoothed her blankets and fixed the tray so it set up over her legs. With a dramatic flair worthy of Tinsel Town, he pulled off the silver lid covering her plate, revealing her favorite omelet and toast.

"Eat, wee one. I don't know what they feed you out here, but you look disastrously thin. Where are all those womanly curves you used to wear so well? Hell, I'll have to have all your clothes taken in."

"I've been under a lot of stress at work trying to get a bunch of Hollywood holiday events ready."

She didn't waste any time devouring her breakfast.

It was so wonderful to have Jeffrey here. And his cooking for her again was over-the-top surreal. To think Grant would go to all of this trouble for her. He knew exactly what she needed to enjoy the holidays.

"At least you still have your appetite." Jeffrey sat down on the dressing chair across from her bed and crossed his legs, taking in the surroundings of her room. "No wonder you haven't sent for more of your clothes. I don't know where the hell you'd put them. You so need a larger room."

Harper ignored Jeffrey's displeasure with the size of her room. She'd chosen a regular room instead of a suite on purpose. She preferred its quaint charm to the estate's barren over-sized master suite.

"I can't believe Grant did this for me," she said to Jeffrey, between bites of omelet.

"In case you haven't figured it out, Mrs. C., Mr. C is not the same man you walked out on." Jeffrey uncrossed his legs and moved to the edge of the chair. "Take for example, the fact that he now dresses himself each morning."

"You don't lay stuff out for him?"

Harper was shocked. She'd thought for sure that was one thing about him that would never change. He'd never given a damn about his clothes, as long as they were well-fitted and top of the line materials and brands. Not to mention, he'd always been clueless as to how to combine them into fashionable ensembles.

"Well, I, along with Reggie, may have given him a few tips, but he's been doing it pretty much on his own ever since."

Jeffrey moved over and sat on the end of Harper's bed.

"We've all missed you, my princess. It's just not the same without you. And I'm not sure that the old chap's told you yet, but he loves you, Harper, and he's fighting so hard to try to show you."

Jeffrey got up and kissed her cheek, then straightened her sheets and carried her tray to the kitchenette.

"I know he's trying. More than I ever thought possible from him."

Harper reached out and touched the blue suede pouch holding her wedding rings, just to make sure they were still securely stowed in the plush cushioned folds.

Grant. Sweet Grant. He'd not only admitted to her how emotionally inept he'd been, but he'd also let down his guard in front of Jeffrey and Reggie. Harper never thought he'd go that far to find a way to reach her.

But even more than winning her back, she was thankful that Grant was getting to know the man buried deep inside himself. She'd been buried too, unable to recognize who she was and what she wanted out of life.

"Well, Mrs. C., I hate to run, but I've got stuff to do for Reggie in the kitchen."

Judging by the size of his eyes, and the hand clamped over his mouth, he must have been sorry that he said that.

But Harper wasn't. She jumped out of bed and hit the shower running.

"I don't believe this. He didn't. Grant flew Reggie here too?! Jeffrey, find me something to wear, would you, please?" She poked her head out of the bathroom door while she waited for the shower to get warm.

"Merry Christmas, Jeffrey."

"Merry Christmas to you, Mrs. C," he hollered back from somewhere inside her closet.

An hour later, Harper ambushed Reggie in the inn's kitchen.

She'd had Jeffrey go ahead of her and keep him occupied while she snuck up on him. Once directly behind Reggie, as he bent down to examine something smelling sinfully delicious in the oven, Harper clapped her hands twice with so much gusto her palms burned. She'd always wanted to do that to him. He jumped so far off the ground that he lost his grip on the oven door, causing it to slam shut with a wicked bang.

"Girlfriend, that was sooo uncalled for." Reggie wiggled his finger at her. "C'mere, you. Give your favorite decorator a holiday squeeze. Lordy, it's good to see you, girl."

Harper held onto him, almost afraid to let go, as if he'd vanish with a bewitching wiggle of his nose. Until she'd seen him and Jeffrey too, she hadn't realized how much she'd missed them. They had been the only sources of joy and much-needed sass that she'd been able to consistently draw from when she lived in Briar Creek.

Just as she let Reggie go back to his oven, she smelled the familiar scent of Grant's cologne behind her. She'd never been able to resist its soft, spicy allure. Turning around, she melted into his arms, surprised that when her skin touched his, desire buzzed through her body.

"Merry Christmas, Grant." She kissed him on the lips, unable to hold back her passion—passion she probably shouldn't have let him see. But feeling his strong response to her, her doubts vanished and pleasure ripped through her. "This is the best gift you've ever given me. I don't know how to thank you."

"From where I'm standing," Reggie piped in, "I'm thinking another one of those hot smooches would work just fine."

Good idea. Harper leaned up to Grant and closed her mouth around his, basking in his warmth. She knew she should break free of him before she lost control, but she didn't want to.

"Now that's what I call showing your appreciation, Mr. C," Jeffrey said, followed by a low whistle. "You'd better keep this idea in your repertoire for future reference."

"Yeah, she's a keeper. I mean the plan's a keeper. Oh, hell, you know what I mean." Grant's face was now the same red as Reggie's crushed velvet shirt.

Harper tried to save him from Reggie and Jeffrey, who wouldn't quit harassing him once they saw how much fun it was.

"So what else do you three have in store today?" she asked.

Jeffrey and Reggie deferred to Grant with regal bows that more than mildly amused her.

Grant opened the oven—as if he knew what the hell he was looking at. But it was cute all the same.

"Just a little family dinner…the four of us," Grant said, a crimson hue returning to his cheeks.

Harper looked at Jeffrey, who then looked at Reggie. All of them smiled together at Grant's choice of words.

"What?" Grant lifted his hands into the air in mock surrender. "Did I say something wrong?"

"No way, Mr. C. In fact, I could just hug you myself right now," Jeffrey said and threw a dishtowel over his shoulder.

He shook his head and checked Reggie's crumpled up, food stained piece of paper on the worktable to see what he was to do next.

"Save yourself the trouble. I'll hug you," Grant said, and he did.

There was no mistaking how much the three had bonded while Harper was gone. Once, they'd shared nothing more than employer-employee relationships, politely strained at best. Now, she saw the genuine friendship cemented between them.

Grant moved across the kitchen to the cabinets lining the wall on the opposite side of the room. "Harper, why don't we leave these two geniuses to their work and have a cup of coffee and a piece of Reggie's famous Swedish tea ring out on the deck?"

He reached into one of the cabinets and pulled out two dessert plates.

"You thought of everything, Grant. Christmas wouldn't be Christmas without that scrumptious treat. I knew I recognized that glorious smell."

Harper followed him out the kitchen door, stopping at the buffet to fix them both a cup of coffee.

Reggie hollered after them, "Don't give him credit for that idea. He's not that well-schooled yet."

"Well, he's sure on his way to making a run for valedictorian."

Harper winked at Grant on their way to the patio, determined to learn more about his schooling. He'd evidently had one damn-fine tutor since she'd left.

Settling into the deck furniture, Harper couldn't help but think about the unfamiliar setting of Christmas morning, Southern California style. She'd never imagined she'd be sitting in a summer-like heat surrounded by palm trees and the Pacific on Christmas Day, with sailboats cruising by instead of sleds.

She wished herself back to the estate, where she'd be enjoying the same breakfast set against the backdrop of a blustery Tennessee winter morning. And if she were lucky, she'd be watching a light snow-fall, covering the rolling hills and blanketing their woods with a thin, white coat.

"Not exactly our normal holiday view, huh?" Grant must have read her mind.

"No, it's not." Harper took a warm sip of coffee, trying to visualize snow. Christmas just wasn't Christmas to her without snow or the promise of it being at least a climactic possibility.

"As much as I love it here, the holiday just doesn't resonate with me as much as it does at home."

Grant hesitated a moment, fidgeting with his cup before he spoke. "I like that you still think of the estate as home."

"In some way, I probably always will. I know it's been your family home for generations, but I came to think of it as mine too."

She just wished that, when she'd lived there, he'd made her feel as if she were a vital part of it.

"You're certainly welcome anytime. It is your home too, Harper, and it always will be." His voice continued to get lower, so soft that Harper could hardly hear him say, "You can come back whenever you want to."

"That means a lot to me," she said and took his hand. "You mean a lot to me, Grant. Just because I left you, like I tried to say in my letter, doesn't mean I don't still care about you. You do know that, don't you?"

Grant nodded. Harper could see the frustration on his face as he struggled to come up with something to say in return.

She gave him the time to find his words. She needed to know where he stood, where she stood, and how he felt about where they were headed. And she didn't want to read about it in the documents his attorney forwarded her. She wanted to hear it from him.

"Harper, I want to tell you how much…"

"Merry Christmas, luv."

Jake burst through the patio doors and swept Harper off of her seat and into his arms, almost knocking the wind out of her.

"Jake," she gasped, while she struggled for air.

Before she found her breath, Grant was out of his chair, reaching for her arms to steady her.

"Mr. Benton, I don't believe we've had the privilege of a formal introduction."

Grant reached out his hand toward Jake, which thankfully meant that Jake had to let go of her to respond.

"I'm Grant Cantwell, Harper's husband, and this is a family day. I don't recall inviting you."

Harper stepped away from Jake and closer to Grant, shocked by Grant's forceful presence. She had to do something or the clash of the two men's titan-sized egos would send the day hurtling into a steep spiral, if not one of them over the railing and into the marsh.

For once, Jake was momentarily speechless. But Harper wouldn't be lucky enough for that to last long. She steadied Grant, trying to back him off, by placing her hand on his forearm.

"Jake, Grant's right. Why are you here?"

"You invited me, luv," Jake said, pushing out his chest like one of those puffin birds Harper had seen at the Nashville zoo.

"Harper?" Grant asked with a tempered edge to his tone.

"Jake, I told you that we were hosting a small gathering tonight, not this morning. You know exactly what I said." He'd opened the wrong emotional floodgate with her, and he was going to be sorry. "Then again, with your listening skills, you probably don't know what I said."

Judging by the tension locked firmly across his set jaw, Grant was about to explode.

"Let me handle this," Harper said.

"If you say so, but I'm not going anywhere or leaving you alone with him," Grant said.

"Fair enough."

She motioned for both of them to sit down, but neither one of them did.

"Please, sit, both of you…now."

That got Grant's attention. But not Jake's, who kept standing, although the air had since left his over-inflated chest.

"Jake, for God's sake, sit the hell down. This won't take long, even by your standards." Harper waited, although very impatiently, never taking her eyes from Jake's until she'd stared him down into the seat cushions. "Thank you."

He started right in on her, "Harper, let me…"

"No, Jake, this isn't about you this time. You're going to hear what I have to say. And don't you utter a sound until I'm finished."

Grant shifted in his chair, anxiously rubbing his hands back and forth on his pant legs. Harper felt sorry for him, knowing how much he wanted to jump to her defense. But he was trying to let her do it her way, and for his gracious acquiescence to her request to stand alone, she was deeply touched.

She wasn't alone though. He was right there with her, his willingness to stay giving her the strength to continue.

She turned on Jake and let loose. "You always know the perfect words to appease me, Jake. But your actions never fit your empty syllables. I can't, and I won't be your keeper or anyone else's. Not any more. I need to put myself first. And I'm sick of standing by and watching you rob me blind."

"But the money…"

He just couldn't stop squeezing his needs into every conversation.

Grant put his hand in front of Jake's face. "Let her finish."

"It's not just the money, Jake. Although I will be in touch with you about how that is to be returned." She paced the deck floor, trying to end his hopes as easily as he'd crushed hers. "You've stolen my dignity as a woman. Not every woman is going to be there for you, only when you need her, Jake. At least I'm not. I want a partnership, not a limited liability love-and-leave-me."

Grant took a drink of coffee, his hands shaking the cup all the way to his mouth and back to the table.

"So this is it? We're done?" Jake got up from his chair and ran his fingers through his hair. "Just like that. Curtain down. Show over. No encore."

"Jake, that's my point. Love isn't a road show. It's an everyday act of faith and commitment. Some day, I hope you believe in someone enough to share that."

Harper looked at Grant and smiled.

He met her grin and matched it with his own.

Jake scuffed his shoes against the deck railings and put both hands into his pockets.

Harper had hit her mark and got him good. She'd kept her pride intact, while he squirmed. She may have been shaking on the inside, but on the surface, she was rock solid.

Knowing one final way to make her point, she said, "On your way out, stop by the kitchen and grab the chart on the refrigerator. Save it until you figure out what it means."

Jake nodded and wrapped his fingers through hers. "I'm sorry, Harper. I really do care about you."

"I know." She kissed him on the cheek. "But caring isn't the same as love."

Jake squeezed her hand and turned to Grant.

"Don't be a dumb ass, man, and lose her again. She's a keeper."

"I know she is, and I don't intend to lose her again. In my life, she's first," Grant said.

Jake walked out the same door he'd barged in, leaving them staring after him.

Grant walked up to Harper and quietly slipped his hand into his jacket pocket. He pulled out a bundle of mistletoe and dangled it above her head. He caught her in his arms and pressed his mouth over hers. The heat she offered was almost more than he could take without carrying her straight to his bed. He held her close against his hardening body, reveling in her explosive warmth.

Before he was unable to wait any longer, he gently moved her away from him enough so that he could look into her eyes. Trying to get his breath and wits about him, he put a finger to her lips, wanting nothing more than for her to take it into her mouth.

She nibbled at his finger and pressed herself against his groin while he summoned the strength to speak. "I love you, Harper. I always have and always will. And I can't live without you in my life."

Harper bit down harder on the edge of his finger, causing him to gasp for the restraint he needed to keep from taking her there on the deck.

"I don't have anything else to give you other than my love, if you'll accept it."

She wrapped her tongue around the length of his finger and worked her hand across his fully swelled length.

"God, I hope that's a yes."

She nodded.

He couldn't stand it anymore and scooped her up into his arms. His body throbbed, aching desperately with the intensity of his need for her.

Holding onto his neck and shoulder with one hand, she slid the other one down his chest to the top edge of his pants. By the time they'd made it to the elevator, she'd worked his belt free. Her hand firmly gripped him through the opening of his briefs.

He wasn't even certain he could make it to his bed without having her first. He'd never felt such an intense desire. He wanted nothing more than to bury his inhibitions deep inside her, releasing them forever.

When the elevator door opened to his floor, she had her tongue running along the outside edge of his ear, sending him into dizzying whirlwinds of fading control.

She whispered into his ear, "Reggie is going to be in a major uproar if we're late for lunch."

Grant gave her a taste of her own sensual tease by sliding his tongue down her neck.

"Well, then, I'll just have to pay him extra to reheat it."

Harper laughed and threw back her head, her hair falling over his arm. "Now that's a great way to use your money."

Grant set her down so he could open the door to his room, silently praising Chick Tricks Inc. for teaching him how to be an emotionally wealthy man. No monetary amount could match the value of his heart with Harper beside him.

CHAPTER TWENTY-SIX
FREEDOM

Even with the craziness of crunch week at the shop, Harper couldn't get Grant out of her mind. Making love to him, after thinking he had nothing left to give her, or she him, was more than she knew how to deal with.

If there was any doubt in her mind that she still loved him, spending the rest of the weekend in his bed freed her from wonder. The creative passions she'd rediscovered over the last few weeks were second only to the passion she felt for him.

But if she were to go back to him and the life of being Mrs. Grant Cantwell, she feared she'd lose the personal power she'd gained. There had to be a balance. But how was she supposed to take the time to find it when she was knee deep in garland, strands of pink pearls and gigantic, iridescent pink Christmas bulbs?

Since Grant had so selflessly taken stock of his life and reorganized it, making her its center, he deserved to know her thoughts and fears. Like the new man he'd become, considerate of her needs above his own, he hadn't pushed her for answers.

She wanted to remain his wife, but only if there was room for the new person she'd become.

Time was running out. She tried to close her mind to her personal distress and focus on her work.

After testing each strand of miniature pink lights, she strung them on the pieces of garland, then set them aside so she could lay out the pearls that she'd use as fillers. By the end of the afternoon, she'd have the balls attached. Each piece could then be loaded into the vans and delivered to the event site early the next morning.

The final countdown had begun. She had two days of preparation left, and she'd be ready for the largest gala she'd ever planned. If she could manage to pull off this last big one, she'd be able to give

Robert back his shop, making it quite possibly even more of a success than it already was.

Several of her soirees had made it into the calendar section of The LA Times. And she'd made it into the rolodexes of most of the personal assistants in Tinsel Town. She'd ensured that The Bloom Factory remained one of the party planners of choice in Hollywood.

Ironically, as she twisted the floral wire through the hangers on the bulbs and fastened them to the garland, she wasn't sure she wanted to take on the job full time. Funny how once she'd gotten what she wanted, and, in her case, exceeding her wildest expectations, she wasn't so sure she wanted it.

Her goals and priorities had unexpectedly changed. She was finally ready to admit as much. She wanted Grant, just not at the risk of losing her hard-earned sense of self.

Why everything in her life had to be such an all-or-nothing was wearing on her big time. In the meantime, if this last big Christmas ball would fit where it was supposed to, she'd be much happier.

She tried to shove it into the space she'd left for it in the center of the swag. Instead she pierced her finger. Shit. Trying to ease the throbbing pain, she stuck her finger in her mouth.

She yanked her glue gun off its stand on the table and gave the trigger a healthy shot. That oughta hold it in place. Screw the floral wire.

With the final piece done, she stole a peek at her watch. She swore aloud at the time that had passed since she last looked. She was due home and presentable for dinner with Grant in forty minutes. Time flies when you're in a lovesick hullabaloo.

She gave her staff the instructions they needed to complete the day's work, then practically ran back to the inn, forgoing her tote bag, which would only slow her down.

When she got back to her room, a note was taped to her door. Opening it, she couldn't hide the excitement nor the trepidation surging through her.

>Come to my room as soon as you read this.
>Do not pass go and do not collect any money.
>I'm not supposed to be giving you that as freely anymore.

Only love, Harper, which I have plenty of for both of us.
Grant

Harper went up to his room and knocked on the door. She could hear soft music playing and the shower running. And something smelled delicious. She was famished and couldn't wait to see what Grant had up his sleeve.

He'd been busy and unusually secretive about his plans. Unable to bring her anything to eat, he'd arranged for Glen to see to it that both breakfast and lunch were delivered to her desk. Without Grant there to make sure she'd eaten, though, she'd skipped both meals. She'd had too much to get done in order to make it back to the inn as she'd promised him.

While she waited for him to answer his door, she glanced down at her watch for what seemed to be the fiftieth time today, swearing under her breath. She was fifteen minutes late. She hated being late, and seldom was, but she couldn't leave the shop until that last blasted piece of garland had been completely finished.

She raised her hand to knock again. Just as her knuckles were about to meet the door, Grant opened it, wearing nothing but a bathrobe.

"Hi. You must have gotten my note."

His warm smile melted the day's anxieties to a puddle of nothingness. Harper could get used to coming home to this.

"That I did."

She attempted to straighten her hair and brush off the glue that had missed its intended mark and landed on her jeans.

"I'm rather a mess, so I hope this isn't anything fancy. I didn't even have time to change."

"Tell you what. Why don't you come in, have some wine, and relax."

He stepped back so she could come in.

A bottle of her favorite Plantation Red sat on the wet bar, along with two glasses.

"And don't worry about your work clothes. You won't be dressed for long."

Grant came up behind her and rubbed her shoulders with his broad hands while he leaned in to kiss her ears.

A new kind of tension filled her—one there was only one way to release. She stood still as he moved his hands from her shoulders, letting them drift down to cover her breasts.

He reached his hands under her shirt and gently, with a tentatively contained intensity, squeezed her breasts, working his hands to their tips, causing them to tighten with anticipation. Lifting her shirt over her head, he bent down, working his mouth over each mound until they were both ripened into sensual bliss.

"Grant, I want you so bad," Harper groaned in his ear as she flicked her tongue over the places she knew drove him wild.

"Patience, my dear."

He unzipped her jeans and slowly let his fingers fall until he cupped her warmth in his palm. With a single stroke of his finger, he almost sent her plunging over her threshold. She begged for her control to return. She wanted him to continue to tease her before she gave into him.

She untied the belt on his robe and let it fall around his hips. Running her hands along his chest, she slowly worked her way lower. He sucked in his stomach, his muscles tightening under her hands. She moved away his robe, exposing him, full and ready to please her. She gently teased his hard length with her palms, wanting him to suffer the need with her.

As she opened her legs to better accommodate his commanding hands, he continued to touch her. Just a little while longer, and she'd be where she longed to be. She eased him away and bent down on her knees, wanting to give him a sense of where she wanted to take them.

Taking him in her mouth and working him until she knew from his trembling legs that he could no longer stand, she got up and stepped away from him, inviting him to make the next move.

He took her hand and led her to the shower.

The bathroom was steeped in steam. But nothing filled her with more heat than when he undressed her—piece by piece, letting his fingers and lips cover every inch of her.

She melted into him, clinging to him, too overcome with desire to stand on her own.

He maneuvered her behind the glass block walls of the shower. With the water cascading over them, he knelt onto the floor and pleasured her to the point that she could no longer hold herself together.

"Please make love to me, Grant, please."

She pulled his face deeper into her and glided across the waves of his exploration. He rose up off of the shower floor and sat down on the corner seat with his fullness beckoning her.

Following his lead, she slowly lowered herself over him, taking him deep inside her. Once she'd covered him completely, she started a gentle rock that soon became a desperate ride.

"I love you, Grant Cantwell."

Those were the only words that mattered as she plummeted toward her pinnacle of satiated desire and took him with her.

Two hours later, her appetite filled by him as well as by the five star meal he'd had catered for them in his room, Harper pulled on the tassels of the belt of her bathrobe as she relaxed against the headboard of Grant's bed.

After dinner, something had changed in him. Gone was the wildly sexual man who'd seduced her when she'd come home from work, and in his place was a deeply introspective man. She wasn't sure what was bothering him, but something was.

She had him sit between her legs and rubbed his back, trying to relieve the tension she'd thought would have disappeared following their activities. Instead, he was nothing but tiny knots, so she went to work trying to dissolve them.

"What's wrong, Grant?"

She turned him to face her and was shocked to see him wiping away a tear. Only one, but it could have been a thousand and still caused her the same panic.

He rose from the bed and went to his desk. Picking up a large legal-size envelope, he returned, sitting back down on the edge of the bed, tapping the package against his leg.

"What's that?"

Seeing the return address, she knew there wasn't anything else it could be.

Harper's heart fell into a death spin. Her head pounded to the pulse that her heart seemed to have forgotten to initiate.

"I had my attorney send these." Grant opened the clasp on the envelope and pulled out the documents in one neatly clipped stack. "Harper, I don't want this divorce. I love you more than anything in this world. But I'll be the first to admit that I'm not good at loving you. I don't want to hurt you again."

She wiped away her tears with the corner of a sheet. He couldn't do this to her. Not now. Not after how far they'd each come. Not yet. Why couldn't they just wait, take it for a few more days and see where time took them?

"This is our divorce decree. You'll see that it has everything our attorneys have agreed to for each of us."

He set the pile of paper into her lap, and then took her face between his hands.

"All you have to do is sign it, and you're free."

Grant watched her fight her feelings. He couldn't bear to watch her go through what he'd struggled so desperately to find for himself. He got up from the bed and turned his back to her, looking out the window toward the jetty in the distance.

He loved her enough to let her go.

He didn't want her backed into a corner, saying to him what she probably knew he wanted to hear and not what came from her heart.

Before she could speak, he turned back to her and said, "I'll be leaving for Briar Creek in the morning. I know how busy you'll be the next couple of days getting ready for your last event, and I have a ton of work waiting for me to start the new year."

Harper reached for a tissue and wiped her nose and eyes.

Dammit. This was hell. But he couldn't give up now. He had to see this through to the end. He'd come too far to quit.

"Take your time with these. And let me know when you're done. I'm in no hurry."

He went over to her, pulling her into his arms, letting her cry on his shoulder as he did on hers.

She broke away from him enough to steady herself, and then looked deep into his eyes.

"I love you, Grant, and I don't want to hurt you, but I need to think this through."

"That's fine. Take all the time you want. You know where to find me." He kissed her forehead. "I think if you don't mind, I'm going to take another shower and get packed. You're welcome to sleep here tonight if you'd like."

She pulled herself off of his bed, almost in a daze, and gathered her clothes. "No, I think I just need to go to my room. I've got some things I need to finish up for work tomorrow anyway."

"I understand."

Holding her one last time, Grant wasn't sure how he was ever going to live without her. He hoped beyond all possibility that he'd finally proven his love for her and that it would be enough to make her come home. "I love you, Harper. And I always, always, regardless of whether you sign those papers or not, will be here for you."

"I know that. And I love you to." She quietly opened and then shut his door behind her.

He sank onto his bed and cried like he was never allowed to do as a child. He'd balanced his heart with his wallet and now faced the biggest risk of his life. Letting her go was the first debt he'd ever been forced to absorb with no guarantee of a good return.

CHAPTER TWENTY-SEVEN
GOING HOME

Harper packed the last of the decorations onto the shelves in the rear of The Bloom Factory van. She'd done it. Every last party was over. Every last one of them had been a major success. She'd taken Robert's shop to a whole new level.

As she hit the gas and drove onto the freeway, she did what she'd done every day since Grant had left almost a week before, she cried like an idiot. No matter what she did, she cried. When she completed the next task on her master shop plan, she cried. When she went to dinner with Stace, she cried. When she sat at the K.O.W. with Stokey and Glen, she cried. When she made arrangements with Robert regarding his first week back at the shop, she cried.

Everything in her life ended with her in an emotional uproar. Grant was the one who couldn't get a grip on his emotions. But he'd never been this far gone, that she knew of. He couldn't feel anything while, she hung out her shipwrecked heart for everyone to witness. What a pair they made.

Harper only had one option to stop this insanity. She knew what it was, but she hoped everyone would understand her decision. Most of all, she hoped that Grant had planned for things to end up this way. Until the last couple of weeks, she sure as hell hadn't.

Pulling into the shop, she was surprised to see Robert's car in the parking lot. She hadn't planned on seeing him tonight. But it would be best to get everything worked out with him now. She could use a good night's sleep and wouldn't be close to getting one until her plan was in motion.

The staff pulled into the lot behind her, and she asked them to unload the trucks. She went straight in the back door to find Robert.

An hour later, and a few thousand tears lighter, she handed him her keys and walked back to the inn for her final night as a guest. She had packing to do and a husband to return home to.

• • •

Harper pressed her code into the front security panel, hoping Grant hadn't changed her access PIN. Relieved to hear the latch give, she quietly pushed open the door and set her laptop bag on the floor next to the marble entryway table. She picked up the package she'd arranged for and the new Chick Tricks kit from the table, making a mental note to hug Jeffrey for his help with her plan.

Shivering beyond control, not sure whether it was because her body was no longer used to the Tennessee winter nights or because of what she was about to do, she hugged her long wool coat close to her. She went up the stairs, sure she'd find Grant in his study. Seeing the light underneath the door, she tiptoed to the open crack between the door and the frame and knocked.

"Thanks, Jeffrey, but I don't need anything else for the night," Grant said, his voice weak and worn, not at all the force of the man he once was, with the world at his feet.

"You don't, huh?"

Harper kicked open the door with her foot, revealing nothing but her black silk stockings and stilettos.

She flaunted her left hand in the opening, showing him the perfect platinum and diamond bands that had found their way back home on her ring finger.

"Well, I guess it depends on what it is. And you're definitely not Jeffrey," Grant said, amused.

Harper opened the door all the way and gave him her best Playboy Bunny pose. She dropped her coat to the floor, revealing the black leather negligee she'd picked up at Frederick's of Hollywood. She threw the legal-size package on his desk, then closed the door behind her and locked. She sauntered the rest of the way into his office, handing him the Chick Tricks Inc. box.

"What's this?" he asked, a sheepish grin spreading across his face.

"Continuing education," she said and smiled.

She sat on the corner of his desk, acting as if she were interested in the documents he'd been working on. Bending over low so her breasts fell in front of him in full view, she reached for his tie and loosened it.

Grant put the Chick Tricks Inc. box on the credenza behind his desk and got up from his chair. In one fluid motion, he swept everything off his desk except for the package Harper had thrown there. He was no longer interested in the deeds to the inn in Playa del Rey or the documents he'd had prepared to purchase the controlling shares of Chick Tricks Inc.

His father had taught him to invest wisely in products he believed in—the only lesson of his worth taking to heart. And Grant planned to invest a lot heavier in his wife, what he most believed in.

Harper reached for the packet of papers and pulled them out, removing the clip that bound them together. She extended her leg around the side of his chair and turned on his document shredder with the toe of her shoe. She fed the papers through, one-by-one.

When the last sheet was swallowed whole, she took Grant by his tie and pulled him to her, noticing he offered no resistance to her efforts. She moved herself onto the center of his desk and lay back, pulling him down on top of her.

When he moved on top of her, pressing her back against the desk, a loud crack broke their heated silence. She leaned up. He reached behind her and removed two shards of wood.

Their eyes met in wicked unison. They'd just broken the Cantwell check register ruler into two pieces.

Grant ceremoniously tossed both pieces into the air like a graduate at commencement, then he went back to the business at hand.

• • •

Harper smiled to herself as she buttoned her coat. Leaving Grant's office, she vowed to pop in and visit more often.

She had unpacking to do and then plans to review for the design shop she was going to open in Briar Creek.

As she stepped into the master suite for the first time since she'd left, she realized that Sartre was right. In love, one and one are one. But only as long as she remembered that it took her satisfying her 'one,' plus Grant embracing his 'one,' to make the equation work.

THE END

NOTE FROM D. D. SCOTT

Happy Holidays!

Whether you're brand new to my books or you keep coming back for more, cheers to you and your families this wonderful holiday season!

Nothing beats treating you to books that are all about spreading the love of the season, and I'm looking forward to sharing these kinds of stories with you for years to come.

To be the first to hear about all of my D. D. Scott-ville books, sign up for my newsletter at www.DDScottville. com . (***Note: your email will never be shared, and you can unsubscribe at any time.)

And please share your love for my D. D. Scott-ville books! Word-of-mouth is vital for an author to succeed. If you enjoyed the book, please leave a review on the store site from which you purchased it, even if it's just a sentence or two. That's how other readers find my books! Your reviews make a ton of difference and are so appreciated.

Also, feel free to email me at dd(dot)scott(at)live(dot)com . I do answer each and every email—unless you're spamming me (LOL!).

You can connect and hang with me in and on…:

www.DDScottville.com
Facebook DeeDee Scott
Twitter @ddscottromcom
Pinterest DeeDee Scott
Instagram ddscottromcom
Goodreads D. D. Scott
Google+ D. D. Scott

Happy Holidays again…from my home to yours.

Cheers! —- D. D. Scott

P.S. As an extra treat for you this holiday season, I've included an excerpt from another one of my humor and heart-filled Christmas Books—**HULLABALOO AND HOLLY TOO** (A Cozy Cash Mystery Christmas Novella). You'll find the first three chapters following my Bio. Happy Reading!!!

ABOUT D. D. SCOTT

I'm D. D. Scott, an International Bestselling Author. With over 300,000 books sold, including 30 titles in 5 genres and chart-topping audio books, I treat my readers to stories with loads of laughs and a bunch of heart. You can get the scoop on me, my books and my adventures as a new, vegetarian (almost vegan) yogi in my new cyber home...www.DDScottville.com .

Full Bio:

D. D. Scott's bestselling books start out a bit Chick Lit, Gone-Country (The Bootscootin' Books). Then, they take on a Will and Kate gone-Bond, as in James Bond, twist (The Cozy Cash Mysteries). Next up, try Castle and Beckett, Gone-Country, with Bewitched tossed into the mix (The Stuck with a Series), followed by The Good Witch meets The Three Stooges and Tinker Hell (The Belle Bishop Books). In her latest series (The Royal Heirs), she's taking you behind the palace doors of the royal family of Kristianico, a tiny French Riviera country that, she wishes was real so she could visit.

She's a four-time Amazon Movers & Shakers List Author (making it all the way to #2 on that prestigious list) and both an Amazon and Barnes & Noble Top 100 Bestselling Author.

Her books have been Top Picks—including one of the Top 10 Books for Mother's Day 2011—for major reader blogs like Ereader News Today (ENT), Kindle Nation Daily, Cheap e-Reads, Pixel of

Ink, The Frugal eReader, Indie Books List, Only Romance, and Bargain eBooks.

She co-founded the one-million-hits-per-month grog The WG2E, a writer's destination site for all-things epublishing. Whatever you want to know and/or cuss and discuss about E-publishing, it's right there at The WG2E waiting for you as well as in her latest bestselling non-fiction book 10 YEARS AND 24 HOURS TO INDIE EPUBLISHING SUCCESS.

When she's not writing, she's busy luuuvin' on her real-life hero (her DH-Darling Husband) and their beloved shelter-rescued dog Buckley and his new playmate Siggy the Affenpinscher.

She's a new, vegetarian (almost vegan) yogi who spends tons of time on the beautiful beaches of her new home in Sarasota, Florida. Follow her adventures on her blog in D. D. Scott-ville.

She's gotta have her Yoga Mat, Organic Food and Love and Gratitude.

An Excerpt of

HULLABALOO AND HOLLY TOO

(A Cozy Cash Mystery Christmas Novella)

By:

D. D. Scott

CHAPTER ONE

And here I thought livin' in a castle was gonna be rough.

Want to know what's worse?

Or at least has the potential to be worse?

Goin' home for the holidays.

That's my current crazy trip...and when that trip includes your new fake husband, who has yet to meet his crazy-ass in-laws, the threat to your sanity ratchets up to unheard of levels.

But wait...there's more.

And no, that's not a line from my favorite infomercial, no matter how much I wish it was.

This is reality. My quirky-crazy reality.

So what happens when your pretend spouse finds out his in-laws are not your average in-laws?

What if...and I'm just gonna toss this idea out there.

What if...they're Mr. and Mrs. Claus?

At least that's who they think they are.

I know, I know...it sounds like something from a Tim Allen Santa Claus movie, right?

Well, it ain't.

It's my hullabaloo of a Whoville life.

Think of my world as a for-real Dr. Seuss Whoville, but one with a cast of characters makin' it feel very Christmas with the Fockers...all year long.

And I know what you're thinkin'...

More egg-nog, please.

And cheers to that...'cause y'all are gonna need it.

CHAPTER TWO

I'm Zoey Witherspoon, Duchess of Caserta, and I'm about to take my pretend husband, Prince Roman Bellesconi Umberto-Vittorio Emanuele Vanvitelli, the Duke of Caserta, home for the holidays.

We're Italy's version of Will and Kate.

And we're headed to the States and my childhood home–the Midwestern suburbia version of Whoville–for one helluva holiday hullabaloo!

I'm about to tell my prince about my parent's mental issues, and it ain't gonna be easy. But that's okay. 'Cause, for me, life has not been easy since the age of five, when my parents stopped being the Witherspoons of Lakeshore Drive.

That's when they decided they were Mr. and Mrs. Claus, who lived in a new version of The North Pole along the fabulous shores of Lake Michigan.

My parents, George and Suzie Witherspoon, suffer from a delusional disorder.

Well…that's not exactly correct either.

Theydon't suffer. They have no clue their beliefs are delusional.

I'm the one who suffers. I'm the kid who's always simply smiled and shrugged off their eccentricities.

I mean really…what's not to love about living Christmas all-year-long?

Okay. So maybe our family elves and reindeer have been a bit much to reconcile with John Q Public. But other than that, life in Santa and Mrs. Claus' workshop ain't all that bad, as long as you're on "the nice list".

I thought about all this and how I was gonna break it to my prince while I snuggled up to our pot-bellied pig's cozy warm snout. Soaking in the love that his squirms and happy-go-lucky ouff-ing noises stirred in my soul, I did find some comfort. But I could use a bunch more.

"We'll be landing in about a half hour," Roman said, as he returned his cushy seat to its upright position aboard our private jet.

Thank goodness he was tired from our stop-over in LA. We'd been there just a few days–long enough to help-out Lily Vaughn, one of our Mom Squad Members, and her brother, Wayne, deal with some Hollywood film industry thugs.

Thanks to their predicament, I'd managed to prolong the obvious for as long as possible. But my time had now run out.

When Dad came to pick us up from the private airstrip near our home in one of our reindeer-drawn sleighs, I was gonna have some major explaining to do. I might as well get a jump on our out of the ordinary greeting committee.

"So, yeah…about meeting my parents," I said, deciding to just go for the gusto.

It's not as if I could somehow get out of the spectacle Roman was about to become part of.

"Are you finally going to tell me about them?" He asked.

The genuine kindness I'd come to expect and adore from him lit up his eyes brighter than the lights on all thirty-nine Christmas trees my parents had in their home.

"Have you ever heard of delusional disorder?" I asked.

While I tried to explain my parent's condition, the age-old knots in my stomach tightened in a very familiar way.

"You mean like a person thinks something is true that the rest of society doesn't? Kind of like when you're a child and believe in St. Nick?"

Oh boy. How do you explain that your parents don't just believe in jolly ol' St. Nick and his Mrs., they think they are ol' Nick and his Mrs.?

"Yes, that's it. And it's funny you should mention the St. Nick delusion…"

I looked straight into Roman's extra-shot-of-espresso brown eyes, knowing his warmth would always be there for me, but still hating like hell to have to burden him with my family's insanity.

"Go ahead," he coaxed me, totally unaware of what he was about to get himself into.

He took a seat next to Vinnie the Swine and me on the vanilla-colored leather sofa in the jet's spacious cabin and put his arms around both of us.

"My parents definitely believe in Santa Claus," I began, taking one last and very deep breath before I unloaded the whole truth. "They believe…because…they also believe they areMr. and Mrs. Claus."

Trying to purge my fears along with the extra carbon dioxide from my last air intake, I exhaled slowly.

"But there's a catch to this kind of illness, right?" Roman asked.

I tilted my head, not sure I'd heard him correctly, but knowing that if I had processed what he'd said in the right way, he'd totally thrown me for a huge loop.

"What do you mean a catch?" I asked.

"Well, I've been doing some reading…"

"On St. Nick Schizoid behaviors?"

I couldn't believe this was happening. "You knew about my parents this whole time?!"

"No offense to your intelligence there, my princess, but I am a princewhich means I have access to just about anything I need or want to know."

I don't know if I should be pissed or relieved. I was pissed 'cause he'd obviously done a background check on me and my crazy-ass family. But I was also relieved 'cause he still chose to make me his fake princess.

"As I was saying, there's a catch to this type of illness. If everybody believes the delusion or acts like they do, then the person doesn't actually have the illness, right?"

Great. Now my prince and primary thug guard was also a pseudo-psychiatrist.

"All of the websites I've visited have said the most effective help for a person suffering from delusional disorder is psychotherapy, not drugs."

"Yeah, I know. But you don't know how many times I've wished they made a little blue pill for this," I said, for comic value only.

That wasn't even close to my true feelings about my parent's illness.

I was just trying to do like I always do and sweep my fears and insane-upbringing under the rug with inappropriate wisecracks.

I would never want my parents to be all doped up. They were the most loveably insane people I knew. In fact, everyone who knew them loved them.

"Seriously, you're right, Roman. There is a ton of research out there advising loved ones not to attempt to argue away a delusion," I said, knowing how tenaciously my parents held to their North Pole fantasy in the face of reality.

"I know about the research. And it's fascinating at that," Roman said, taking from his pants pocket a small folded-up piece of paper.

"Did you know there's an actual empathy model teaching us how to respond therapeutically to their delusions?" He asked.

My prince looked so proud of himself, I didn't have the heart to talk him down from his comfy, on the couch, pay by the hour approach to meeting my parent's mental issues.

"I'm not sure those kinds of therapy work for my parents, but you're more than welcome to give 'em a whirl."

"I think I might. Oh, and one more thing," he said, tilting-up my chin so that my mouth was deliciously close to his, "don't you worry. I have a feeling I'm going to really enjoy getting to know your family."

Our pilot came over the cabin's speaker system and advised us to buckle-up and prepare for landing.

"We'll see," I said, handing Vinnie to Roman.

"I hope Vinnie likes reindeer," Roman said, while shoving him into his carrier.

What's not to love, I thought to myself, knowing this was gonna be a holiday none of us would ever forget…including Vinnie.

CHAPTER THREE

Standing beside Roman in the doorway of our private jet, I watched as the royal-crested, red-and-gold-carpeted stairway unfolded onto the tarmac. Vinnie watched too, cradled in Roman's arms and wearing his own little wool coat.

I breathed in the fresh, ice-cold, lake air.

Nothing beats the crisp chill of winter around Lake Michigan.

Truth be told...I always looked forward to coming home for the holidays. During the Christmas season, it truly is rather magical here.

But for years now, I hadn't dared to bring anyone new into my nutty family mix. I just didn't have the energy to explain my zany childhood.

This time, though, I didn't really have a choice, did I?

Now that my PI Gig had landed me permanently in Thug Guard and Pretend Princess Land, I couldn't very well hide this part of my life from Roman.

He deserved to know everything about his fake wife. So here we go...

Snow swirled through the air, brushing against our cheeks, which must be bright cherry red by now.

Stepping out into the lakeshore's winter fury, it wouldn't take us long to get frostbitten.

Large, white, crystaline flakes tumbled from the sky onto Roman's dark hair then toppled over onto the shoulders of his gorgeous Alpaca wool mohair overcoat.

When I heard the jingling of Dad's sleigh bells getting closer and closer, the snow globe magic of the moment was lost.

Here we go, I thought.

Ho-freakin'-ho.

When Santa's sleigh glided to a stop in front of us, Roman handed off Vinnie to me and dashed down the jet's stairway to wrap my St. Nick Dad in a tight hug. He followed this up with very Italian kiss-kiss sweeps across both my dad's ruby red cheeks.

"God, I love Europeans," my dad said, giving Roman a nice jolly-ho Italian kiss-kiss in return. "I'll have to have Mrs. C break into our stash of limoncello. I always grab a couple cases during my Christmas Eve fly-ins."

While Dad temporarily abandoned his limoncello dreams to scold Vixen for nipping at his ass, Roman looked to me for help.

"You'd best be checkin' your empathy model a bunch more than twice, my luv," I whispered in his ear.

As if he'd forgotten he had that saving grace, he whipped the list of recommended responses out of his coat pocket while I kept dad busy fussing over me being home for the holidays.

Okay. Who was I kidding? Dad was making a bigger fuss over Vinnie than me, or at least just as much.

"Gosh I've missed you, Zoey Bean," my dad said, hugging me so tight to his huge white beard, I was concerned either Vinnie or I could very well suffocate.

"I've missed you too, Dad."

And I had missed him.

For all my parents' craziness, I still love 'em so very much.

They, for sure, have a unique take on the world, but a take full of nothing but love for all mankind and all the world's creatures too. That's something I didn't see much of in my fashion world.

Despite the thugs in my new Princess Diaries lifestyle, being a Duchess did indeed allow me to spread the love my parents raised me on. I was enjoying the philanthropic duties of my new title. With every little bit of goodness I paid forward, I always thought of my mom and dad.

"You say you do Christmas Eve fly-ins," Roman said, evidently checking-off one of the approaches on his empathy model.

"That I do. And oh, they're such marvelous fun. You should join me this year, my son. I'd love the company."

Roman again looked to me, and I again motioned for him to just carry on with his behavior model methodology. The sooner he learned that thing was a huge farce, the better off we all would be.

"I can't see that and the tests don't show any worms in your head," Roman said.

I damn near choked on the warm cocoa my dad always kept in a thermos in our sleigh.

"What?" My dad asked. "I'm sorry, son, I can't hear ya very well with all these damn bells jingling."

By this time I was laughing so hard I couldn't breathe, which delightfully made my prince's cheeks turn an even brighter shade of crimson.

Roman's empathy model was based on subjects with a delusional disorder who thought worms were eating their brain. Not a particularly helpful model for dealing with the St. Nick Schizoid variety of this disorder.

"Roman said he'd love to see that. As in, he'd love to ride with you this Christmas Eve," I said, deciding I'd answer for my prince just this once, before I peed my pants and choked to death on hot cocoa at the same time.

"I imagine I might feel overjoyed to share the adventure with you, Sir," Roman said, beginning to recover, but still relying way too much on his behavioral model's suggested wording.

"No need to be so formal, son," my dad said, patting Roman on the back with one hand while he took hold of the sleigh's reins with the other. "Call me Santa. Or Nick. Or Dad. Why yes, of course…just call me Dad."

With that invitation, he lightly snapped the reins against Donner and Comet's rumps.

Oh boy, I thought. That wasn't gonna sit well with these super-spoiled and ornery reindeer.

Donner turned around and looked at my dad as if to say 'you must be nuts, old man, we don't answer to that trick anymore'.

"These guys can be a bit stubborn," my dad said, his round, cherry-red cheeks glowing just about as bright as Rudolph's nose.

And yes, The Witherspoons' lead reindeer, aptly named Rudolph, also sports a glowing red nose.

You see, my father doesn't just think he's St. Nick, he's also a toymaker and inventor, plus he has a few rather spectacular side gigs as well.

So yep, you guessed it. He designed and made a glowing red nose for our Rudolph. And it's not just your basic, glowing red reindeer nose.

Dad also outfitted our Rudolph's nose with some sort of specialized GPS device. Our Rudy had grown old and developed

Alzheimer's. So my dad added this rather sophisticated GPS system to help Rudy make it around the globe on Christmas Eve. Otherwise, Dad and his sleigh-pulling entourage sometimes got lost between Bali and Belfast.

After five minutes of no onward and upward progress, Dad got off of his captain's bench to have a little heart-to-heart with Donner and Comet, who were always the cause of our reindeer stand-offs.

My guess was that it probably had something to do with Vinnie. I doubt they appreciated that my pot-bellied pig was now riding high and mighty in their sleigh's co-captain's spot.

Whatever Dad said to Donner must have really pissed him off 'cause the next thing I knew, the jerk had bucked his head, snatched the empathy model right out of Roman's fingers, and was chomping on it as if it were an organic carrot, his favorite snack.

"I hope that paper wasn't too important," Dad said, holding his belly full of jelly as he laughed for a jolly bit.

Dad then got back into the sleigh with us, took the reins, and without the slightest grunt or stomp, Rudolph and Company led us home.

On our ride, we weren't just accompanied by sleigh bells, we were also being serenaded by Vinnie's wild ouffs. He was making all kinds of racket while shaking his head back-and-forth, full of melodrama. Obviously, he wasn't all that impressed with the family reindeers' bad attitudes.

And no, we weren't flying today. Dad and his reindeer had started saving that just for Christmas Eve. It was their way of "being green" by helping to save the ozone layer.

How did that work?

Well...let's just say those reindeer eat a ton of cabbage to gear-up for their Christmas Eve flight. So their, ahem, emissions tend to be quite high.

I settled back into the comfy confines of our sleigh with Roman and placed a beautiful blanket my mom had made over our laps.

I love sleigh rides.

We began to follow the lakefront and would continue along its curving shoreline all the way to my parent's house. With the snow falling at a good clip, it was nothing less than a magical journey.

Roman was no longer upset over Donner making a snack of his empathy model, and life just felt right.

I don't know how else to explain it.

"I'm over the moon that you two are finally here, and with your terrific PI skills, I'm hoping you can help me out," Dad hollered over his shoulder from his sleigh captain's seat.

"Sure thing, um, Dad. What can we help you with?" Roman asked, again looking at me as if I could help save the day.

"I swear I'm being phone-hacked."

"What?! By who?!" I asked, glad to pitch-in on Dad's latest crazy-trip theory.

"Father Time, that's who. The bastard has a beef with me and my Naughty List, and now I think he's got me phone-hacked too."

And just like that, my belief in life feeling oh-so-right took a reindeer-sized cabbage crap on me and my prince.

HULLABALOO AND HOLLY TOO is available on Amazon, Nook, Kobo, Sony, iTunes and more!

Happy Reading!!! —-D. D. Scott

ACKNOWLEDGEMENTS

A big thank you to my DH (Darling Husband) who keeps the spirit of the season in my heart each and every day.

BOOKS BY D. D. SCOTT

Welcome to D. D. Scott-ville, where "The First One is On Me!"

In other words, the book that started it all for me is FREE on all ereading platforms (Kindle, Nook, Sony, Kobo, Apple, Smashwords and more)! It's been downloaded over 600,000 times around the world. I'm over the moon to be able to treat you to this special book.

If you're like me and enjoy reading a series in order, from the first book to the last, here's a list of my entire collection, in order:

The Bootscootin' Books
Bootscootin' Blahniks
Stompin' on Stetsons
Buckles Me Baby

The Cozy Cash Mysteries
Thug Guard
Lip Glock
Hullabaloo and Holly Too
Carats & Coconuts
The Royal Digs

The Mom Squad Mini-Mayhem Mysteries
Fluid Fulfillment
Licensed for Love

D. D. Scott Boxed Sets
Bootscootin' and Cozy Cash Mystery Boxed Set
The Cozy Cash Mysteries Boxed Set #1
The Stuck with a Series Boxed Set #1

The Stuck with a Series
Stuck with a Stiff
Stuck with a Spell
Stuck with Sleigh Bells

Stuck with a Slut

Belle Bishop Queen of Witches
Practical Mischief
Practical Mayhem—Coming 2015
Practical Madness—Coming 2016

Home for The Holidays
Hollywood Holidays

The Royal Heirs Series
The Keys' Prince
A Royal Christmas Rescue
Kristianico's Crown Prince — Coming February 2015

Non-Fiction Books
Muse Therapy: Unleashing Your Inner Sybil
10 Years and 24 Hours to Indie Epublishing Success

The WG2E All-For-Indies Anthologies
Winter Wonderland Edition
Viva La Valentine Edition
Spring Hop Edition
Summer Fling Edition
Spooky Shorts Edition
Martini Madness Edition

Audio Books
Bootscootin' Blahniks
Stompin' on Stetsons
Buckles Me Baby
Stuck with a Stiff
Stuck with a Spell
Stuck with Sleigh Bells
The Stuck with a Series Audio Book Boxed Set #1
Thug Guard
Lip Glock
Hullabaloo and Holly Too-Coming soon!

Carats and Coconuts-Coming Soon!
Practical Mischief

Happy Reading and Listening! --- D. D. Scott